Ruth did not speak until they were alone in the apartment. She hadn't decided how she was going to tell Larry the news. Doctors aren't too tactful, and she was no exception. But she wanted to share her fright, her upset, and possibly her dilemma with him. If they were ever going to have a trusting relationship, it would have to begin at the beginning. She didn't want Larry to hear this from anyone but herself.

"What's the matter, honey," Larry said, sensing something was wrong.

"I don't know how to say it . . . Larry . . ." she cried, unable to say the words. "I've got a lump in my breast!"

Ruth laid her head on his chest and sobbed. He heard every sob with pain, every teardrop leaving a sting on his skin. As a physician he could understand why she was crying—she could be facing a life-death situation. As a man he realized how much he cared for the woman who was being threatened. Larry felt cheated too, realizing that he could offer her no help. Ruth knew more about cancer than he did, and unfortunately that was not enough.

He pulled her closer and held her shaking body as if it were a gift from heaven, perhaps a gift that could be taken away . . .

FICTION FOR TODAY'S WOMAN

EMBRACES (666, $2.50)
by Sharon Wagner
Dr. Shelby Cole was an expert in the field of medicine and a novice at love. She wasn't willing to give up her career to get married—until she grew to want and need the child she was carrying.

MIRRORS (690, $2.75)
by Barbara Krasnoff
The compelling story of a woman seeking changes in life and love, and of her desperate struggle to give those changes impact—in the midst of tragedy.

THE LAST CARESS (722, $2.50)
by Dianna Booher
Since the tragic news that her teenaged daughter might die, Erin's husband had become distant, isolated. Was this simply his way of handling his grief, or was there more to it? If she was losing her child, would she lose her husband as well?

VISIONS (695, $2.95)
by Martin A. Grove
Caught up in the prime time world of power and lust, Jason and Gillian fought desperately for the top position at Parliament Television. Jason fought to keep it—Gillian, to take it away!

LONGINGS (706, $2.50)
by Sylvia W. Greene
Andrea was adored by her husband throughout their seven years of childless marriage. Now that she was finally pregnant, a haze of suspicion shrouded what should have been the happiest time of their lives.

Available wherever paperbacks are sold, or order direct from the Publisher. Send cover price plus 50¢ per copy for mailing and handling to Zebra Books, 21 East 40th Street, New York, N.Y. 10016. DO NOT SEND CASH!

DIARY OF A WOMAN DOCTOR

BY MARILYN GILMAN

ZEBRA BOOKS

KENSINGTON PUBLISHING CORP.

ZEBRA BOOKS

are published by

KENSINGTON PUBLISHING CORP.
21 East 40th Street
New York, N.Y. 10016

Printed in the United States of America

For my husband, Edward,
who knows all the reasons why

Acknowledgments

The author extends gratitude to the following physicians whose efforts and research provided the medical information for *The Diary of a Woman Doctor*.

Gianni Bonadonna, M.D., National Cancer Institute, Milan, Italy

Susan Covey, M.D., Park City Hospital, Bridgeport, Conn.

Melvin Deutsch, M.D., University of Pittsburgh, Pittsburgh, Penna.

Bernard Fisher, M.D., University of Pittsburgh, Pittsburgh, Penna.

Samuel Hellman, M.D., Harvard Medical School, Cambridge, Mass.

Sydney Salmon, M.D., Arizona Cancer Center, Tucson, Arizona

Umberto Veronesi, M.D., National Cancer Institute, Milan, Italy

Prologue

"I can't be calm, Larry!" Ruth Simson-Stein, M.D. cried to her husband as she leaned her head on his chest. Her salt-filled tears stung like thousands of tiny needles. They pierced her cheeks with the burning memories of the past. . . .

Larry Stein, also a doctor, acknowledged his sense of helplessness in light of her devastating situation. Ruth would be doomed with the diagnosis of "uncertainty" until their child was born. The dilemma arose from her nearness to childbirth, a mere eight or nine weeks away. The needle biopsy would be utterly inconclusive. An excisional biopsy could present a hazardous condition because the anesthesia might pass through the placenta and affect the child.

"What can I say, Ruth. I love you. I've always loved you and I don't give a damn about anything else on the face of this earth. You and our child are

9

my reasons for living." Yes, Larry Stein realized that he could offer her only love and support, nothing more. How does one ease pain? relieve suffering? or bear the burdens of crisis for another? No, he rationalized, that was impossible. But, God, he asked silently, hasn't my wife experienced her share of grief? Where was her physician's bargaining card? And now, with child, Ruth was faced with a life-threatening crisis. Larry knew clearly that both Ruth and their child were in jeopardy.

Ruth walked slowly to the sliding glass doors of the living room of their Riverside Drive apartment. The moon shone brightly on the water giving the liquid a shimmering glow. Her tears blurred the peaceful view of the river. Ruth turned to her husband. "Jim Hayes says it could be normal changes due to the pregnancy," she said, trying to believe it. "But then again, we have no conclusive evidence, at least not for a while." Ruth's lips curled and the tears began to well again.

Larry walked over to the window and stood beside her. He put his strong arms around her and felt the weight of her pregnant body lean toward him for support. "Let's just pray, honey. Pray that we're lucky again." Then Larry became more sensible, more rational. The physician, not the husband, spoke. "This is 1979, Ruth, and the treatment for breast cancer has come a long way."

Suddenly Ruth spun around on her heels and faced him. She was reminded of his physician's attitude of five years ago when she had had her first brush with cancer. That was the beginning of their life together, the beginning of her crusade, the point at which she had become a devoted cancer-activist. But now *she* was the patient! The rules shouldn't apply when it's your wife, Dr. Stein. Ruth felt angry, cheated. "That doesn't change *my* feelings, Larry. Our child might grow up without a mother!" Ruth cried.

The discovery, the aloneness, the fears . . . God, she knew what it was like! And anyone who had not had the experience would never know the feeling. The moment when the clock stands still. The water ceases to flow. That precise frame of time. The fuckin' moment in a woman's life when she fears she might be the next victim. Older, meaningful memories of five years ago were suddenly as vivid as yesterday . . . as fearful and frightening as the seven days in spring, 1975. . . .

Chapter 1

Spring, 1975

"Fuck off, Donovan. You're the biggest load of bullshit in this hospital," Ruth Simson, M.D. thought. She didn't dare say it aloud. Somehow the only time a man could accept and enjoy the word *fuck* from a woman was when she went to bed with him. Ruth Simson had no intentions of going to bed with her chief of staff. She did have intentions of giving him a good fight on a matter of extreme importance to her: methods of treating breast cancer.

"I've reviewed your request, Dr. Simson," he was saying, "and I feel that at this time it would be impossible to consider such a radical procedure in this hospital. Memorial does have a reputation to live up to."

"If you had read through the program, Dr. Donovan, you would have realized that the request was for study *only*, not participation in the trial.

But now that you bring it up, I must admit that my long-range goal is to evaluate the possibility of employing that procedure in my department."

"Look here, Dr. Simson. At this point we are not ready to plot new paths with radiation therapy. Interstitial implants are out of the question; it's an infant theory," Alvin Donovan replied rather heatedly.

Ruth did not want to lose her cool tone. She tried to be ladylike and patient with her colleagues, but now that Donovan was refusing to recognize the value of a very reputable study, she took the liberty of abandoning her polite approach in favor of something more realistic and rebellious.

"That's the trouble with this goddamn hospital," she told him. "It's one of the most conservative places I've had the misfortune of working in!" As the words spilled out, Ruth experienced immediate feelings of regret. She *did* like Memorial Hospital and many of the physicians she worked with. It was the administration which was her chief target, her real source of frustration! This was the year 1975, hardly the dark ages for medicine. Yet a hospital the size of Memorial, slightly over five hundred beds, still refused to make the appropriate advances in medical practice. If New York City proper was experiencing the "cultural lag," she thought, what could be expected of all the rural hospitals?

"As a community hospital we are not set up to make human guinea pigs out of our patients, Dr.

Simson. That's for the university hospitals. Believe me when I say that I would not care to be a patient in one of those institutions."

"Dr. Hillman is not using his patients as human guinea pigs," Ruth retorted. "The reports I showed you indicate a five-year follow-up study, and the statistics are significant."

"In this hospital, Dr. Simson, the Halsted Radical Mastectomy is still the standard treatment of choice for carcinomas of the breast. And until proven otherwise, that is, *proven*, Dr. Simson, I will not have you or any other physician handing out alternatives!"

Ruth felt urgency for her cause, anger at the man she was answering. "May I ask why you insist on ignoring the new theory of the biology and treatment of this disease?" she asked.

"Because it's *only* a theory! You have no proof."

"May I remind you, Dr. Donovan, that you do not have any proof either. The fact that you still hold strongly to a theory that's a hundred years old, without question, despite failure rate, leaves grave doubts in my mind as to your ability to keep abreast of the newer developments in medicine."

"And who are you, doctor, to question my abilities and sound judgment? I have a lot more experience than you!"

"Of course, you've had more experience. And that's precisely why you should acknowledge the failure rate of the radical mastectomy. The 'en bloc' dissection just has not yielded a cure rate for the majority of patients," Ruth insisted.

15

"But we are curing *some* patients, Dr. Simson! And that's the most we can hope for at this time. All this perplexing and confusing literature on the possible systemic nature of breast cancer can become devastating!" Donovan threw his hands up in the air. "How many women are going to consent to such treatments? Radiation therapy, drug therapy, needle implants—it's all too radical!"

"And how many women are refusing the radical surgery and going untreated, Dr. Donovan? Do we have to take a census of the number before you realize that the radical, for some patients, is worse than the disease?"

"That's their problem, Dr. Simson. We did not give them the cancer."

Ruth's blood began to boil; her heart raced. How could any sensitive physician make such a statement! Donovan was cold-blooded, aloof, and removed from the human element in illness. Was he assigning blame and guilt to the patient? Could he not realize the raging inferno through which these women walked? The shattering of their divine universe which always comes with a diagnosis of breast cancer? No cause, no cure, no hope! She chose her words carefully.

"Dr. Donovan, what the hell are you treating? A human being or a goddamn disease entity?"

"I'm practicing medicine, Dr. Simson, and that's exactly what *you* should be doing. All of you young snips coming out of medical schools today think that the core of medicine is change, change,

16

and more change. Jim Hayes and his simple mastectomies, you and your implants! Are you trying to tailor medicine to the patient or the patient to the procedure? Answer that, please?" he demanded.

"I'm not tailoring," Ruth said loudly, "I'm respecting the fact that medicine is a science as well as an art, Dr. Donovan. As a science it should move forward. If cancer research remains stagnant, we'll never find the answers. And if we ignore the art of medicine then we aren't respecting the fact that our patients have two distinct sides. As physicians we should not ignore the psychological implications of their illnesses. We must communicate with them and respect individual differences to achieve a healthy balance."

"What differences, Dr. Simson? A breast cancer is a breast cancer!" he replied, pounding his fist on the desk.

"False!" Ruth screamed. "A breast cancer represents an individual patient. Christ almighty, who the hell are you to tell someone how to live? This place is crawling with omnipotent chauvinists, and personally, it makes me sick!" She paused, gathered her thoughts and went on, now speaking more calmly;

"You know that the ninety-one percent survival statistics for a five-year period on the interstitial implant are remarkable."

"It's not sufficient time and trial to evaluate the side effects of the treatment. To deliver five thousand rads of cobalt 60 and another two thousand rads with interstitial implants is definitely a radical procedure."

"But this is not an infant theory. Interstitial implants of iridium 137 filaments have been used for fifty years," Ruth continued to argue.

"Not in the radiation unit of this hospital!"

With Donovan, Ruth felt that it was not only a battle of a progressive viewpoint coming up against an ultraconservative one, it also became a battle of the intellect. In that respect Ruth Simson felt that she had the brain power over him. Alvin Donovan might be chief of staff, but as a physician, Ruth thought him to be incompetent. Perhaps, for the sake of humanity, he was best off remaining in the ivory tower pushing his paper work. To her, Donovan was one of those die-hards who refused to move forward; every hospital had its share. She resumed:

"Dr. Donovan, when are you going to move out of this ivory tower and get down to the floors where the real people live? Try it some day when you can make the time, Dr. Donovan. There's a lot to learn there."

"Are you questioning my capabilities as a physician, Dr. Simson?" he asked angrily.

"No, sir. I'm questioning your capabilities as a person!" she answered. "Would you like to meet one of my patients who refused a radical mastectomy, Dr. Donovan?"

"Women's liberation . . . moving into everything. Now they want to pick and choose their medical procedures! Damn! I remember the good old days when the doctor was God. We made all the decisions!"

"And you goddamn well took the blame for every one of them," Ruth retorted. "Patients know more today, and the mass media is not keeping secrets from the public. It wouldn't surprise me at all to see a patient's rights bill come into being in the near future, Dr. Donovan. If you don't move ahead you are surely in for a 'leveling' from the medical community as well as the public."

"Is that a warning, Dr. Simson?"

"No, it's a promise. Look back into history, Dr. Donovan. Gods have been 'leveled' since the beginning of time. Physicians are a prime target now," Ruth stated firmly, turning toward the door. "Let's go. I have to see a patient, and I think you can learn a lot from her."

He relented. "Mary," he said to his secretary, "I'm going up on the floors with Dr. Simson. Hold my calls for about half an hour."

Once they left the confined walls of Dr. Donovan's office, both physicians used less heated language. Ruth tried to gear down from the charged battle. She did not want to leave Donovan in a fighting mood. Her purpose was to educate both of them, not to cause more dissension among the medical staff. That would defeat her purpose. She turned to him as they waited for the elevator to take them to the fourth floor.

The elevator arrived. It was full. Ruth decided it was better not to pursue the conversation further for the moment. They were among a group of orderlies, nurses, and visitors. People outside the physicians' community liked to think that doctors were a most harmonious group, working together toward one goal: good health for all mankind! It gave them confidence in their ability to live and survive! "What a crock of shit that is," Ruth thought. "If only they knew all that we don't know, we would not have to play God."

Janet Doyle was in her bed. She was feeling weakness from her intravenous "feedings" of anticancer agents. A tray, filled with food that to her was offending, lay untouched on the table. "Why do hospital dieticians insist upon sending up trays like this for sick people?" she asked herself out loud. For the past three weeks she had sent most of her meals back to the kitchen untouched. She thought eventually that someone would ask her why she wasn't eating, but that never happened. Janet realized that people became anonymous in many ways in the hospital setting. They were diseases with room numbers! With the exception of a very few professionals, there was little personal interest.

Janet depended on Woody, her former husband, to bring her a more palatable snack. He would arrive for a visit momentarily. She hobbled to the bathroom to wash and change into fresh clothes. As she began to wash, she heard a knock at the door. "Damn it, he's here before visiting hours," she thought. Janet needed time to do a complete toilet before she felt comfortable with anyone. Vanity had never left her, even in the darkest hours of her illness. She tried to look beautiful, for that was her business, and she would not drop down from this position because she was hospitalized. It was all the more reason to look well, because she felt awful!

"Come in," she yelled from the bathroom. "I'll be with you in a minute."

"Take your time, Mrs. Doyle. It's me, Dr. Simson," Ruth answered.

Janet rushed. She had just seen Dr. Simson that morning. Why another visit? Could something new have turned up? Her hands felt cold, her stomach a bit queasy. Was it fright, or simply the reaction to the medication? She did not want any more bad news, especially now when Woody would be arriving. Janet had always tried to play lightly on her afflictions. This gave her the opportunity for periods of denial, which were valuable—time in which to gather new means of coping with her problems. She washed up quickly and combed her hair. She noticed that it was thinning now from all the drugs. Still, she could not tolerate the weight of a wig when she had to remain in bed.

As Janet walked from the bathroom, Dr. Donovan rose from his chair to greet her.

"I'm Dr. Donovan, Mrs. Doyle, chief of staff. I wanted to speak with you for just a few minutes, if that's all right."

Janet looked to Ruth, and saw her nod affirmatively.

"Surely. I have all the time in the world now. What would you like to ask me?" Janet said politely.

"I was discussing your case with Dr. Simson this

morning. I understand that you knew that you had a lump in your breast three years ago. Is that correct?"

"Yes, that's correct," Janet answered.

"May I ask what you did when you found out that it was a malignancy?" Donovan continued.

"Nothing. When I was told that I would have to undergo radical surgery, I refused. I decided that if I had one life to live, doctor, I was going to continue to live it my way," Janet said courageously.

"But you were aware, were you not, that you could have been saved from this progressive illness with radical surgery?" Donovan pursued his questioning.

"No, doctor. I was not told that I would be cured. And even if I had been told this I would not have believed it. I knew enough at the time to be aware of the high failure rate of this treatment. Whatever time I had left to live I wanted to continue with my career. With a radical mastectomy it would have been out of the question. Besides, I could not live with myself after an amputation. My beauty is my life, doctor!" Janet stated firmly.

"And what is your line of work, Mrs. Doyle?" Donovan asked.

"I'm a high-fashion model. How do you think I would look on camera with a concave chest and a 'milk-maid' arm?" Her voice broke.

"I'm terribly sorry, Mrs. Doyle. I did not mean to upset you. Are you feeling well now? I see you haven't touched your lunch." Dr. Donovan tried to seem concerned and apologetic for his aggressive questioning.

"When the hospital chooses to continue to send me food that I cannot eat, I send it back. About the only thing I feel I could tolerate is a milk shake," Janet told him.

"I agree. There must be something done about the inappropriate diet we serve patients receiving chemotherapy. I'll speak to the dietician today," Dr. Donovan stated with a firm voice of authority. "The nurse will bring you that milk shake, Mrs. Doyle. And thanks for allowing me to speak with you."

"Dr. Simson, I'll see you later. It's time for me to meet with the surgical staff. Good day, ladies," he added as he walked from the room.

Janet turned to Ruth. "Why did he come here?" she asked.

"He is the chief of our staff. I asked him to make some rounds with me today to meet some of my patients. You were very kind to him, Janet, and I appreciate it very much," Ruth told her.

"Well, I told him the truth," Janet added. "I really don't care what he thinks. I don't believe that I would have made another choice today. I've had three excellent years, and I have faith that this radiation and chemotherapy will help my lungs as well as my breast."

"Good girl. When is Woody coming?" Ruth asked. "I'd like to meet him sometime."

"Soon, I hope. We have had some very interesting talks lately. You know, I really like that man very much in spite of all we've been through. I never believed he cared that much for me until he found out how ill I was. After our divorce I'd hear from him occasionally. He always kept in touch. I realize now that I hurt him deeply when I left, but I just couldn't take his way of life. I thought it was the best solution for both of us," Janet told her.

"Perhaps you may look at him differently now, Janet. He certainly spends enough time with you."

"He's the *only* one who spends time with me!" Janet said. "A model lives a rather hectic life. I have an agent who gets the assignments. There's a lot of frenzied activity at the TV stations and the ad agencies. I used to be very popular. I receive oodles of cards, but that's about it. Woody is the only one who really cares."

Ruth patted her hand.

"I'll see you in the morning. Same time, okay?"

Janet nodded as Ruth left the room.

Ruth felt renewed ability to fight for her cause after Dr. Donovan interviewed her patient. He had seen for himself, through a patient, that surgical procedures could not be pushed onto all people. Patients had to feel some sense of authority over their own lives, and Janet Doyle certainly asserted hers. Let Donovan think that one over for a while.

As Ruth waited for the elevator she saw Mark Fenster walk by. He was the psychiatrist she most often consulted for her patients. He was a middle-aged man, extremely personable, and very good in dealing with people, especially patients and their families in the cancer crisis.

Ruth had always been of the opinion that all her

cancer patients should be seen by a psychiatrist. Unfortunately, many of her colleagues disagreed. Not that all families facing the crisis needed intensive care, but Ruth knew that the majority desperately needed to talk. She felt that Janet Doyle needed to talk to someone. Ruth was planning to discharge Janet within a week and she was unsure about the condition of her health. Janet, having no family at this point in her life, needed to make plans.

"Mark," she called, as he passed her.

"Ruth Simson, I have been meaning to get down there to see you about one of your patients. But it seems that the only time—"

"—that you get down to the sub-basement is when you want a coke," Ruth said, finishing the sentence for him.

"How did you know?" Mark asked, laughing.

"Because Donovan gives me the same story."

"Well, if that's all we have in common, then I'm thrilled! Is he giving you a difficult time these days?" Mark inquired. "He's been putting the heat on Jim Hayes."

"I know why Jim is having a hard time," Ruth said. "He's another rebel."

"I'm going to see a patient of his, Sarah Roget. She's an artist. Ever hear of her?" Mark asked.

"No, I don't know anything about her, as yet. She must be new. What's the problem?"

"The woman is refusing a radical mastectomy. And you know Jim. He's been fighting for the past year to change the policy in the hospital about these radicals. He wants to present the case to the

25

Tumor Board. You'll see what's up there. Any-how, Donovan is fuming because his old conserva-tive buzzards will be on his back if Jim Hayes starts with the 'revolutionary' treatments."

"I know what you mean, Mark. Unfortunately I'm finding the same resistance. I think I'll talk with Jim. But what I wanted to ask you is, if you have a chance, could you stop in and see Janet Doyle? She's the beautiful model who refused the radical three years ago; upped and left the hospital and unfortunately went untreated. Now she has metastases to the lungs, and some local node problems. I'm treating the nodes and Dan Drieden is giving her chemotherapy. We are hoping to discharge her within a week. God knows what she'll do. She has no family. Her ex-husband is now back on the scene. I'd hate to see her alone. One never knows the turn that might take place. If therapy works she'll be all right for a while. If we fail, then she'll have other plans to make. I'm sure she needs someone objective to talk with."

"Ruth, you are a one-woman team. You never overlook any side of the patient," he compli-mented her.

"Hell, Mark, you know these people need help in getting back into society again. We surgerize them, radiate them, pump them full of poisons. How the hell can we expect them to feel like 'normal' people after that?" Ruth shrugged.

"You're right, Ruth. That delicate balance must be restored. The emotional aspects of the crisis can't be overlooked. Sure, I'll see Mrs. Doyle. I'll do whatever I can. What's her room number?"

"Four-oh-eight and read the P.H. folder first. She's quite an interesting woman, and she has a strong constitution!"

"Ruth, you're so unconventional that it's refreshing!" Mark called as he entered the elevator.

Chapter 2

Ruth was unconventional, there was no doubt about that. She knew it, her family knew it, and all her friends knew it. And what was most important to her, just about everyone at Memorial, a fine, well-staffed, community hospital, knew it.

Ruth was in medicine to fulfill a need, a very personal need to excel. From early childhood Ruth had had to find a way to draw attention to herself. She was the younger of two daughters. Her sister had been the easy, talented, and more favored child. Ruth was the rebel. She threw tantrums when she disagreed with her parents. In this way she could best manage them; they were afraid of her! The more attention her older sister had, the stronger were Ruth's vows that she would find a way in which to make herself the more successful one in the family. She would punish her parents for making the gross error of investing their lives in their older daughter rather than her. Ruth succeeded. She was an excellent student, worthy of scholarships, and she went on to medical school to compete with the best.

In a whirlwind romance one summer her sister Amy had seemingly lost her senses and married. She left her bohemian flat in New York's Greenwich Village and traded it for a split-level suburban trap. At least it represented a trap for Ruth. She was careful not to fall into the same pit. Ruth kept arm's distance from men, especially those who seemed to have only marriage in mind. She would not ruin or even compromise her career. Medicine was more suited to her need to excel. She left super-mom and super-cook to her sister. It seemed a short time before Amy had six children.

When Ruth arrived back in her office, the anteroom was filled with patients. There was a message on her desk from the president of the hospital Medical Association.

Dear Doctor: Tonight there will be a meeting of the medical and dental staff in the doctors' cafeteria. We urgently need to discuss the possibility of our participating in a new cancer protocol. Your attendance is requested.

As Ruth read the note she quickly glanced at her calendar. As usual, she had several committee meetings to attend, all related to her cancer work. It was why she had declined Larry's invitation to dinner. But now she would have dinner with him anyway. He'd assume she'd drop everything to hear what was going to be said about a new

29

cancer protocol.

Ruth attended to her patients with expertise developed after a few years of practice. She spent some time going over cases with her resident physicians, cleared her desk, and made notes to herself for the next day's work.

"Anne," she said to her secretary, "if anyone calls I'll be in the cafeteria at this meeting until eight. You can have them page me there. I'll see you in the morning."

"Good night, doctor. I'll take care of the messages. Do you want me to hold your service calls until after the meeting?" her secretary inquired.

"That will be fine, Anne; I'll pick up the messages here until eight," Ruth replied as she left her office.

Most of the staff was assembled and eating dinner when Ruth arrived. Larry saw her and motioned to her. He had saved her a seat next to him, as she had expected.

Ruth thought at times that she could write a best-selling "sexy novel" about her relationships with men. On the one hand, she gloried in being a *woman;* on the other, there was the *doctor* part. That had to come first—always. She did not want any permanent relationship. When one seemed in the offing, she put up her defenses. Larry—Lawrence Stein, M.D., neurologist—posed a threat to her security. Oddly, because he was sweet, charming, and considerate. And he professed to like her. Could she like him? She wondered as she

30

walked in his direction.

"I was beginning to think that you weren't coming. I'll get you a plate," Larry offered.

"Please, Larry, eat your dinner. I'm not helpless," Ruth said.

"That's your problem, Ruth, no one can do anything for you. Suit yourself. I'll hold your chair. . . ."

But Ruth was already gone. He watched her walk quickly toward the buffet table. He wished that he could make her relax so that they could start something other than a professional relationship.

They worked well together so long as they kept the professional status; but once he began to speak to her on an intimate level, Ruth felt torn apart. She wanted both to be yielding, and yet appear invulnerable.

Within minutes Ruth returned to the table with her dinner plate. Larry rose and held the chair for her. As she sat down, Dr. Donovan approached the front of the room and began to address the group:

"Good evening, Colleagues," he started routinely, warming to his subject as he went along. "As president of the medical and dental staff, I have asked that you join me this evening for a very last-minute engagement. I am pleased to see that so many of you have elected to give up your evening at home to be here. Before we begin the program, which comes as a surprise to all of us, I would like to say a few brief words about our guest.

"Dr. Engelman is a physician who has devoted

much of his medical career to cancer, primarily breast cancer. With the passage of the President's new cancer bill, more funds will be devoted to research protocols in a strong war against malignancies of every type. Dr. Engelman most fortunately was able to receive a grant from the National Cancer Institute to pursue his research. Without further introduction, I should like to present Dr. Engelman, who may be a familiar figure to you, and allow him to proceed with his program. Dr. Engelman."

"Ruth, this is right up your alley. I heard about it today on the floor. I think Engelman is looking for physicians to take part in his new project, but he's sure as hell going to have a hard time here with all the old stuffed shirts," Larry whispered.

Dr. Engelman was a tall, robust-looking man well into his fifties. He commanded attention by his physical stature alone. Ruth had read many of his articles about breast cancer treatments; she knew him through *Cancer Journal, The New England Journal* and other medical books on cancer. He practiced surgery at the local university and had received much national attention with what was considered to be a rather radical approach to malignant diseases. He had a difficult time in his own city, where the older, conservative group seemed to rule the roost. Ruth wanted to hear him; she felt excitement as he approached the microphone. It was about time medicine moved on from the hands of the conservatives. Cancer research had not been making the progress it should have been making for all of the monies that had been spent on it. The public, too, was getting restless. Perhaps it was time for another look at the picture. She listened to Dr. Engelman with hope.

"Thank you, Dr. Donovan," he began. "Gentlemen, and ladies, it is indeed a pleasure to be here this evening. I asked Dr. Donovan to give me this time with you so that I might share some innovative therapies for cancer treatment, to which I have been devoted for many years. Unfortunately, my fellow physicians, breast cancer still remains the number-one killer for women over thirty years of age. We have not seen any marked decrease in the death rate from this disease since the days of Dr. William Halsted. New knowledge of the biology of cancer seems to indicate that this disease is, in most cases, systemic long before we have the chance to operate on our patients. We therefore remove the primary tumor, but leave behind small micrometastases, capable of forming new tumor sites within a short time after surgery. It is becoming more apparent that the treatment of cancer will have to be aimed at its systemic nature if we are to see a greater number of women surviving breast carcinomas.

"The National Cancer Institute has granted the National Surgical Breast Project a vast sum of monies to explore various surgical and adjuvant therapies in order to determine whether better results may be seen from a multimodality approach. We at the university health clinic have devised the protocol for this research. I am now actively soliciting your enrollment in this cause, which is an attempt to attain more promising results than the radical mastectomy has given us. Women selected for enrollment in this research plan must present early-stage breast cancers. We cannot consider those with widespread disease. Surgery is contraindicated where we find evidence of widespread distant mestastases. It would be useless and quite inhuman to put these patients on the surgical table.

"I am proposing that we backtrack in a stepwise fashion. We shall consider two surgical modes of treatment in conjunction with adjuvant radiation and chemotherapy. . . ."

Ruth listened eagerly. Here was a man of great medical authority, a pioneer with respect in his profession, asking for much the same privilege she had asked Dr. Donovan for that morning: the right to learn. And Donovan was present! He had to listen. Perhaps now he would recognize the need for change, and the fact that the "big people" were doing it might make him more receptive and appreciative of *her* efforts. She glanced in Donovan's direction. He was saying something to John Davis, one of the older, conservative surgeons on the staff. Neither physician looked pleased.

"I'm going to play this down, John," Donovan was whispering. "We do have a few of these radicals on our staff, and I don't want them getting the idea that we are about to join in a protocol study."

"It's not the time, Al. And this is not the place.

I prefer to leave this experimental stuff to the university."

Dr. Bruce Thompson, seated directly in front of them turned his head in their direction. "I agree with you, Al. One hundred years of Halsted can't compare with these five-year studies. We know that women can survive the disease for at least that time without treatment."

"And these new therapies bring up other problems, too," Davis added. "Radiation and chemotherapy will scare the shit out of my patients!"

Alvin Donovan looked reassured. "You're both right. And a bigger issue for me is that participation in a protocol might interfere with our rather independent position. Once a bureaucracy walks in here with grant monies, we lose control."

"Control of the hospital policies *and* control of *fees!*" Thompson added. "The market is killing my pocket. I need my medical practice to fill it."

"I agree, Al," John Davis continued. "We need to maintain control in the department of surgery. That's where cancer treatment should begin and end at this time. And those news blurbs lately about the dosages of x-rays from the mammograms should keep the radiation therapy unit where it belongs. Can you imagine the response of the public to large doses of this stuff? God almighty, they'll think we're about to kill them! I don't feel that we have a rational basis for going ahead with this. I think that you should make some comments that are rather noncommittal."

Dr. Engelman was still speaking. Some of the audience was captivated, others seemed disturbed. Donovan was aware of the conflicting feelings around the room, and this gave him confidence that his conservative views could survive.

"Radiation therapy and chemotherapy will both be considered in this randomized clinical trial," Dr. Engelman was saying. "We hope to have at least three hundred oncologists in every subspecialty participate. You, as individual physicians, may consider joining the protocol in your practice with the good wishes and blessings of the administration. . . ."

Dr. Engelman paused for a moment. There was some laughter in the room. He was acutely aware of the confusion he was causing. This was not a new experience for him and he realized that he was throwing bombs at the administration. But this was his job, his duty, and he was totally dedicated. That reason alone was overpowering, and a group of conservatives would certainly not put him down. As an educator and researcher he had spoken to audiences many times before. He continued his talk after a pause and a sip of water. His throat was parched from the heat of the room and the heat generated from his own anxiety.

"I realize that many of you here tonight will consider what I have to say rather radical, and for this reason alone you will decide not to participate. However, I am going to supply you with the information on the study which will give you in-depth details of the way in which we have elected to set up this trial. You may then review the data personally and consider its worth. I am delighted to see that so many of you were able to join me on such short notice. It is my hope that many of you will decide to look toward these newer horizons. Thank you."

Dr. Engelman walked back to his seat. A small amount of applause was heard, and a greater amount of confusion and small talk was audible.

Ruth turned to Larry who had been looking around the room at the others to see some signs of the reactions of his colleagues. Larry knew most of the staff quite well. He had been a resident physician at Memorial, and later a Fellow in Neurology. He had personal contact with almost all the physicians. Ruth nudged him.

"Larry, I admire that man; he has guts and determination. This is exactly what I have been hoping for myself. Why, just this morning I was doing my own personal pitch with Donovan about interstitial implants. He was vehemently opposed to everything I said. He acted as if I had come up with some new way-out hoax in cancer therapy. Now at least I feel as if I can find support through Dr. Engelman."

"Hold on a minute, girl," Larry answered quickly. "You don't know enough about this protocol yet. And I'm willing to wager that Donovan discourages everyone on the staff from joining. He's so conservative that even the 'conservatives' have problems with him."

"From my heated talk with Donovan," Ruth pursued, "I felt that he conducts himself like an omnipotent bastard. Yet you just heard him.

Larry, please explain to me why he allowed Dr. Engelman to come here tonight to speak on this issue?"

"Ruth, my dear," Larry whispered, "you still don't know anything about politics in cancer, no less politics in hospitals. Donovan doesn't want to look bad. If he doesn't allow Engelman to speak then he looks like a sucker in the eyes of the N.C.I. He can't afford to do that for the sake of his own reputation, nor will he allow his staff to join the protocol at risk of the reputation of the hospital. He was taking the course of least resistance. Let the man have his say; then use the power of the conservatives, and dissuade all of us from joining. Remember, malpractice suits scare the hell out of chiefs of staff and administrators."

Almost as soon as Larry finished giving Ruth his explanation, Dr. Donovan rose from his seat to address the staff. Dr. Engelman had already shaken his hand and left the conference room. Ruth thought that Dr. Donovan looked confused, puzzled, and rather put upon. He did not have his usual air of controlled confidence. She hoped that this was because he was beginning to doubt his own position on the issue.

"Thank you all for attending tonight," Donovan began. "You may, or you may not elect to read the literature that Dr. Engelman so kindly gave us. Decisions such as these should not be made in haste, but should be given your most attentive consideration. I should be glad to assist any of you who may still have questions.

"As the hour is growing late, and most of you

will wish to leave for home, I feel that private conferences with each of you would be the best solution. If you should make the decision to consider this protocol, I wish to see you before you sign the final papers for enrollment. Good evening."

Ruth was no longer surprised by Donovan's statements; he certainly was not in favor of change. The fact was clear.

Larry rose from his chair and held Ruth's for her. "Well, what did I tell you? He's going to try everything in his power to keep things at the status quo."

"Larry, I just can't see what it is that makes these people so smug and so sure of themselves. Can't they recognize that we have been failures to our patients for this very reason? Engelman is offering women a reasonable, well-established alternative to a radical mastectomy. Why the hell does he continue to insist upon keeping to these antiquated ideas?" Ruth asked.

"Sweetheart, I told you before. It's politics on the one hand, training on the other, and the God almighty buck on the upper hand."

"I still don't understand completely, Larry."

"Look, when those guys were in medical school, William Halsted was their God. Why should they give up on firm beliefs and years of training for something they have no assurances about?" Larry asked her.

"Because these people have shown that the radical mastectomy is antiquated! The survival rates are equal for all of these newer, less devastating treatments. One hundred years of precedent which includes needless amputation after needless amputation, is an issue that has to be addressed. We, as physicians, owe this to ourselves, as well as to our patients," Ruth retorted.

"Ruth, are you aware of the money factor here? If the surgeons give up a piece of the pie to the radiation therapist and the medical oncologist, there is all the less for them. Besides, they get more money for a radical than for a simple mastectomy, more money for a simple than for a partial, and nothing if you go into interstitial implants! Come on, Ruth, realize the dollar game."

They walked toward the parking lot together. For a few moments there was a silence between them. Ruth was trying to digest what Larry was telling her without feeling disgust for some of her colleagues. If he was correct, then physicians were killing patients needlessly, for profit.

"Donovan didn't look too good when I took him to see Janet Doyle today. She's the model who refused the surgery and now, three years later we are trying to save her life with local radiation and systemic chemotherapy. And it's simply because the two surgeons she consulted told her that she had no alternative to amputation. That's death by neglect! No, Larry, that's wrong. It's murder by neglect!" Ruth said loudly.

"Ruth, that's medical practice here! Get that much through your beautiful head. I've been here at Memorial longer than you. . . ."

"And what, may I ask, is that supposed to mean?"

"It means that I am a lot more aware of the feelings and attitudes of the administrators and the Board of Trustees."

"And who the hell are they? The Board is made up of men who are in large corporate businesses, bankers and the like. Tell me what they know about medicine?"

"They know nothing. But they run the business, and that *you* should know. This community hospital has conservative policies. Leave the experiments to the universities."

"You sound more like Dr. Donovan than an intelligent physician, Larry. That really shocks me. Where is your human side, or did you lose that when you came to Memorial? Did you trade it in for a seat among the majority conservatives?"

Larry had always been sure of his status as a doctor. He thought he was a good one, good to his patients, considerate of the policies of the hospital and the other members of the staff. Ruth was putting him on the defensive. He didn't feel that he deserved to be there, no more than he deserved to defend the position of others.

"Ruth, let's change the subject for a while, okay? Why don't we go out for a drink?"

"Sure, Larry, I feel rather keyed-up anyhow and a drink will help me settle down. Where to?" Ruth inquired.

"There's a small disco-bar near my place. Let's give it a try. My residents tell me it's good. Of course, they are a little younger and their eardrums are used to the blasted music. I enjoy the dancing, anyhow. Do you?"

"I never had much time for that, Larry," Ruth answered. "I always had my head in some book or another. There wasn't much time, and now I feel that I have even less."

"How did you ever get into medicine anyhow?" he asked as they got into his car. "A pretty woman like you must have had quite a social life, and yet you've managed to remain out of the mainstream of husband and family. Since your father isn't a doctor," Larry wanted to know, "what was the influence?"

"I had an uncle who was a wonderful internist. He had the most bearing upon the decision. He was so proud when I decided to go into medicine. None of his children wanted it, and I guess he wanted to be a mentor. He took me under his wing and encouraged me. Another factor," Ruth admitted, "was my great need to prove myself to my family."

Larry swung the car into the parking lot. He got out and held the door for her. She tried to let her defenses down for just an evening and enjoy male company. Ruth had to work hard at being dependent.

They took a booth toward the back of the tavern. The lights played havoc with their eyes so that any contact was impossible. A waitress, scantily clad, approached them.

"Ruth," Larry asked, "what would you like to drink?"

"A gin and tonic will be fine," Ruth said, directing her glance at the waitress.

As they waited for their drinks to be served,

Larry said, "I was going to ask you if you had signed up for that medical conference in Montreal. It sounds exciting, and I especially love to do that city in the spring."

"No, Larry, I haven't as yet. I'd like to, but the program at Harvard takes precedence. I'm going to study the interstitial implants for at least a month. My residency training program is also up for accreditation soon and I want to have everything well planned for the Board. That means many crash hours with the residents."

"Wow! If your program is coming up for evaluation then you had better cool things between you and Donovan. He's the big man around here, remember."

"The Board of Radiation Therapy will be evaluating my worth and my program, not Donovan's personality rating sheets, Larry. They are a lot more progressive, and I am sure that their wish is to see our specialty in a strong position, too," Ruth answered.

Larry reasoned that she was right. The Board would probably favor expansion in the field. He was going to speak, but Ruth spoke first.

"I asked Mark Fenster to see Janet Doyle today. I have to discharge her soon. I don't know what the future will be for her, and she's all alone. I hate the feeling of 'throwing a patient out,' Larry. And I feel that Donovan was especially hard on her today. He wanted to prove a point to me and he used her. I felt ashamed for myself that I allowed it but I didn't think that he would be so cruel. He prodded her as much as he could, hoping that she would admit she was sorry that she had not submitted to the radical three years ago."

"What did she say to him?" Larry asked.

"That she'd still do it the same way all over again. She expressed no regrets. She even came back at him, telling him that she was well aware that the radical cured only a small number of patients. She didn't feel that she could have lived with the grief of amputation."

"To each his own. I can't refute that. I've seen sure bets turn treatment failures in no time, while bad cases took a turn uphill and continued all the way to recovery. It is a chancy situation," Larry admitted.

"Enough of my patient problems. I'm sorry I burdened you, Larry. I just wanted to know what was going on in other parts of the hospital. I'm very concerned and confused myself after tonight's program."

"Confused?"

"Oh, no, Larry. I'm not confused on the new treatment methods. I'm very much in favor of looking in new directions. And all the research seems extremely promising. My confusion is in how to sway Donovan and the others to begin work in this area. He really laid it on me today, and I think that even if I do take the training with Dr. Hillman, he'll see that I don't get the machinery to carry out the procedure," Ruth told him with a slight tone of resignation.

"Cheer up, dear. Tomorrow's another day and another battle."

Ruth looked at her watch. It was late, and she

had to be in early. She would be at the Tumor Board meeting if only to hear Jim Hayes speak.

Ruth decided not to invite Larry in to her house when he drove her home. He could take it to mean she was being aggressive. At least that's the way she saw it. More time with him would tell her more about her feelings. They said an easy good night.

Chapter 3

Sarah Roget's room was located on the fourth floor of Memorial Hospital. Her window faced the dreary courtyard, hardly a pleasant site for someone in her frame of mind. But she had requested a private room for her two-day admission. Tomorrow she would be going home. She had already decided that. She was sick of hospitals and of the physicians who manned them.

"Goddamnit," she mumbled to herself, "I'm ready to face the illness and face what I must. Why do they have to make the fool's attempt to give me added years? I've had good ones, and perhaps some bad ones, but I'd rather go out on my feet singing, then on a stretcher croaking!"

She threw herself onto the bed. There was something farcical about being ill when you didn't feel sick! Time, time, time, it was all a matter of time. And Sarah thought she used hers well and wisely. That is why and how she had managed to accomplish so much in a relatively few years. Now, in her forties, she could enjoy the limelight of her fame as an artist, indulge herself in lavish material objects which pleased her, and entertain a vast array of friends in a very continental style. She had attained what she wanted out of her life.

"Radical mastectomy," she had said to the surgeon when he first told her that the lump in her breast was probably malignant. "There will be none of that for me, doctor, and you can take that as a final answer. I don't believe in amputating breasts."

"Mrs. Roget, I think that you're being unreasonable," he advised her.

"Listen, doctor, in plain English; how would you like to live without balls? Do I make myself clear?" she snapped at him.

"This is an entirely different question, Mrs. Roget. A prosthesis takes care of the way you look, and it can be very adequate," he remarked sharply.

"About as adequate as a cyclops when I'm in bed with a man, doctor. Put that in your book of jokes!" Sarah growled.

"But it's your only chance, and I feel that it's a good one," the doctor told her.

"Good, my ass. I've read your medical literature on breast cancer. The survival rates don't look promising to me. So please spare both of us your 'statistical data.' I know it. And what the hell do you think my life would be like if I went along with that surgery? I'm an artist, I do large metal and stone sculpture. What mobility would I have in my arm when you surgerize me to that extent?

Very little, doctor. I've seen the effects."

"But you can live and do other things, Mrs. Roget," the surgeon told her.

"Yeah, you're right, doctor. I can get a second opinion or I can take my own life now!"

The doctor was aghast. Sarah hadn't intended to shock him, but she meant what she'd said. In a matter of minutes she had fled his office.

Independence of mind, ability to guide one's own destiny, and a great deal of personal dignity were innate in Sarah's character. She was a self-made person with a strong will to live, but only so long as *she* determined how she would like to live. The diagnosis of cancer had only accelerated her pace and accentuated her already determined desire to be the sole guide of her destiny. Her husband and children were well aware of this. But they had not come up against the problems involved in the possibility of Sarah's potential actions. She spoke a lot about the right to self-termination after her mother's prolonged death; she had even written a living will. Whether or not it would be applicable in the eyes of the law was another point. But Sarah did not care. She would never endure what her mother had suffered, and she would not put her family through the horrible ordeal of watching a loved one tortured for the sake of another day, another week.

Sarah was ready to sign her "resignation slip" when her husband insisted that she seek a second opinion.

"Sarah," he pleaded, after a few weeks had passed and she seemed back to herself. "See another doctor!"

"I don't care if I see another doctor! There are no real cures for cancer. You act as if I'm fighting a common cold. This is ridiculous. I'll live until I'm ready to die, and you know that. If this doctor was right, then I'll know in due time what my course of action will be. If he's wrong then I have nothing to worry about."

"But I'm concerned. Please, for my sake, see someone else."

Jim Hayes was suggested to her as a "second opinion" surgeon specializing in cancer of the breast. She made the appointment to see him. After the usual amenities, examinations, and history were squared away, Dr. Hayes had spoken to her in his office. He took time with her, not like the other physician had. He seemed positive about his attitudes toward her illness and offered her hope for a possible "cure." Sarah still felt pessimistic despite all of this.

"Dr. Hayes, I wish that I could consent to the radical mastectomy and feel 'right' in my own mind about the outcome. But, you see, I know the odds are not in my favor with a strong history of cancer in my family. My attitudes are influenced by my past as well as yours are by your medical training. The quantity of my years is not as important as the *quality* of my years. This is probably difficult for a physician to understand," Sarah told him.

"Suppose I look into a less radical procedure combined with radiation therapy? Do you think that you could consider this, Mrs. Roget?"

"I have heard of the simple mastectomy, doctor. I realize that there may be gains here, but I don't feel that I trust radiation as yet. And all of this is so time-consuming. For what end, doctor? Five years at the most?"

"Today medical oncologists are employing adjuvant chemotherapy, and I feel that the trials are promising," Jim added, trying to reassure the woman.

"I'll go ahead with the biopsy, doctor. But you must be honest about the tumor pathology. I understand that it's possible to know, in many cases, from pathology alone whether the chances are good for cure."

"That's been a theory that hasn't been tested long enough for us to be sure as yet. However, it is more valid when we consider these 'indicators' with pathology of the entire area involved. That's why I want to do a complete biopsy, Mrs. Roget," Jim pleaded again.

"I'm sorry, doctor. I refuse the radical. I will permit a biopsy, and give some thought to the simple operation. But my gut instincts are to say 'no' to all of it."

Ruth awoke to the sound of her alarm at six a.m. She took a warm shower, dressed, and gulped a cup of coffee. Her mind focused on the Tumor Board meeting and the possible problems that were likely to be stirred up with the presentation of Jim Hayes' patient. She wanted Sam Ray, her junior staff physician, to be there with her. Sam was the type of man who had to hear everything directly from the source. Ruth didn't object to this; she respected him for it. Sam made sound judgments. He complemented her in many ways which added balance and leverage, to the climate of the department. When Ruth had first hired him for the position, she had wondered how he would feel working for a female chief. It was not easy for a man to find himself "below" a woman in rank, taking rather than giving direction. But Sam had adjusted quickly. They didn't agree on everything, but then again, find two doctors who do! They were both good listeners as well as learners; they found they could share information, discuss procedures, and split the teaching and conferences with efficiency. To Ruth that was miraculous. The jealousy that she had expected from their differences in rank never occurred.

And Sam, she knew, enjoyed working with her. He never felt that he was working *for* her. He respected her as a teacher and admired her as a physician. She knew he thought she was also a good sport, a quality that Sam found to be a rarity in women physicians. He had come to Memorial directly from training at a university center. Ruth allowed him to use his expertness in the areas in which he excelled. She imagined that Sam thought that some day he would be taking her place. He probably figured that a good-looking, bright woman like Ruth Simson couldn't remain single for long. Ruth laughed that one off.

Sam was looking for status as a physician. The money aspect of the profession was not foremost in his mind. He had married a woman who had money, and she spent it! It was a dazzling and different way of life for Sam, who had been the only son of immigrant parents. They had sacrificed everything for him, footing his bills through college and medical school. He was grateful that he now had some money to give them some rewards in their old age. But their greatest reward had been his fulfillment of *his* goals. From that, they, too, gained stature. Sam had little to worry about other than his job, and that certainly gave him pleasure. His wife, busy with her personal activities, gave him space to grow. Ruth knew he was counting on growing, on making it to the position of chief.

An hour later Ruth knocked on Sam's door on her way down the hall.

"Come in."

"Only me, Sam," she said as she opened the door all the way.

"You're early today," he said, looking at his watch.

"Tumor Board, Sam. You didn't forget?"

"No, as a matter of fact that's why I'm early this morning. We should be in for a heated debate . . . after the way you took on our chief of staff."

"News travels fast around here."

"Always. Especially when some bloody noses are in the offing. Drs. John Davis and Bruce Thompson have a position to defend; you, I, Jim Hayes, are the opposition."

Ruth looked a bit dubious. "Hospital talk, like my session with Donovan, why am I the last one to know about these things?"

"Because you're always racing around at a frantic pace, Ruth. You have to listen carefully for the undertones."

"You mean the gossip?" Ruth asked carefully.

"No, I mean the currents. You can almost tell from the emotional climate of a hospital when factions are forming. Just take the dining room. Now there's the place to see the action. . . ."

"Okay, Sam, that's your arena, not mine!"

"You're on alone this morning, Ruth. Both of us can't leave. We're stacked high with new patients," Sam advised her.

"But Sam, you're the one who always wants to hear everything firsthand!"

"I trust you, and your memory. I'll still be working here when you get back," he said, laughing.

"You're sure you won't quit if things don't go our way?"

"Between you and Jim Hayes, things will begin to move ahead for the therapy department. I'll be patient. And that's what you'll have to be, Ruth . . . a little more patient. Don't get all worked up. You'll never win the battles that way."

Ruth smiled. She knew that Sam was aware of her outspoken and rebellious personality. That was another arena in which Sam balanced her; he never allowed himself to be provoked. He didn't lose his patience quickly, as Ruth often did.

"You're right, Sam. I'll harness my impatience."

"Are you taking any of the residents with you?" he asked.

"Can you spare Tom this morning?"

"I think so. For a short time, anyway."

"Good. I think that Tom needs some experience with the political aspects of hospital life. He'll be on his own soon."

"That's something else we'll have to . . ." Sam's words ended abruptly when he became aware of someone listening at the door. Ruth had left it slightly ajar.

Larry knocked quietly, then entered. "Well, a meeting before the big meeting!"

"Just to get the record straight!" Sam said, rising from his chair to greet Larry.

Larry motioned to him to sit down again. "Don't let me interrupt. Stay where you are, Sam. I was just looking in Ruth's office for a moment. When I didn't see her there I was curious."

"You didn't think I wasn't going to show this morning, did you?" she asked.

"Certainly not, Ruth. How about a cup of coffee before the inquisition . . . rather the meeting?"

"Great." Ruth got up from her chair. "Sam, just tell Tom to meet me in the conference room, please."

"Absolutely." He turned to Larry. "Watch out for this woman today. She's overstimulated."

"Don't worry, Sam. I'll save that for the evening." Both men had a hearty laugh. Ruth thought it was at her expense. She just didn't have their sense of humor at seven-thirty in the morning.

"It's time for my exit," Sam said with resignation. "Have fun!"

"Sam," Ruth called, as he was making his way

toward the door, "Don't forget to tell Tom to meet me at eight."

"Straight away, chief!" he replied, giving her a salute.

Ruth and Larry took a small table toward the back of the doctors' cafeteria, well out of hearing distance of the crowded areas. Ruth wanted to talk to Larry about the patient whose case Jim Hayes would be presenting at Tumor Board. She knew that Jim and Larry were close friends as well as associates. If anyone had insight into the problem, it would be Larry. But Ruth also knew that Larry did not invite her for coffee to discuss hospital business. She'd have to be cautious in her approach. She planned her attack while he ordered their coffee.

"Larry, what's the trouble with this patient of Jim's?" she inquired.

"You'll hear about it at the Tumor Board meeting. I don't want to spoil your surprise," he answered.

"Surprises are the last thing I need today, Larry," she begged.

"I only had a few minutes to speak with him this morning. He was in early to prepare the presentation with the radiologist. God, Jim goes at such a pace I often wonder how he survives," Larry told her. "Did you know that his wife is also a physician?"

"No." Ruth realized that Larry was once again getting off the track that she wanted to pursue.

"She's not practicing now. They have four little ones at home. I guess that Jim has a lot of responsibility on his shoulders. They both worked damn hard putting themselves through medical school," Larry said.

Larry intended to speak about this for a while longer. Marriage and a family were more to his liking for social conversation. He wanted to get closer to Ruth. He liked her very much, liked the way she moved, talked, and her intelligent mind. She stimulated him.

"Then Jim can't afford to compromise his position here, can he?" Ruth was asking.

"No, he certainly can't, Ruth. And Donovan is giving him plenty of flak with this case. Jim even feels there are stirrings among the conservative surgeons to push him out!" Larry told her confidentially.

"Why would they want to do that? He's probably the most competent surgeon on the staff," Ruth said.

"Because of the commotion he's arousing with the patient he's presenting this morning. Funny thing, that story. All the while that Jim and I were talking about her I had absolutely no idea who the woman was. You know how we tend to keep patients anonymous? But at the end of our talk he told me her name. It rang a bell; I had met the woman, socially that is, and now I'm really interested."

"One of your long string of female followers, Larry?" Ruth said cuttingly.

"Are you being intimate or exhibiting jealousy?" he asked smiling.

"I'm being Ruth. But I'm sorry, Larry. Please go on."

"Sarah Roget is the patient. She's an artist by profession. I met her many years ago. When I was a resident I had been invited to her gallery opening, and like the scrounger I was at the time I decided to go for the free wine and cheese. But I loved her work and I bought one of her etchings, a lovely piece.

"She had gone to a surgeon at another hospital a while back when she discovered a lump in her breast. He performed a needle biopsy and the pathology was positive for malignancy. She refused his treatment, which was the radical mastectomy; she claimed that the surgery was worse than the disease. Anyhow, her husband was really concerned and he finally pushed her to get a second opinion. She was given Jim's name through the medical hot-line. Jim subscribes to that program, but, of course, he could only perform the full biopsy. . . ."

"That's the stinger of the program, Larry. The second-opinion man can never perform the surgery. But I guess that it's important to keep the program free of abuse. What was the pathology report?" Ruth asked.

"Positive. The cephlo-caudad and lateral views on the mammogram revealed a mass density in the upper outer quadrant. There was calcification seen within one centimeter of the mass. But there was no evidence of skin thickening or nipple inversion. Jim thinks that he has an 'early' and 'localized' cancer in this case.''

"Then what seems to be the problem?" Ruth asked.

"The malignancy is in this gal's dominant side. Jim is hoping to get approval for a simple mastectomy, but since he can't perform the surgery he'll have to solicit the other surgeons," Larry told her.

"I can guess the rest, Larry, spare yourself the energy. Donovan won't approve the procedure, and most of the surgeons on the staff are his little Indians.''

"You got the picture, baby. Jim is going to bat for a patient that isn't his, and he's putting his professional position here in jeopardy," Larry continued.

"But I'm willing to bet that this single case is not the entire issue, Larry. It's more than Sarah Roget; Jim is fighting a principle. The problems with the cancer field today, especially breast, are so numerous. We just don't have the answers; we only have theories! And the fights and dissension among the various factions have done nothing for the patient," Ruth added.

"You're right. It only adds to the patient's burden. The patient suffers.''

"What is Jim planning to do if he can't get her a simple? Will he send her to a cancer clinic?" Ruth asked.

"If he can't get another surgeon here at Memorial, then for our purposes the woman goes untreated. It will be up to her to seek out another institution, and from the manner in which she's been responding, I don't think she'll carry it any further."

"So," Ruth said, feeling uneasy, "we give her the death sentence by neglect. Is that progress, Larry?"

He was beginning to see some light on her side of the picture. Nothing was black and white. Sometimes the causes and treatments for a specific disease remained in the dark, in that vast "gray" field for a long time. Perhaps the only way to go now with cancer was intensive study and trial. But would the public stand for this? Could the medical practitioners be persuaded to see other viewpoints?

"No, Ruth, it's not progress. Not yet. But these things take time—especially changes in medical policy and practice."

Ruth glanced at her wrist watch. She had five minutes to get to the meeting. "Thanks for the coffee, Larry. Are you going to the meeting?"

"No, I have a consultation and teaching rounds. I'll await the news from you later," he replied.

"Then I'll hear from you?" Ruth asked smiling. She wanted to hear from him.

"You bet," he told her as they went their separate ways.

Tom Kresh, senior resident, joined Ruth at the meeting. Ruth liked Tom, although they sometimes clashed. Their personalities were so much alike; fire met fire when they argued a point. They challenged each other frequently, but these were intellectual challenges, hardly vicious arguments.

Tom's background was unique, and Ruth admired him for his courage and stamina.

Tom came from another world than most middle-upper-class physicians. He had been brought up by his mother, who had divorced her husband when Tom was quite young. Tom was more trouble than most kids, but then again what does a child do who is left to run loose in a big city ghetto? Ruth recalled vividly the first interview she had with Tom after he applied for a residency in her program.

"And what are your long-range goals, Dr. Kresh?" Ruth had asked him.

"To alleviate some human suffering, Dr. Simson. I've seen too much of it!" he told her in his straightforward manner.

"And tell me, Dr. Kresh, what do you know of human suffering straight out of medical school?" Ruth asked. Most residents knew nothing, but Tom Kresh was the exception.

"A hell of a lot. I'm thirty-six years old, Dr. Simson. I came up the hard way. I had no father; I dropped out of school at sixteen and joined the Navy. There was nothing else for me with any appeal. I served my four years. When I got out I was equipped to do absolutely nothing. I drove a cab."

Ruth sat back in her chair and smiled. She already liked the man. "And how did you get into medicine?"

"I had the good fortune to meet a woman who was in a rush to work. She was a schoolteacher. On her way to school she had a flat tire and she hailed me down. She was beautiful and interesting. I asked her out to dinner that evening. Within three months she became my wife. Her goal was to get me a high school diploma. She worked with me at night and I passed the qualification exam easily. I applied to Columbia University and they let me in for a year as a nonmatriculated student. My grades were very high, and after the first year I became full-time. I gave up my cab, and my wife gave up everything!"

"You're a lucky man, Dr. Kresh. I admire your wife's sacrifices as well," Ruth said.

"I went on to medical school at Columbia University, then a rotating internship at P. and S. And now it's my turn to do the work in the family. My wife is about due to have our long-awaited first child!" he said, smiling.

"Well, congratulations, Dr. Kresh!" Ruth said. "You're hired."

And Tom proved to be an excellent choice. He was intelligent, personable, and conscientious, and had made his way to chief resident in three years. Tom would be in practice at the end of the year, and Ruth wanted him to have exposure to hospital politics, an arena in which she knew he would be an effective physician.

"I hear we're in for some fuss this morning," Tom whispered, leaning his head close to hers.

"Let's hope for our sake and the sake of humanity that there is no fuss, Tom."

"I only wish we had more of the young bloods here," Tom remarked.

The meeting commenced. Jim Hayes was about

to make his presentation. A radiologist on staff was speaking quietly with him near the podium. The radiologist sat down and Jim began.

"Good morning; an early good morning. I'm glad to see such a large turnout today. I'm not quite sure why we have so many in attendance, but I'll take a guess that the attraction was not the free coffee and doughnuts. . . ."

Tom leaned toward Ruth. There was a short period of laughter among the physicians. "I guess that there's nothing like some humor to warm up an audience."

"He's going to need that sense of humor in order to survive at Memorial. Remember, Tom, he was a university-trained physician," Ruth commented.

Jim continued. "This thirty-nine-year-old white female presented a tumor one centimeter in size. Mammogram indicated a neoplasm with slight calcification; no indication of skin thickening or nipple inversion. She was seen by a surgeon at another hospital who performed a needle aspiration and a needle biopsy. That biopsy showed a malignancy. She was offered a radical mastectomy. The patient refused for many reasons, however they are not pertinent to the case for our purposes. The important thing to remember is that she refused treatment.

"As a 'second opinion' subscriber, I was consulted. For this reason I shall not be able to take her as a patient. However, presentation of her case is extremely important because I feel that there are many surgeons at Memorial who are capable of offering this patient options to the radical mastectomy.

"Because of the nature and location of the mass, I feel that the patient would benefit from just a simple mastectomy."

Ruth could hear small talk begin among the audience. They were charging themselves up for what was coming.

"It does not make sense to remove the muscles underlying the breast, or the supraclavicular node chain. As you realize, this would leave the patient with a concave chest, perhaps severe lymphedema, and probably lack of mobility in her dominant arm.

"In a recent article in the *Surgeons Journal,* a group of researchers in a midwestern city reported five-year findings in over a thousand patients receiving simple mastectomies and radiation therapy. When compared to a similar group receiving a radical mastectomy, the results were equal. There seems to be justification for limited surgery, employing radiation therapy as an adjuvant. I propose that this patient be given the option to have a simplified operation. My fear is that she will otherwise go untreated. Thank you."

Jim Hayes took a seat. There was commotion in the room. Dr. Thompson asked to be recognized.

"My fellow physicians. I too have read this study in *Surgeons Journal,* and I am sure that many of you have seen the article. I ask you to bear in mind two loopholes in that study. First, it was not a randomized clinical trial. How can we be sure of their patient selection? Secondly, we are becoming aware of the fact that patients are leery of the carcinogenic effects of x-rays. What could be the rational basis for employing x-ray therapy if there was the potential danger that it could *in*duce that which we hope to *re*duce?"

Jim Hayes was up from his seat. His face appeared stern, ready to take on the task. The meeting was turned into a battleground. The floor recognized his appeal to answer the surgeon.

"Fellow physicians, we are not here to fight, but to make intelligent inquiries and facilitate answers to medical problems. Unfortunately, our predecessors were unable to conduct many randomized clinical trials due to lack of funding. But we must still consider the work that has been accomplished, and to overlook this study would be a gross mistake. If you are saying that the simple mastectomy plus radiation therapy versus the radical mastectomy does not make sense because you are gaining nothing, then gentlemen, you know nothing of the female species or the physical and psychological problems of your patients living with cancer. Where you have saved a part of the human body you have gained a great deal!"

Applause rang out from the small radical group. Ruth Simson and Tom Kresh were among them. Ruth got up slowly and beckoned to Tom. They left the conference room together.

"What do you think, Dr. Simson?" he asked.

"Let's get closer to the department before we discuss it, Tom. The walls have ears here," Ruth replied.

They took the first elevator down.

"Tom, ask Dr. Ray to come into my office for a moment, will you? You can take over for a while. The schedule is tied up with new patients today."

Tom nodded, and left Ruth's office door open. Sam Ray entered within moments.

"Well, how did it go?" Sam asked as he entered the room, closing the door behind him.

"We didn't stay for the entire meeting," Ruth began. "Jim presented first and that was what I wanted to hear. I'm glad that I took Tom with me. The residents need more first-hand experience in this arena."

"How did the presentation go, and what was the outcome?" Sam questioned. Ruth relayed the story, adding the fact that nothing had been solved, that the staff had displayed mixed reactions.

"But, of course, now this woman must wait for one of the other surgeons to come forth and agree to do the simple surgery. Who is there, Ruth?"

"I don't know, Sam. I just don't know," she said pensively. "I can tell you this for sure, it won't be Thompson or Davis! Thompson made himself perfectly clear this morning. He's opposed to radiation therapy."

"He doesn't even know if he's opposed to radiation therapy, Ruth. If you ask me that's a load of bullshit. What he's really opposed to is called loss of income!"

"How do you go about educating a pocket?" Ruth asked.

"You don't. Thompson is deep into gambling, Ruth. It's like a disease with him. He needs money."

"And what's Davis's motive?"

"Also money, but probably not for the same

65

reason as Thompson. What the hell does it matter? Their financial problems aren't helping medical practice, and that's our problem."

"Well, there are still a few others around, Sam. That's probably where our best chances lie. Those that aren't really committed to a procedure but would like to practice good medicine are the souls that are redeemable!"

"From your mouth to God's ears!" Sam said, looking toward the ceiling.

"God may give us strength, Sam, but we still have to do the work. That's what we're here to do. I really want to discuss the role of adjuvant radiation therapy with you. If the simple mastectomy becomes a reality then we may hopefully look forward to enrollment in the protocol."

"That's in the future plan, Ruth. First the procedure must gain some acceptance."

"I realize that, Sam. But this is the time to act . . . when there's action going on. I don't want to wait! When things calm down we won't have support. Everyone will go back to the old ways and then we won't have our foot in the door. That's why I want to use this time wisely. We're going to present the interstitial implant, now, while the heat is on!"

"Wow!" Sam replied, throwing his hands in the air.

"Save the reactions, Sam. What do you think?"

"I don't know what to think! I know a lot about them. I keep up with the studies and journal reports, but there are very few places that are doing implants, Ruth. We aren't even sure how they work."

"But the studies indicate that they *do* work, Sam. That's the important issue. And for patients like Sarah Roget and Janet Doyle, this may be the answer."

"Did you propose that to Donovan yet?"

"Yesterday morning, and he nearly hit the ceiling. But I did take him to see Janet. He wanted to be convinced that some women were still sticking to their decisions regardless of whether they became failures."

"Maybe it's best to see the outcome of the surgical war before we begin to throw x-ray beams into the picture," Sam suggested.

"Perhaps you're right, Sam, but I am going ahead with that course I applied for next month. I will get the chance to spend time with Dr. Hillman and review the patient data firsthand. We have to understand a procedure and exhibit expertise with it before we can convince the hospital to condone it."

"I'm with you on it, Ruth. I'd like the opportunity to share the experience with you, but unfortunately we can't go together. I'll have to request it sometime in the fall."

"I think that we should share this with the residents, Sam. They should be doing as much research as possible while we are learning how to teach them," Ruth stated emphatically.

"Fine. I'll get to the literature tonight and have it · prepared for the teaching rounds in the morning."

"Thanks, Sam. That will save me the pleasure

of asking Donovan for my papers. He still has them, so perhaps that's a plus."

"I only wish sometimes that we had more women out there who were afflicted with the disease fighting for their rights. After all, aren't we keeping sacred knowledge from them?" Sam asked.

"Of course we are, Sam, but go find the women to fight! Most of them are so overwhelmed with fear when they hear the word *cancer* that they don't have the emotional energy to search for alternative answers to their problems. And the media haven't been kind to us either."

"Just think of what it would do to the breast prosthesis business if we were to save breasts!" Sam laughed at his bit of humor.

"They'd fold; the government would have larger unemployment rolls; and as someone said to me just yesterday, that's the politics in cancer!"

Chapter 4

Woody Doyle took a seat at the cafeteria counter. He was tired, tired of the routine that he had followed for weeks now since Janet had become ill again. The counterman approached him hurriedly. Every stool in the seedy-looking parlor was taken. It was twelve-thirty in the afternoon.

"The same?" the man asked politely.

"The same," Woody replied. As he waited for his order, Woody noticed a foursome of young nursing students across the room. One of them reminded him of Janet—the Janet he had met thirteen years ago. It was a day in spring, much like today, he remembered, when he had gone to Steve Gross's modeling agency to make inquiries on behalf of a client. Normally Woody left the scut work to one of his staff, but he had decided to do this job himself out of deference to Steve. He and Steve had been fraternity brothers in college, and although they had not kept a close relationship when Woody went on to law school, he still saw

Steve every now and then at reunions. His client, a model, was filing a suit against Steve for a broken contract.

He had entered the building and was making a quick step toward the elevator when he first saw her. Her strawberry-blonde hair was pulled severely back from her face, showing nearly perfect features. Her tight slacks and sweater exhibited a beautiful figure. The girl was striking. She entered the same car as he did, and when she left the elevator at the same floor, Woody felt a shiver pass through his body. He'd like to meet her. She entered the door of the modeling agency, and he followed.

The girl continued on her way and was soon lost behind a closed door.

Woody turned to the secretary at the desk. "Tell Mr. Gross that Mr. Doyle is here, please."

He took a seat and waited, hoping the girl would make an appearance; she didn't. Within a few minutes he was sitting in front of Steve Gross.

"It looks like you're doing pretty well, Steve," Woody commented. The decor of the office was modern, somewhat garish, but nevertheless impressive.

"Hey, buddy, remember we sell beauty here. That's our commodity."

"That was evident from the minute I walked into the building today!" Woody said, his mind still on the girl.

"You haven't had a chance to see anything yet. All the best is behind the scenes."

"The girl I followed up to the office . . . is she

one of yours?" Woody asked.

"Which girl?"

Woody went on to describe the girl. Steve threw both arms up in the air and laughed. "A mere child, my friend, but one of the best in the business. You still have good taste."

"What's her name?"

"Janet Walker. She's only part-time now, but I hope to get her full day soon. A face and body like hers should be in the best magazines."

"I'd like to meet her, Steve."

"Come on," Steve said, rising from his chair. "She's in action now." They walked out of the office in the direction of the camera room.

"One more take, Miss Walker," the camera man yelled.

Woody continued to stare at Janet. He thought she was the most striking woman he had ever seen.

"She's almost finished," Steve said, interrupting his thoughts. "Want to wait around?"

"Absolutely!"

When Janet emerged from the dressing room, Steve introduced them. Woody asked if he could take her home.

"He's straight, Janet," Steve assured her. "An old fraternity brother."

"On your say-so, Steve," Janet agreed, picking up some school texts she had left on the bench near the camera room. She turned to Woody and handed him the books, put her jacket on, and the two of them left the agency.

Woody at once felt foolish carrying the books. It made him aware that there must be at least ten years' difference in their ages. Janet read his mind. "How old are you?" she inquired, "or shouldn't I ask?"

"That's all right. I'm thirty-one. Is that too old?"

"Not at all. I rather like older men. They're more respectful. What do you do?"

"I'm a lawyer. And a bachelor," he added quickly.

"You're safe!" she exclaimed. "You know in this business a girl has to be awfully careful. You wouldn't believe how many men hang around modeling agencies looking for fast pick-ups. And most of them are married."

"I guess that's one of the hazards of being beautiful."

"That's why I'm trying to keep my scholarly image. It serves a good purpose, although I don't think I'll stick with it."

"Why not?" Woody asked. "There's nothing wrong with an education."

"Because I can make a hell of a lot more money in modeling. It's as simple as that. Steve has offered me full-time work soon and I want to take it." They were in the car and leaving the parking lot.

"Where to?" he asked.

"In the direction of the university. I have a small apartment that I share with another girl."

Roommates spoil plans, Woody thought. He'd ask her out for dinner.

Janet was at no loss for words. She was comfortable with men, that was obvious to

Woody. She had her life's history capsulized within the forty-five-minute ride home. She had been orphaned young, brought up by an aunt now deceased. She liked to have money and thought that capitalizing on her beauty was the surest way to attain her goal. Woody thought that for a girl of twenty, she was conscientious and well-directed. She had been alone most of her life which probably made her grow up quickly. Janet had experienced her share of sorrows and hard luck at a young age. He felt a compulsive need to cater to Janet, serve her, and fill her life with happiness. Janet needed to be protected.

By their fifth date, Woody grew anxious about her roommate. Jane kept the "Good Housekeeping" rules and never invited him in. It became a source of frustration for him.

"Where to tonight?" Janet asked as she closed the car door. He had picked her up after work.

"My place. We'll cook dinner together."

"So, now we get serious!"

"That's right. I'm dead serious and tired of your roommate!"

Janet gave her roommate notice and moved in with Woody. Although she agreed to live with him she didn't want to be forced into marriage. Woody consented to wait until she was ready. He only wanted to be in her company, be seen with her, and delight in the benefits of living with her. He gave her everything to keep her happy.

Yes, that was the beginning. He was still staring at the student nurse when the counterman pushed the paper bag at him.

"Pay the cashier," he said, interrupting Woody's thoughts.

"Thanks," Woody said as he left the cafeteria. He walked across the street to the hospital.

He tried to concentrate on the Janet of today. His thoughts were lingering on the girl of yesteryear, and that wasn't reality. "But what is reality?" Woody asked himself as he entered the hospital elevator. He knew the answer. "Reality" was that Janet had left him; he had never abandoned her. For years now he had constantly asked himself whether she had ever really loved him, or whether it was the circumstances of their married life that had caused her to leave him after ten years. He pressed the button for the fourth floor.

Woody knew that his feelings of guilt were a catalyst in the situation. He still felt responsible for the fact that Janet had never attained motherhood; never felt a complete woman. But what else could he have done, given their circumstances? He couldn't find the answer; he only knew that the compelling need to protect her was still there. He felt resigned to do what he felt was right; take care of her as he had promised to do from the very inception of their relationship.

When he got off the elevator at the fourth floor he quickened his step in the direction of Janet's room. The door was closed, and respecting her privacy, he knocked.

"Come in," she called out.

Woody entered the room, trying to smile. He

knew that what he had to say to her would have to be said properly with just the right tone in his voice. Would she suspect that he felt sorry for her? Surely, it would occur to her that many acts are performed for the sake of pity. Or could Janet truly believe that she was still the princess he had idolized, despite the fact that they had been cruel to each other more times than he cared to remember? Oh, shit, he thought. Did it really matter? Nothing mattered so long as he could have her back. And then things would be "right" again; "right" in his duty to her; and "right" in the eyes of the church, which had never given sanction to their divorce in the first place.

"Janet, I've made some decisions. They're not rash. I've given everything a lot of thought," he said as he approached her. She moved her legs to make some room for him at the foot of the bed. He realized that she wanted him close to her.

"What's on the great attorney's mind?" she asked, taking the milk shake from his hand. "I'm starved here!"

"I want you to come home—to be my wife again," he said, almost choking on the words.

There was silence for what seemed like hours to Woody. Janet did not respond to his proposal. Then tears formed in her eyes. She leaned against the pillow with a look of total despair on her beautiful face. "Woody, how could you ask that of me now? You're in the prime of your career; I fucked up your life more than once. I don't know what the future holds for me!"

"Janet, no one has assurances for a future. But

we do have a chance to begin again. That is, if you still care for me."

"Of course, I care for you, Woody. You know I do," she said, taking his hand. They shared a few moments of warm comfort, a sharing of deep human feeling which both needed desperately.

"Then if you care for me, Janet, there's the answer. We should be together. We need each other."

"Woody, please give me time. I need to think this through; I want to know the course of my illness. I don't want to go home an invalid. That's not the way to start over again."

"You can't go home alone, Janet. You need to have someone with you!" he cried.

"There you go again, Woody, playing father with all the answers. Do you want to care for me like a child again, too?"

"No, I don't think so, Janet. I've had a lot of growing-up time. I guess you have, too."

"Yes, I have. And if I do go home with you Woody, things will have to be different. We never led an honest life, did we?"

"'Honest' is not the word I would choose, honey. 'Realistic' would be my choice. It was unrealistic for me to fence you in. It was unfair of me to think I could be everything to you. One person can't deliver a lifetime of happiness and fulfillment to another person. You needed other people."

"Our life as a family never turned out that way, did it?" she asked. But the answer was interrupted by a nurse at the door.

"Time for x-ray, Mrs. Doyle," she said, strutting into the room. "Oh, I didn't realize you had a visitor. He can stay. We'll be only a short time."

Woody helped Janet on with her dressing gown and into the chair. "I'll be here when you get back," he reassured her as the nurse began to wheel her down the hall. He kept his gaze in her direction until the two disappeared. Woody walked in the direction of the nursing station.

"Excuse me," he said to a nurse who sat at the desk, buried in patient charts. "Would it be possible for me to speak with one of Mrs. Doyle's doctors?"

"Just one moment, please, Mr. Doyle. I'll have to check her chart. Do you know who her in-house physicians are?"

"No, I'm sorry. I don't."

"Why don't you have a seat in the waiting room. I'll see what I can do."

Woody found an oversized armchair and sank into it. He glanced at the table in front of him, hoping to find a magazine he had not already read. As he flipped through the stack he saw that everything was outdated by more than six months, true to the pattern of hospital waiting rooms and clinics. He tried to relax, get away from his uncomfortable feelings. It seemed impossible. The depression was slowly setting in; now he would face spells of self-incrimination. Why the hell was he trying to make things right between himself and Janet? She had made herself very clear three years ago. Was he opening up old wounds? Did he feel guilt and responsibility for her illness? "No," he thought. "I am not responsible. There is nowhere to assign blame for illness." But, on the other hand he felt responsible for the mode of living that Janet had become addicted to. She had been an excellent fashion model, and he had been very proud to possess a beautiful woman. She gave him much pleasure from her beauty. It seemed that they had everything going for them as a couple. Except for the one thing they wanted to share: a family. After four years of yearning for a child they had begun to consult one physician after another.

"No problem, Mrs. Doyle," they all assured her. "Just go home and relax!"

"Woody, I'm sick of their advice. 'Just relax, and you'll get pregnant!' That's absurd. There must be something wrong with me."

"Janet, they must know what they're talking about. It's just taking longer than we hoped." When her periods were late she would call in sick, and Steve would excuse her absences, delaying her work until she reluctantly had to conclude that she was once again not pregnant.

Woody remembered their summer vacation at the Cape the year before she finally left him. She had missed her period again, but this time she seemed to exhibit all the signs and symptoms of pregnancy. Her breasts swelled, she ate constantly, and her face had a "flush" of motherhood. She spoke her dreams to him as they sat together on the beach.

"What do you want, Woody?"

"Just you and a healthy baby."

"No, really. You probably want a son. All men

do. But if you told me that then you would feel guilty if he turned out to be a she, wouldn't you?"

"I'll take anything, honey. So would you. If it's ours, we'll love it." They sat in silence for a few moments. Both were lost in thoughts of their child to-be—their flesh and blood, their baby to hold and love. Janet interrupted the silence.

"I'm starved, Woody!"

"It's only five, Janet. I made dinner reservations for seven-thirty."

"I'll never make it. Can I get a sandwich now?"

"Why don't you go back to the room and relax. You've had too much sun for the first day. I'll bring you a snack at the cottage."

He was erect just watching her beautiful body pass him. How he would love to nourish her with his love. But that was impossible now; she might be pregnant. He couldn't take the chance of upsetting a pregnancy. He dove into the cold water. His erection shriveled.

Woody bought a sandwich and a coke and strolled happily toward the cottage. As he approached the door he heard screaming and the pounding of fists against the wall. He rushed to open the door but it was bolted from the inside. He screamed to her, but she would not respond. Her sobs were stings in his ears.

"Janet! For God's sake open this door!"

She finally did. When he saw the traces of blood on her thighs he knew what had happened. "Dear God. Why did this happen to us?"

He tried to comfort her, but she refused him and pushed him away from her, as if he were to blame.

"My baby! It's gone . . . gone . . . I can't stand this torture anymore!" She threw herself on the bed, banging her hands against the headboard. Woody grabbed her by the shoulders and tried to calm her, but she screamed louder. Finally he realized what he had to do to bring her out of the crisis. He smacked her fiercely across the face. Suddenly the hysterics subsided. She was exhausted and defeated. Only soft sobs were audible.

"I was so sure, Woody. This time I was so sure . . . why me?" she asked him.

"I don't know, honey . . . I don't know. Jan, why don't we consider adoption? You know that many times after adoption women conceive their own children. And we could have a child to love and care for if we don't ever have one of our own."

"I want *my* baby! I want to be a woman. Every cow can have babies. Why can't I have mine?"

The doctors confirmed the fact that she never had been pregnant. "There is such a thing as false pregnancy, Mr. Doyle. Your wife, given her psychological condition, is a prime candidate. She wants a child very much. With her irregular periods it's possible for her to fantasize."

After that episode, Janet changed. She wanted to prove her own femininity and sexuality. She felt robbed, cheated of her motherly role. She would get her attentions elsewhere. She severed her ties to their married friends. She loathed being in the company of wives with babies in their arms, when she, Janet Doyle, could not have one.

Janet quit her job with Steve's agency that summer. She needed the time to herself to feel sorry for herself and angry with Woody. But there was little to do in the suburban Long Island environment but watch mothers stroll the streets with their children. She decided to go back to work in the fall.

"I took a job today, Woody," she told him one evening.

"Why the heck did you do that? We don't need the money."

"Because I'm bored as hell with this neighborhood!"

"Are you back at Steve's?" he asked.

"No. I need a change. I look better without my clothes."

"In front of me, yes. In other places, no."

"I'm going to do centerfolds now," she said carefully. She knew that he would explode, but she didn't really care.

"Janet, you can't be serious!" he cried, getting up from the table. "That's for other women, not my wife."

"And what's wrong with your wife? Why shouldn't I do something with my body? That's my talent. Besides, this is more of a challenge," she retorted.

"Listen, Janet, you're the decent young wife of a prominent lawyer. I don't want your body up for public exhibition!"

"It's not good for anything else, is it?" she screamed at him.

"That is the screwiest way to show off talent, Janet. If you want to model then go back to Steve's."

"Why? Because you trust Steve?"

"Yes. At least there I know you're doing work."

"Don't you trust me?" she asked.

"I don't trust the people involved in the kind of work you're after. They're a flaky lot at best. And you know that."

Janet pursued the job despite Woody's objections. She enjoyed the attention she received from other men. She substituted this for Woody's love. He became depressed, while she felt angry. One night he wanted her very much and she pushed him away, professing a headache.

"I'm your husband, Janet! How long am I supposed to go without you? Are you getting all your love and attention at work?" He was immediately regretful for the accusation. But it had coursed through his mind so many times that it came naturally to his tongue. She turned on the lights and sat up in bed glaring at him.

"It's *you* who can't have children. *You*, not me. You never once, in all this time, had yourself checked. You dragged me from doctor to doctor for years, Woody. You put me through torture! And for what? Tell me, my big sexual hero! Go screw yourself!"

The pains were knife wounds in their relationship; each one was torn to shreds, neither knowing how or where to approach the other. Communication was closed. Their life as husband and wife ceased to have meaning, and each felt the burden of guilt. Woody tried to absolve himself of guilt by seeing the doctor. It seemed ridiculous to him, but, nonetheless, Janet was right. He had never had a sperm count, but he was relatively sure that he wasn't sterile. Wasn't it usually the woman?

"Mr. Doyle," the nurse had said, "this is Dr. Howard's office. We received all your test results back today and the doctor asked that I phone and let you know that everything is normal."

"Hold on a minute. Does that include the sperm count?"

"Yes, Mr. Doyle. It does. Have a nice day."

Nice day, Woody thought. That was a laugh.

His cigarette burnt his index finger, snapping him back into the present. "Damn habit. When will I have the sense to give it up?" he asked himself. A young woman in a white coat approached him.

"Mr. Doyle?"

"Yes, doctor?" It almost sounded as if he were asking a question about her profession, rather than answering a call. He could not quite get used to the idea of women physicians, although he knew they were an up-and-coming breed.

"I'm Dr. Simson, Mrs. Doyle's radiation therapist," Ruth told him, taking a seat on the sofa. "The nursing station advised me you were here and looking for Janet's physician."

"I appreciate your coming, doctor. I realize how busy you must be. But I think I have some plans to make and I would like to solicit your help."

"What can I do for you?" Ruth asked.

"Exactly what is my wife's, or rather my former wife's, condition? You know that we have been divorced?"

"Yes, Mrs. Doyle told me. I have been her doctor

for a while. We've discussed her problems quite candidly," Ruth admitted.

"Is she bad, doctor?"

"I can't really say, Mr. Doyle. I know that to the layman that sounds evasive, but it's not meant to be. It's the truth. Cancer is a difficult disease to determine. And breast cancers come in so many garden varieties that it's almost impossible to give an accurate accounting. Honestly, we just do not know enough."

"I appreciate your honesty, doctor. It's refreshing."

"I try never to make promises I can't deliver, Mr. Doyle, and Janet's health is too precarious at this point for me to be accurate. However, I feel extremely hopeful. I just had her down for x-rays. If the radiation and chemotherapy work, she'll be in a state of remission. I consider this a good possibility. We have to hope that her lungs will respond to this drug."

"And what will she be like if she doesn't respond, doctor?"

"Why be pessimistic, Mr. Doyle?"

"Because I have to make plans for her, doctor. Janet has no family. I'm it! And I want to remarry her."

Ruth looked shocked; she knew she did. Janet was a lucky woman to have a man so devoted. In most instances, cancer tended to tear families apart. Ruth had seen it many times in her patients' relationships. Role changes caused stress; others had to pitch in and take over the responsibilities of the sick loved one; there was always one martyr in the family who later tended to make everyone, including the patient, feel guilty. "Boy, what I sacrificed for all of you!" was the classic line. It was refreshing for Ruth to hear something to the contrary. Woody seemed to know what he was talking about; what's more, he expressed intense interest in her patient.

"Mr. Doyle, I greatly admire your courage. I don't know your motives, but I do know from Janet that you're a daily visitor. If she doesn't respond, it may be a straight downhill run for Janet. It will take a lot of caring and devotion on your part to do this. We'll try everything possible to keep her comfortable, but palliative care is all we can offer if treatment fails."

"I see," Woody said. He was obviously lost in his thoughts. Ruth was feeling uncomfortable. She was embarrassed for Woody, who was trying his best to sort out the needs of two assaulted human beings.

"Doctor, I was going to ask you when you were planning to discharge Janet. I know that she isn't going to stay here indefinitely."

"I was planning to complete my therapy by next week. Dr. Drieden will have to give us the word on her response to the drugs. If it's good I don't see any reason why she can't go home as soon as she likes. She can get around fairly well, and much of the listlessness and fatigue that she's experiencing are due to the radiation therapy; they'll disappear shortly."

"Could you put in a few good words for me, doctor?"

The beeper rang; Ruth was grateful. Saved again.

"That's my call, Mr. Doyle. I must go. I'll try my best to help if I can, but I do try to encourage my patients to make their own decisions," Ruth told him as she began to walk toward the elevator.

"Thanks," he said, looking helplessly into the busy corridors of the hospital.

Janet returned to her room after her visit to the x-ray unit expecting to find Woody waiting for her. He wasn't. She assumed he had gone to the cafeteria for some lunch. Feeling exhausted from the therapy, Janet lay down and dozed for a while. She ignored the stack of letters and cards still sitting on the tray. Well wishes from her colleagues; fan mail from the magazines. It didn't matter, she realized. None of it mattered anymore. Friends and acquaintances had become penpals. They absolved themselves of guilt with their steady stream of correspondence. No one came to visit. That might be too painful! "Isolation," she thought, "is the mark of the condemned! Those condemned to cancer!" When she heard a knock on the door she didn't get out of bed. There was no need to be formal with Woody. "Come in."

She was surprised to see a total stranger.

The stranger was more surprised. Mark Fenster knew the woman in the bed. He had seen her many times in the magazines he chose to read alone, before he put them on the waiting room tables. She was even more beautiful in person. He liked women without all the make-up, with a more

86

natural beauty. And Janet Doyle possessed just that. Only her thinning hair detracted from the picture, he thought.

"You look almost as surprised as I do," Janet said candidly.

"I am," Mark told her. "I know you."

"Not me. Just my pictures. Correct?"

"Correct. May I come in?"

"Sure, I was expecting a visitor. I guess he was detained."

"I won't take much of your time, Mrs. Doyle. I just stopped down to see you on Dr. Simson's referral."

"That was most kind of her. She seems to be taking care of my social life these days," Janet remarked.

"I'm Dr. Fenster, one of the few psychiatrists on the staff," Mark said, pulling a chair closer to the bedside.

"Well, thank you for making the time, doctor. Hospitals are lonely places. Seems all I have is mail," she said pointing to the unopened stack on the tray. "Dr. Simson was here this morning with another doctor. I've never seen him before, but he gave me the impression that I was an exceptional case."

"How so?" Mark asked, knowing about Donovan's tactless remarks. He, too, had thought Janet Doyle to be exceptional, but only in her beauty. Mark had been a womanizer in his younger days, and his wife had told him that his marriage to her would give him stability. It did. He became an exemplary psychiatrist; he didn't screw around with his patients. He had straightened out. But that didn't keep him from fantasizing, or from reading the girlie magazines.

"He made me feel terribly uncomfortable about my treatment decisions, Dr. Fenster. But perhaps you can understand that a woman in my position couldn't cope with a radical mastectomy."

"I do understand, Mrs. Doyle. Amputation is difficult to deal with. But let's discuss you now, not two years ago. How are you getting along?"

"I think I could use some help in finding direction. There are many pressing problems. I'll have to make many changes in my life and that frightens me, doctor. I don't know where to begin."

Mark sat back in the chair, ready to listen. "Start anywhere. It really doesn't matter; the pieces will fall together eventually. What's troubling you at this moment?"

"My future," she told him. "I'm very uncertain about the future."

"How so, Mrs. Doyle?"

"About my health, naturally, but there's little I can do about that myself. I have to depend upon my doctors for help."

"From what I have read in your chart, things seem to be going along well," Mark assured her. He always promoted a feeling of confidence among his patients facing crises. Mark held to the theory that a healthy mental outlook often aided the course of recovery from illness. That was not to say that cancer patients were cured by healthy minds; certainly not. But it seemed to him that those who were able to accept their problems well, to assume some responsibility for their bodies, to make their time count, and to reconsider their priorities where necessary, seemed to do better than those who immediately threw in the towel. Mark was a fighter and he liked to see that spunk in his patients.

"That's just it, doctor. I will be going home soon and I have to make some big decisions. My former husband has been visiting me every day, and just an hour ago he asked me to marry him again," Janet blurted out.

"And how did you respond to him?" Mark asked sitting straight up in his chair. He wanted direct eye contact with his patient.

"I told him I wasn't sure. It's so new to me. True, Woody and I had some good years, but somehow the bad ones always seem to stand out more in one's mind. I was a bitch to him because I was looking for myself, and when I couldn't have what I wanted, I acted like a spoiled child." Janet told him of her inability to have children and her decision to leave teaching, Woody, and everything that represented the stable, conventional life.

"And you're surprised that he wants you back?" Mark asked her.

"I can understand things only from a 'sick' point of view, perhaps a little from a religious angle. But the whole thing seems to boil down to guilt and pity, doctor. For what other reason would he want to be tied down to a terminal patient?"

"Mrs. Doyle, we are all terminal. I can't say that

I don't agree with your reasoning. It's all perfectly logical from where you stand. And, of course, you're going to need some time for all of this to affect you. I think that once you begin to speak with your husband—your ex-husband—a little more intimately, you'll begin to realize his motives."

"And what else could they be?" Janet asked puzzled.

"If he has never remarried, Mrs. Doyle, the chances are quite good that he loves you very much. We all make mistakes, take and give abuse. It's human nature. A mature outlook makes us realize our own roles, and then allows us to piece life together again."

"Are you saying that I should consider marrying him, doctor?"

"No. That will have to be a decision based upon your responses. You must have the confidence that you're doing this for the right reasons, and then have the energy and desire to make it work. I'm sure that neither of you wants to face failure."

"I don't want to make his life miserable again, doctor," Janet said as she began to sob. "He doesn't deserve it! God, he was always so good to me; perhaps that was the problem. He gave into my every wish and when I didn't get what I wanted I blamed Woody."

"We all make mistakes, Mrs. Doyle. I'm sure your husband is feeling just as guilty in many instances. Marriage is a two-way road, and usually where there's trouble both partners have put in their share of bad behavior. Why don't we all get together? Perhaps we can all work this out?'' Mark suggested.

"Oh, would you really, doctor?'' Janet asked eagerly. "Woody and I have needed counseling; that's a fact. It's only unfortunate that we didn't seek help when our marriage began to go sour. Perhaps we could have salvaged it the first time around.''

"That's in the past, Mrs. Doyle. Let's look to the future. You seem very eager for the three of us to work together. I think that shows your interest in Woody.'' Mark was aware that he was pushing his personal preferences upon his patient. He was very conventional, so his patients told him. He liked to see homes intact; children living with their parents. In general, he felt himself identified with an image of a more stable past in this liberal decade of the Seventies. Divorce, suicide, drugs, and alcohol were all too much a part of the modern American scene. By his personal moral standards, Mark Fenster condemned all these, rarely taking exception. One could rightly conclude that, although middle-aged, he was a man who believed in the traditions of the past.

"Suppose I'm a failure on this treatment regime, doctor? That's the other side of the coin. Then what does Woody have left but a life of grieving! I fucked up my own life, but I can't play with his anymore. Excuse my language, please,'' Janet said, somewhat surprised. She hadn't meant to allow the word to slip from her tongue. She was too comfortable with Dr. Fenster.

"That's quite all right, Mrs. Doyle,'' he assured

91

her. "The word 'fuck' is in my vocabulary, too."

"Thanks. I didn't mean to sound coarse. And please, call me Janet."

"It's more professional for me to call you Mrs. Doyle. In that way I give you the same respect you give me when you say Dr. Fenster. It gives us an equal level. But watch out! When and if I ever call you Janet, it's a crisis! The familiar is meant to shake the hell out of you."

"Here's hoping you continue to call me Mrs. Doyle!"

"Is that the ex-Mrs. Doyle, or the new Mrs. Doyle?"

"I think I'm going to give it a lot of thought."

"Good," Mark said, rising from his chair. "I'll drop in to see you again tomorrow. Say about lunchtime?"

"Yes," Janet exclaimed. "That would be fine. Woody is usually here by noon."

"Good. I'll see you both then. And should you need anything before that time, ask the nurse to call my office. I always answer when service rings through."

"Thanks for caring, doctor."

"That's my business, Mrs. Doyle, as well as my nature."

Chapter 5

Ruth went up on the floors to see her in-patients, and check charts. The elevator stopped at three and Larry Stein entered. They were alone.

"Well, Ruth, how did things go this morning? I haven't had a chance to speak with Jim."

"Classic, Larry. But that was to be expected. Where are you going now?"

"To the x-ray reading room. I sent a patient down for a G.I., and I need the results before the reports are typed. And you?"

"Just to check on some charts. Seems we have more in-patients this month."

"If you're going up to six, I'll stop and have a soda with you in the solarium. I think that's the most beautiful part of the addition to the hospital. Did you ever just sit up there and stare out at the view? Inspirational . . . positive for thinking; especially in the middle of the day when everything seems to be piling up."

"Actually, I could use the break. And, no, I've

never taken the time to see that room. I think it's been open only a month." They got off at six.

"Here, this way," Larry told her. His arm was around her shoulder, and he was leading her in the direction of the solarium. Surprisingly, there were only two patients there. The glass-enclosed room was filled with flowers and plants, no doubt from patient contributions. They sat on the sofa out of listening distance of the patients. Ruth commented on the view of New York City.

"Yes, it is really beautiful and exciting. I don't think any other American city offers all that New York can. That's probably why I never looked elsewhere for a job," Larry told her.

"There's little that would tempt me either, Larry. But I must confess that during the long gray winter I occasionally look south. By the time I get finished reading the vacation folders, the spring has come and I put them away for another year."

"What would you like to drink?" Larry asked, walking toward the soda machine.

"Pepsi light, thanks."

"You really have your share of depressing work, Ruth," Larry told her, opening both pop cans. He handed Ruth hers.

"I don't find it terribly depressing. Actually, today there are many more patients benefiting from radiotherapy. And remissions are always possible. It's enough for me to see that much being accomplished. Now we can begin to look to the quality of time for these people."

"How did you ever make the choice? There are so many residencies that seem easier."

"You mean less draining?" she asked.

"I guess you could say that. Working with 'healthy' patients."

"Honestly, I did get into radiotherapy by default. I had wanted dermatology when I was an intern. But there were very few openings at the time. Was neurology your first choice?" she asked.

"Yes, it was. But, of course, women usually make choices for reasons other than men do in medicine."

"I guess in some way you're right. I tried to select a specialty that would give me the time to pursue motherhood—the great American Dream. In radiotherapy I am hospital based; I have a junior staff, and a residency program. They really can't miss me too much!"

"But you haven't gone after that great dream, have you?"

"Oh, heavens, no!"

"Tell me something about your father."

"Dad worked in the garment center, here in New York, for most of his life. He died recently. He was a very colorful and lovable man. Oddly, he was born on the Mississippi River. . . ."

Larry began to laugh. When Ruth described her father there was so much love and admiration in her voice, so much excitement and happiness in her expression. He wondered whether father love could ever be replaced by husband love.

"You really are stuck on one man, Ruth. I'd hate to compete with his image!"

"Larry, he was a prince in every way. He always took my side when I argued with mother. And that was all too often. We never agreed on anything, still don't. She worked all her life, in excellent positions. Now she's in Florida, bored to tears and constantly complaining."

"Tell me about the uncle who was so instrumental in getting you into medicine?"

"He was another delightful person. He had two children of his own; neither wanted to follow in his footsteps. When I began to do well in the sciences, he began to speak to me about being a doctor." Ruth sat back, reflecting upon the image of her uncle. Then she asked Larry about himself. She hated one-sided conversations.

Ruth felt a slight flush come to her cheeks. "No. I guess I deliberately haven't let the right man come my way as of yet. As you know, I feel a very deep commitment to my work, Larry."

"You're an exceptionally competent doctor, doctor!"

"Thanks. You're not bad yourself!"

"Now that we've elevated the egos, tell me more about your start as a doctor. Was it gratifying? I recall your saying that you wanted to prove yourself to your family. Did getting that shingle do it?"

"In a great many ways." She wanted to change topics. "Where's your family, Larry?"

"I've only my mother and one sister. Mom still lives in Brooklyn—against my advice. I would have liked her to move to a better neighborhood, but I could see her point of view. When my father passed away she had only those friends who surrounded her for years."

96

"Does she live alone?"

"Yes. My sister is married and has two children. She's quite a little spitfire, my sister. She got married directly after college and put her husband through law school. She even managed to hold down her job after the kids were born. It takes a long time to become established in a law practice. But they're doing well now."

"My sister is also the productive, or rather the *re*productive member of our family. She has six children!"

"Hurray for sisters!" Larry exclaimed.

"Well, they keep grandmothers in business. That's for sure."

"Well, beautiful, it's time for both of us to work. I'll see you later."

"Wait, I'll go with you. I have to get back to four. Mrs. Parrish is having trouble with her diet."

"Have you ever looked underneath the lids on the meal trays? I did once, Ruth, and that was enough to put me off," Larry told her as they parted on the fourth floor.

Dan Driedan, M.D. sat in his inner office drinking his cup of coffee. He needed the break, the thinking time, alone. His position at Memorial Hospital had always been a respected one. He had begun practice there twenty years ago as an internist, and his patient following was good. Late in the Sixties he began to see more and more cancer patients. His interest in their management, through the use of chemotherapy, grew. In 1972, he had asked for a grant to begin research on these agents in order to develop tests on human tumor cells. The inaccuracy of animal modalities was a constant source of concern to him. He had presented the research program to the hospital administrators. Even Donovan had a hopeful outlook. But the grant was running out; Dan was losing time. If he didn't show progress there was little chance that it would be renewed.

The phone rang before Dan had a chance to glance at the *Medical News*, a publication that he read every week. He was looking, searching, for others who were into chemotherapeutic experiments.

"Dr. Driedan," he said softly.

"Well, Dan, how are you? Are things moving there in your department?" It was Alvin Donovan's voice.

"Oh, fine, Al. Yes, things are moving."

"I don't mean with the patients, Dan. I'm talking about the drug experiments," Donovan told him.

"There's some progress, Al. But I need more time. In vitro experiments are a difficult problem." Dan realized what Donovan was getting at. The grant. It was up to the hospital administrator, who relied upon the chief of staff for advice, to evaluate the program.

"You know that grant of yours is up for renewal in the next few months, Dan. And, of course, you will have to submit the progress reports for review."

"Al, I need time. I'm getting close. We just can't afford to lose now!"

"There's a lot of rumble here on the cancer therapy, Dan. It is going to be scrutinized very carefully. I have upheavals in the surgery department, the radiation unit, and I can't afford to have any more. I need to see some progress somewhere." Donovan was pleading, and at the same time threatening. Would he really pull back on the monies? Dan, being rather uncertain, pressed his case.

"Look, Al, this is a very difficult task, but it's going in the right direction. We're losing cancer patients every day to unorthodox therapies, downright hoaxes! We have to work on the legitimate programs and make them better. It only takes publicity to make a hoax look attractive, but it takes years of labor to make a 'cure' that's time-tested a reality."

"Time is what we don't have, Dan."

"Well, we've got to make it, Al. Here's another one. Right here on my desk this morning; *AMA News* is running the story. Some practitioner in the Far East claims to have come up with a cure for cancer. Says it's so simple someone can make it in their kitchen. And listen to this, and I quote: 'The world will be astonished to learn how simple cancer is. It is caused by a deficiency of a single substance which can be corrected by injections!' Bullshit."

"I guess there are many of those out there, Dan. But we can't stop them."

"Al, there are three thousand cancer patients from one state in this country who are being treated in this so-called clinic. They're being ripped off by someone who doesn't really give a goddamn. Another laetrile experience. We can't ignore this. To turn our backs on legitimate research and allow this nonsense to continue is condoning these quacks."

"You think it will dig into our pockets?" Donovan asked.

Money talks, Dan thought. Donovan was worried about money, Dan was worried about losing patient treatment time.

"Al, maybe we've lost the essence of medicine here; involvement in people's lives! We've got patients copping out on these unorthodox treatments, and you're worried about the income loss?" Dan said, trying to control the impatience in his voice.

"Well, it's not exactly that, Dan. . . ."

"Sure it is, Al. It's the money game. There are a lot of hungry staff members, and you know it. If that's the way you want to present it, then it *is* so. If we don't discover the 'cure' that's legitimate then we'll lose money. Think of it that way if you like. I'm thinking of the human beings; you concentrate on the money!"

End of conversation, Dan thought, putting the receiver back on the phone. Donovan wasn't any more a physician today than he was twenty years ago. The money aspect and the showmanship were foremost in his mind.

It made Dan angry to know that many of his fellow doctors came to medicine only for the financial rewards. The intangibles—concern, attention, worry, and emotion sharing, none of which could be measured—seemed important. He tried to forget the conversation, to read some *Oncology News,* and gear himself up to more time in the lab. Then he saw the article:

"German Oncologist On the Track
To Chemotherapy Testing."

There was his counterpart! Here was a connection. Perhaps a possibility of working out a technique. The report sounded so promising that Dan immediately wrote out a memo for his secretary. He needed the German reports. Sharing information, working in units just might make this a reality. He felt somewhat less defeated by lunchtime.

Chapter 6

It was rather late and Ruth thought she'd skip lunch. But her usual breakfast of juice and coffee was not holding her over today. Besides, she needed breathing time away from her department after the morning's explosive events. Ruth had the feeling that there were going to be radical changes in hospital policy, and when that happened the staff tended to form factions. The real question from which all these events were arising was becoming quite evident to her: Was surgical oncology really a specialty unto itself?

She pondered the question as she entered the doctors' dining room. She took a tray and went to the salad bar, added a cup of coffee, and paid the cashier. She was looking around for a table when she saw Dan Driedan and Jim Hayes stand up and wave to her. She was glad for some company of her own kind and she walked in their direction.

"I think that your presence here closes the circle on the cancer team, Ruth," Dan said smiling.

"You sound like our formal chief, Dan."

"We were just discussing the case that Jim presented this morning, Ruth. Have you any comments to make?" Dan asked. The three had a hearty laugh.

"I have more than 'comments' to make, gentlemen," Ruth said. "But uppermost in my mind right now is the big issue, the one which is inevitably going to give rise to the rumbles in this hospital as well as all institutions caring for cancer victims."

"And what *is* that ultimate issue, doctor?" Jim asked.

"I think that all this confusion and commotion about treatment modalities, patients' rights, informed consent—the whole basket of oncological problems, will lead us to ask ourselves whether surgical oncology is a separate specialty."

The two men chuckled at her remark, and Ruth asked indignantly, "What's so funny about it?"

"Nothing's funny, Ruth. You have just hit on the issue we were debating. When I was a resident at the university," Jim began, "we were involved in various cancer studies. Many of the surgeons had advanced training in the field, and were committed only to oncology; research and teaching were their specialty. But the dilemma here is that there is no special board certification in surgical oncology, and in a general hospital like Memorial you have every surgeon on staff performing cancer surgery, when in fact he is simply a general surgeon. You just can't win these guys over to new ways of thinking, Ruth. It's virtually impossible for them to move from square one. They haven't the education." Jim rubbed his hands in disgust and frustration. "Maybe I don't belong here," he added.

"Jim, you can't give up at this point," Dan advised. "What you can potentially do for patients and physicians at Memorial no one else on staff can accomplish. What they have to begin to realize is that you are not about to steal their patients. That's not the issue. Your presence here is one of leadership!"

"And whom do you propose that I lead, Dan? They resist me, both me *and* change! If you think I can use my training here you're mistaken, Dan."

"I think it's a matter of time, Jim. Dan is right. Our concepts of the biology and treatment of cancer are only beginning to make changes. There's always a lag between research and education. The management of the cancer patient is going to become more and more complex. But that doesn't mean we give up. Other hospitals are starting to step up their pace, and Memorial will have to go through the regular growing pains, too. Harness your impatience, Jim," Ruth advised.

"If anyone should be impatient now, it's me!" Dan stated.

Ruth and Jim looked at him in disbelief. To them, Dan Driedan was probably the most patient guy in the world. He was older, wiser in hospital politics, and generally had the capacity to keep himself composed in the light of stress. And he was a dedicated researcher, a respected man in medicine.

"What is your problem?" Jim asked. "I didn't think that men like you ever got into trouble."

"It seems that I'm in the pressure cooker now, friends. And I'm not enjoying one minute of it!"

"You always got along well with everyone, Dan. Why would anyone want to give you flak?" Ruth asked.

"Because it seems that the money people in medicine control research. That's an established fact. When these people don't see progress on the data sheets the monies are withdrawn from a specific project. This morning our chief informed me that my oncology grant might suffer if I couldn't document sufficient progress," Dan told them.

"They can't do that, Dan," Jim cried. "It's no secret that chemotherapy is a hit-and-miss thing. And what you're trying to accomplish takes time and patience—two attributes that you lend to medicine."

"Don't argue with me, Jim. I know that. Every day I encounter another therapy hoax; each time I take it like a dose of poison. I know why patients feel a state of hopelessness. I can understand their flight in search of magicians. But how do I make men like Donovan realize that this is inevitable when you cut legitimate studies?" he asked.

"Is he threatening to cut off the grant?" Ruth asked.

"Well, he certainly won't go to bat for it. The only way I hit him was in the pocket!"

"How did you do that?" Jim asked.

"I told him that the less we know about chemo,

the more we'll see patients going for hoaxes. And that, my friends, happens to be true."

"How much longer does the grant run?" Jim asked.

"Another six months. But I may have hit something this morning. There's a researcher in Germany working on a similar project. I'm going to try to make contact. Perhaps we each can contribute to the other's findings, and get this project on firmer footing."

"Oh Father," Ruth said in a most theatrical tone, "do guide us through these rough times."

"And what rough times are you experiencing, little Princess?" Dan asked.

"I was discussing two issues with Sam Ray this morning after the Tumor Board meeting. First was the prospect of employing radiation therapy as an adjuvant with the simple mastectomy. I agree with Jim; this is our first forward advance."

"You heard the answer this morning, Ruth," Jim told her. "It was very plain that the other surgeons are going to constantly attack us on the issue of large dosages of radiation. They can't sell their patients on the value of the mammogram! Do you think they're going to show faith in radiation therapy? Ruth, you're dreaming! Even I saw that this morning."

"Well, then, let's go back some fifteen years. Long before you or I went to medical school, Jim. In this very city an innovative female physician conducted a study on sixty-seven patients considered 'too far gone' by the medical community to be put to the radical mastectomy."

"I remember that study quite well, Ruth," Dan chimed in. "I was in practice then—internal medicine and a little chemotherapy. But anticancer agents were truly in an infant stage at the time. Being interested in oncology, I followed that study quite closely."

"And the results were astounding, weren't they, Dan?" Ruth did not wait for his response. "This physician treated her patients with supervoltage radiation alone for a five-week period. And, at the five-year mark, fifty percent of these women were alive!"

"That's a remarkable study in favor of radiation therapy, Ruth, considering the fact that they knew so little about it at the time. And, of course, the machinery was not so nearly sophisticated as what we have today. There's certainly been a lot of progress in your department. But it's been fifteen years since that study was published and I don't think we've made progress in teaching these methods. Which brings us back to the initial point of the conversation. Oncology, in all forms, should be a separate specialty, my friends."

"I asked for a leave of absence to study, and I think Donovan is going to try to block it somehow," Ruth blurted out.

"Which course?" Dan asked.

"Harvard. Interstitial implants."

Both men looked at her and laughed heartily. They couldn't resist. Not that what she stated was particularly funny, but they were always amazed at

Ruth's spunk. She was a rebel with force, force from within, and they admired her for it. Ruth was competitive. She would someday make her mark on the condition of medical practice. They only hoped that she wouldn't strangle herself doing it.

"You're a gal with guts," Jim was saying. "I admire you."

"Well, Donovan can't stop me, really. He can just make it difficult for me," Ruth replied. "I'm not intending to cut in on your territory, Jim, but I think that interstitial implants are just as valid for clinical assessment as the simple mastectomy."

"Hey, Ruth, you know me. I'm not opposed to anything that shows promise. That could be a very good option for women like Sarah Roget, or even that model you treated. These women want the entire breast preserved, and they make few concessions," Jim admitted.

"Speaking of concessions," Ruth said, turning to Dan. "What do you think about discharging Janet Doyle?"

At that moment the paging system rang out: "Paging Dr. Driedan, Dr. Dan Driedan. Please call four-oh-eight-four. I repeat. . . ."

"Well, that's obviously me, folks. Ruth, I'll speak with you about Mrs. Doyle as soon as I have the x-ray report. Thanks for the conversation." Dan left. Jim turned to Ruth.

"Have you read over Dr. Engelman's protocol yet, Ruth?"

"No, Jim. I'm afraid I've been pressed for time in the department because of the evaluation coming up," she admitted.

"Don't worry your pretty head about that too much. The board will be concerned with your merits as a teacher, not with your popularity with the administration. You could see from our meeting with Dr. Engelman that being an innovative physician negates your possibilities of becoming favored by the administration. Dr. Engelman isn't exactly Mr. Popularity, at least not in this city. But that hasn't stopped him, Ruth, and it shouldn't stop you."

"Are you trying to advise me to use the protocol to further the position of my department?" Ruth asked, looking very surprised.

"It's exactly what I intend to do, Ruth."

"Engelman's protocol will have a multidisciplinary approach," Ruth responded. She was thinking, now. The wheels were turning. She realized what Jim was trying to tell her. The protocol might just be the place to begin.

"You're right, Jim. Cancer is one disease where we need the team approach. Completely."

"And that encompasses psychiatry, too. I need a little of Mark Fenster on my side with patients like Sarah Roget. She's the kind of patient who's most difficult. She knows everything and she's bent on making all of her own decisions. But I fear greatly for patients like her. Sometimes they take their lives into their own hands, refuse everything."

"Mark has helped me with patients many times, Jim. I have implicit faith in him. Jim, why can't you send a patient like Mrs. Roget to Engelman, or even Hillman?"

"I'm the second opinion doctor, Ruth. My hands are tied."

"Jim, if there is one thing I'm learning from this heated battleground, it's that the patient winds up on the short end of the stick. They are the objects of our medical dissensions. There is no one in this hospital who would prevent me from telling a patient to go elsewhere if I were not at liberty to deliver the service they needed. And Memorial Hospital is not ready to deliver the service that Sarah Roget needs. Every woman is different, Jim. What will suit one woman will not be the choice for another. The patients have rights, too!"

"You're right. We can only offer an opinion. After that the decision is theirs," Jim said taking the last sip of coffee. "I've got to get to the OR, Ruth. Have a good day!"

"I've got my hands full, too. Let's get together another time when we can really hash this out."

"Fine. My wife would love a social evening out. A quiet evening away from four lovely, loud kids!"

"Sounds good to me," Ruth replied.

"Perhaps Larry Stein would like to join us. I'll try to get something together."

"And what makes you think I want to have dinner with Larry Stein?" Ruth demanded.

"Parking lots have ears," Jim said smiling.

"This hospital can be worse than a college dormitory!"

"Conversation often gets dull in the OR, and Larry and I spice things up."

"I hope you haven't picked me apart to the

core," Ruth said sarcastically.

"Nonsense. We just have a good sense of humor, and a good feel for sex!" Jim told her.

"Dirty old doctors!" Ruth admonished him.

"See you later, sexy," he called, as he ran for the elevator.

Chapter 7

Sarah Roget paced the floor of her small private room, reliving past scenes in her mind. She had vowed to herself for many years that she would make a "grand exit" from living at the time that she chose to do it. Now she was facing the reality of a life-threatening situation. Did she really want to give up and end her life? Would that be a cowardly act? Or was she preserving her dignity, and considering the suffering of her loved ones?

Sarah knew her true feelings, and she had known them for a long time. She had seen much suffering in her family. She had cared for a mother who was no more than a vegetable for years, following a stroke. The woman had suffered a double assault near the end of her miserable life, from cancer. Sarah had been responsible for her mother's care; she alone carried on with the daily drudgery of attending to an invalid. Sarah could never leave the poor woman alone, and the expenses of a nurse were more than she could afford. Her father's illness and early death had left her mother destitute. Sarah suffered in those years, not only because she loved and cared for her mother, but because she had allowed doctors to prolong the woman's life when it would have been a blessing to let her go. Now Sarah knew that neither she nor her children would ever suffer those indignities. She continued to ponder the reality of the closing chapters of her life. They would be bound between leather covers for all the world to read, but only after she committed the finale. There was work to be done.

The door opened slowly. Sarah turned from the window to view her visitor. "Mrs. Roget? I'm Dr. Fenster. May I come in for a few minutes?"

"Why not? Seems that everyone else has . . . I must be some kind of freak around this place," she said angrily. "Oh, hell. I'm sorry, doctor! I'm just faced with so many perplexing problems, and all these interruptions aren't making matters better. Excuse my cutting remarks."

"That's quite all right. I'm used to them. People facing crises are usually anxious, and you are no exception. Sometimes it's necessary to let some of that anger out."

"What do you want to know?" Sarah asked tonelessly.

"Just what is the dilemma? If you don't mind talking about it."

"My immediate problem, doctor, is that I would like to get the hell out of this place! I'd prefer a delicious meal with wine and champagne. I'd also like to dance with some good company. Does that sound terribly abnormal to you?"

"It's quite an interesting proposition, Mrs. Roget, but aren't you taking things a bit out of logical order? You've a serious health problem, and that should have priority over other matters."

"Look, doctor, I don't want you to think that I'm pushing you or anyone else here around. Please spare me the ordeal of having you try to reorganize my life for me. Why do physicians feel so compelled to impose their own values on their patients?"

Mark felt that she was putting him on the defensive end of a battle that didn't begin simply with this illness. And he did not want to answer for every physician in this woman's life. "I'm not asking you to reorganize for my sake, Mrs. Roget. I'm asking you to consider an immediate problem."

"I don't feel the way the rest of you do about cancer, doctor. I'm not afraid of death, and if this is the way it was meant to be, then so be it and the hell with these debilitating 'cures.' I don't want to have my breast amputated; I don't want cobalt therapy; and no one is going to force anticancer drugs down my throat! I came here feeling perfectly healthy, doctor, and I'll be goddamned if I'm going to allow all of you to make me feel sick. Can you understand me?" Sarah's voice was filled with emotion.

"Mrs. Roget, I am not a surgeon or an oncologist. I don't propose to treat your body at all. I am here because I do understand how you feel about guiding your own destiny. I will certainly respect your decisions. But sometimes people tend to act irrationally during a crisis because there is a threat to their life. I am a psychiatrist. I want to listen to how you feel, and perhaps help you sort out those feelings so that you can make a rational decision." She was a tough woman, Mark thought. There was no doubt about it! He did not want to persuade her to do something she would regret, but the healing instinct deep within him hoped that he could persuade this woman to give the doctors a chance to save her life.

"Well, then, doctor, if you are a psychiatrist, perhaps we can talk," Sarah told him. She relaxed a bit. "None of the other physicians seem to understand my position. They insist on treating my body without giving a thought to my mind! I only want to live for as long as my constitution naturally allows me. And I want to live in the same style that I have lived for the past number of years."

"And what is that style?"

"I've always lived life to the hilt, one day at a time. I live artistically, creatively, and I enjoy each experience as it comes. My life is exciting. My work and my friends are exciting. I'm not worried about tomorrows when life is to be lived today. And everyone knows how I feel about illness. I've experienced it too many times in my life, doctor. I'm going out with my head up while living it up! My husband and children are aware of my plans, and they don't begrudge me my preferences."

"But don't you feel that you're copping out on them when they need you most?" Mark asked, looking for some reason for her to want to live.

"My husband and I have discussed this at length for years, long before this crisis. I planned to take my own life when I reached the age of seventy-two. That's enough years for me, doctor! My children are grown; they don't need a mother to care for them. And certainly they don't need a mother to care for!"

"Seventy-two is a long way off for you, Mrs. Roget. Perhaps your feelings about self-termination are a bit premature."

"Not at all, doctor. I don't fear death. I fear life with pain and suffering. Cancer will do that to me; I know it because I have seen it! I think I will choose a very creative and artistic death to end a most exciting life. Everyone will remember the happy, vibrant, and talented Sarah Roget, not the ugly, emaciated, suffering cancer patient."

"You know that Dr. Hayes is trying to get some help for you, and it's taking a lot of hard work. He very much wants to see you cured," Mark tried to tell her.

"I realize that, doctor, and I appreciate his efforts. But this was certainly not my idea. My husband wanted a second opinion because he feared that the diagnosis might be incorrect. That doesn't change our minds about cancer. The diagnosis is correct. I realize that the treatment might be different, but I do not think that it will change our feelings. The alternative that Dr. Hayes can offer, although far less devastating than the radical mastectomy, still has many draw-backs."

"Why don't you give it some real thought for a while before making a final decision, Mrs. Roget? Speak with your family again. The fact that your husband wanted a second opinion makes me feel that he wanted very much for you to try the alternative."

"There's no trying with amputation, doctor. Once it's done there's no turning back," Sarah replied.

"There are ways to remedy that. Millions of women have done it."

"And go through surgery again? Never! I'm not going to spend the rest of my days in a hospital bed. I want to feel well and be productive."

"May I stop in and see you again, Mrs. Roget?"

"Certainly, doctor. I don't mean to offend you, or your profession. But my illness is *my* problem, and I want to solve things my way."

Mark Fenster left Sarah Roget's room feeling troubled and badly defeated. How many patients like her had refused treatment? Was the therapy too devastating? Only one who had experienced the illness could answer that. Physicians, in their own defense against death, could not properly assess the effects of therapy upon their patients.

Chapter 8

April 1, 1975

Ruth drove into the suburbs, feeling the fresh air spill through the windows of her car. It was pleasant to spend a sunny spring day away from the sub-basement of the hospital.

It was Friday, generally a good day. The radiation therapy unit of Memorial Hospital rarely operated on weekends; Ruth would have two days to herself, which she badly needed. There were many programs to evaluate and plan for. All of these would have great bearing upon her professional future.

She found Chestnut Street. Now she looked more closely for Janet's address. All of the townhouses were identical. When she saw a few cars parked in one of the drives, Ruth was relatively sure she had the right house.

She parked away from the crowded driveway, as she knew her visit would have to be short. It was still a working day. She picked up the elegantly wrapped gift on the seat next to her and got out of the car. As she walked toward the house she began to feel anxious. Had she and Dan made the right decision in allowing Janet to go home? Was the timing premature? They had weighed the decision very carefully with Mark Fenster. He was the one who had persuaded them that Janet and Woody needed each other, and that Woody provided a support system that Janet had not had throughout her illness. Mark felt sure that Janet would fare well emotionally under Woody's watchful care, and that the value of the love he could provide her during this crisis greatly exceeded whatever could be done for her within the confines of the hospital. Ruth and Dan agreed that Janet could be served on an out-patient basis.

The combined therapies had worked well; Janet's lungs were clearing and lymph nodes were no longer apparent. Ruth reasoned that they had made the proper decision, and she attempted to slough off her anxieties so that she might enjoy the festivities.

"Doctors making house calls," she thought, as she mounted the stairs. That seemed rather odd these days. The door was ajar and Ruth walked into the crowded room. She glanced around trying to find Janet and Woody. This was the first time she had attended a social engagement for one of her patients, but Janet's and Woody's wedding was different.

"Janet," Ruth said, approaching the bride, "you look absolutely beautiful!"

"That's only in comparison to those awful hospital gowns," Janet replied, laughing. "Do you really like this dress?"

"It's lovely," Ruth replied sincerely. And Janet was as pretty as Ruth had imagined she could be. She wore an excellent wig made in a fashion that suited her—sophisticated! Her make-up was amazing, Ruth thought. Janet had been transformed in a matter of days. Except for the weight loss, which was apparent, one would never suspect that she had been so ill.

"Have some champagne, Dr. Simson, please. This is a special occasion. I promise we won't let you drink too much."

"I don't want you to overdo it either, Janet. Remember what Dr. Driedan told you—chemotherapy and too much alcohol don't mix." Ruth said in a whisper. "We'd all like to see you through the ceremony on your two feet!"

Woody walked in their direction with a broad grin on his face. "Well, Dr. Simson, my very favorite female physician!"

"Why, thank you, Mr. Woody Doyle," Ruth said with a smile. She allowed him to play "Sir Gallant" and kiss her hand. Woody was a warm and tender human being, and as Ruth had learned, he was a friend for life to those whom he liked. Ruth was among his "chosen" ones, although she suspected that his feeling for her was simply related to her ability to help Janet.

"Well, what do you think of my bride today? A different woman, *n'est-ce pas?*"

"Absolutely a different woman!"

Woody turned to his bride. "Janet, please go easy on that champagne. I've been watching you and you've already gone beyond the limits for at least two days."

"Come on, Woody; if you don't tell, I won't tell. Besides, we have to celebrate all things bright and wonderful today," Janet begged.

"Janet, your doctor is standing right here as a witness." He took the glass from her hand.

"Honestly," Janet said, turning to Ruth. "He treats me like a child. Not differently than before. But I admit that I appreciate him now. I guess it's all position in life. He cuddles me and cradles me and I love it."

"There's certainly nothing wrong with that. I wouldn't mind having that type of man step into my life, Janet."

"Dr. Simson, you have to be more available! Take it from me; I learned the hard way. If you don't give a man the attention and love he craves from you, both of you suffer in the end. You work too hard. Come, I want you to meet some of Woody's associates. Unfortunately, they all have wives!" Janet exclaimed, taking Ruth by the arm. "There are a few neighbors too, but I don't really know any of them well. Woody's been here alone for three years."

"You'll make friends again, Janet. Real people, not those who abandoned you in a time of need. Are you planning to stay here?"

"I think so. For the time being, at least. I

certainly won't be going back to the type of work I was doing. And this is a convenient location for Woody's suburban office. But I will do some decorating. This is truly a bachelor pad!"

They walked toward a handsome-looking woman dressed in a clerical robe. Janet made the introduction. "Reverend O'Hara, I'd like you to meet Dr. Ruth Simson."

"Well, doctor," the reverend said with a smile, "I've heard more about you and Dr. Fenster in the past few days than you can possibly realize!"

"I hope it was good, Reverend. It's not easy for a physician to obtain a positive rating sheet any-more," Ruth said, extending a hand.

"You have it. I think that this couple owes much of the happiness and peace they have found to both you and Dr. Fenster."

"I'm sorry that he couldn't be here today. Crisis intervention keeps him terribly busy."

"I can testify to that," Janet said, leaving the women alone for a few minutes. She wanted to greet Steve, who had just arrived.

"I think that I should ask Woody to get the guests seated. This will be too long a day for Janet," Reverend O'Hara said.

"I'm inclined to agree," Ruth told her, watching Janet with a glass of champagne to her lips. "She's overdoing the drinking." The two women approached Woody, who was now disengaging the glass from Janet's hand.

"I think we should begin the ceremony," Reverend O'Hara advised. "Can you get the guests quieted?"

"Yes, certainly," Woody exclaimed, looking at the three women. "I feel surrounded by outstanding feminists. My wife and teacher; my minister, and our doctor! Who said that women can't make it in a man's world?"

Janet reprimanded him. "Woody is putting on his comical side for you. Deep down he's getting his chauvinist kicks! There isn't one female lawyer working in his office. I can assure you of that!"

"And feel threatened all around?" he told them. "Never!"

The guests took seats quietly and faced the floral canopy where Janet and Woody stood holding hands. Reverend O'Hara spoke:

"Dearly Beloved: We are gathered here today to reunite this couple in holy matrimony. . . ."

As the familiar service began, guests quieted down. Ruth listened closely.

"Blessed *is* he *whose* transgression *is* forgiven, *whose* sin *is* covered . . . O Lord my God, I cried unto thee, and thou hast healed me. O Lord, thou hast brought up my soul from the grave: thou hast kept me alive, that I should *not* go down to the pit. . . ."

The prayers had been spoken with great emotion which brought tears to the eyes of the bride and groom as well as their guests. The room was filled with a pathos that rarely accompanied such an occasion. Woody turned quietly to his bride, and before delivering his kiss, said, "God, I have always loved you, and I shall until the end of my

123

days." Kiss; applause; no music.

"And now I am your *mature* bride, Woody; not the child I was the first time around."

Woody quickly shifted his mood from the serious to the light. They would have a marvelous time today, no somber thoughts would enter their minds. Today was the here and now, tomorrow would always come. He swung Janet up in his arms, and ran on toward the doorway. They posed for pictures in the backyard against a backdrop of sunny blue skies and vibrant red roses.

Ruth looked upon the scene, thinking how right it had all been. The remainder of their lives would be spent in giving love and support to each other, making everything all right. It made Ruth wonder about how the threat of death affected each individual. Some ran from the situation; others did everything possible to cram as much living into the small space as possible; still others chose death long before it came to them naturally. "Coping" was the word she was looking for. Coping was the answer, and each person would choose to cope differently.

Guests rushed to the buffet tables. Ruth stood at a distance savoring the scene, and waiting for the bride and groom to reenter the room.

"Hey, Dr. Simson," Woody said, taking her by the arm. "You must have something to eat." He led both women to the table, asking the caterers to give them each a healthy portion.

"Oh, gosh, Woody," Ruth declared. "Where am I supposed to put all of this?"

"Wait till you taste it. It's a far cry from what

124

we've been eating in the hospital cafeteria, doctor. That's why Janet looks so good these days. I see that her meals are palatable!"

"That's right," Janet added. "Woody and I spend a lot of time in the kitchen. Once you've had really bad food you appreciate good cooking."

"She's learning, too," Woody commented. "Jan will be in that kitchen full-time soon. She really enjoys it." He had a look of delight on his face. Ruth surmised that some magic, a mystical force, a reunion, a finding, had occurred. How rare it was to discover this love in a lifetime. "Does crisis bring renewed caring? Perhaps more enhanced emotions?" Ruth asked herself. Priorities change with the diagnosis of a terminal illness. To Ruth that was evident. Negative friends and acquaintances are put aside, for they are useless and sometimes counterproductive. Janet was reinforcing the one positive, valuable relationship in her life, to make sure that it would have real meaning. Woody was doing the same.

Guests began to approach the bride and groom. Ruth realized it was time for her to leave. "I'll see you two on Monday morning. And, I almost forgot," she said handing them a card. "This is from all of your friends in the unit."

"Thank you, doctor," Woody said. "And tell them we appreciate their love and remembrances."

"You bet. And have a wonderful weekend, both of you. But Janet, remember not to exhaust yourself," she warned. Ruth hated to put a damper on the affair, however she didn't want to see Janet back in the hospital.

125

"I will be the exemplary patient!" Janet told Ruth as they walked to the door. "And thanks for coming, and for the gift. You really didn't have to. . . ."

"But I wanted to, Janet," Ruth told her, giving her a peck on the cheek.

Chapter 9

Ruth drove her small sports car into the hospital lot. She felt rushed now; she had spent more time at the wedding than she had planned. Now it was back to the business of winding up the week and preparing for the long weekend of work ahead of her. Sam would be carrying the entire load of the department work, and the residents would be seeing patients on the floors. This was always a difficult situation, Ruth knew from experience. There was always that one patient who would gape at a resident and screech, "I want Dr. Simson, not a resident!" Residents took abuse, too; Ruth remembered those days well. No matter how capable one was, some patients absolutely refused to be seen by someone who they thought was "in training."

"Good afternoon, Dr. Simson," an orderly greeted her.

Ruth acknowledged him and hurried toward the elevators. One of the doors had just opened and she didn't want to miss the down car. The hospital planning commission had never given sufficient time and thought to the travel service when they expanded and added new wings to the complex. There were too few elevators for the extent of service needed in a five-hundred-bed hospital. If Ruth missed this car it could take as long as five minutes for another, going down, to arrive. She made it before the doors closed, and pressed for sub-level A. Lost in her own thoughts, she hurried from the elevator without looking directly ahead. She bumped into a body wearing a white lab coat.

"Oh, Larry," she said with surprise. "I'm sorry. I wasn't looking where I was going. There's never any traffic here."

Larry looked around. "No traffic in sight. Just me."

"Well, what are you doing down here?"

"Actually, I'm looking for you!"

"Oh?" Ruth questioned. She could feel her heart begin to race.

"Can you have dinner with me this evening for a change? There are no hospital meetings, no staff meetings, and a weekend ahead. I conclude that you have no excuses!"

"Larry," she begged, "this is an awful weekend for me. You can't imagine the amount of work I have to do. There's the review board to prepare for. . . ."

"Hold it, lady," he said, waving his hands in the air. "You have to eat dinner tonight, right?"

"Right."

"I have to eat dinner too. Now, tell me why we can't accomplish this together?"

"Okay, but on one condition."

"And what's that condition?"

"That you don't bring up my work."

"And why is that, Ruth? Are you afraid that I want to sway you from the direction of the protocol?" he asked her directly.

"Truthfully, yes. And Larry, this has to be my decision. I promise not to stick my nose into your department. Let's make that a rule."

"You're cutting the vital lines of hospital communication," he advised her.

"At mealtimes, yes. I like to enjoy my food."

"You win, my lady. Are you afraid that I've been sent from the high and mighty to reform your thinking?"

"Are you Donovan's scout or my dinner date, Larry?"

"Listen, Ms. Chip. I'm your date as well as your protector from all evil," he said with a broad grin spreading over his face.

"Can we make it late? I really need a hot bath and some time to recover from the day's events."

"I'll be at your place at seven. Is that suitable?"

"You're on. Now you better get this car up and I better get to work or there won't be time for dating!"

"I'll see you later. . . ." he called, entering the up car.

Ruth watched the doors close. Larry was certainly the most handsome and the best-liked bachelor in the hospital. The nurses, aides, techs, and Ruth knew it. Any one of those women would have envied Ruth her position with him. It was obvious that he more than liked her, but true to Ruth's character, she hadn't shown him the same attention. Larry was too easy to like, and perhaps love. That would threaten her; it could pose the problems of permanent relationships. Ruth chose to keep her menfolk affairs in a manageable place; her career in medicine came first.

It was almost six o'clock when Ruth arrived at her apartment. She hung her coat in the closet and went directly to the bathroom. Kicking her shoes into the corner of the dressing room, she sat down for a moment to rub her feet. They felt sore and swollen from the high heels she had worn because of the wedding. She usually chose very practical footwear for work because she was constantly on her feet. She bent down and ran the water into the tub. Ruth walked into the bedroom where she carefully undressed and hung her clothes. She glanced at her body in the mirror. Every now and then she liked to give thought to her own sexuality. In defense of her career-oriented life, Ruth had never pursued her love affairs on a serious basis, and they didn't last too long. Long involvements could make serious inroads into her career. She also liked her freedom, freedom to do what she pleased when she pleased to do it! Ruth knew that she needed "space," the kind of "space" that most men were not willing to give a wife. But . . . perhaps Larry would be different. It was difficult to assess just yet. True, they were in the same field. While other doctors had always found Ruth too competitive, Larry hadn't, at least not yet. Ruth competed in a man's world in her profession, and this always made her feel vulnerable. She did not want that to be the case with a husband. Love shouldn't be competitive, she thought. That spoils everything.

She put her hands on her hips, glancing once again at the mirror. They were still slim and curvy in the right places. Her breasts were high and young-looking. Ruth was pleased with her physical appearance.

She removed her undergarments and walked into the bathroom to turn the faucets off. She leaned over the tub and spilled fragrant lotion into the water. Finally, she lay down in the warm water. "Ah, that feels wonderful," she said out loud. She had a sense of floating as the hot water soothed her aching limbs. Her thoughts turned to Larry again. He was handsome, and taller than she by more than a head, but that was how Ruth liked it. She thought of him sexually. He was appealing. But could she really love him? Was he trying to love her? She wasn't sure yet?

Ruth reached for the bath soap and began to cleanse her body. She moved the cloth in large circles, using both hands to rub over her skin. She loved the feel of warm flesh. She reached her breasts and began to soap over her nipples. They reached out to her, young and taut. Her fingers moved gently; she washed the outer side of her left breast and then the armpit. Suddenly she froze!

Her finger stopped between the armpit and the periphery of the left breast. A small lump swelled to her touch. Ruth panicked; her heart began to race and she felt her body become flushed. Again she rubbed her soapy finger over the area; again the pea-sized lump was apparent.

Ruth's mind went blank for just one moment, one moment in time when the clock did not tick, the water ceased to move, and her mind drew complete blanks.

"Goddamnit!" she cried. "This can't be happening to me!"

She tried desperately to calm herself. She had to get out of the tub without falling or fainting. She was a doctor! Over and over again she kept reminding herself who she was. But that didn't stop the terror, it only accentuated the situation. She knew too much, and that set her into a frenzy. It was not a patient who had a swelling in the breast, it was herself, Ruth Simson! Ruth Simson knew the odds, and the odds weren't good. Cancer ran in the family: breast cancer, a familial cancer! Shit!

Rinsing the soap from her body, Ruth held tightly to the side of the tub lest she fall on the tile. She was shaky; she knew that. The bed; that was where she needed to go. Quickly she wrapped the towel over her body and drifted to the bedroom. She slipped into a gown and lay on the bed. Sweat began to pour down her armpits. She wanted only to sleep, her escape from reality. A world of fantasy and denial was what Ruth sought now as she had many times in her life when the situation was too painful to face. As she caressed her body, wrapped tightly in a fetal position, she began her period of denial. This was a cyst; something many women developed. She was too young to have cancer. These things did not happen to doctors. She had the built-in immunity to cancer by virtue of her profession. Denial works wonders!

She tried to sleep but it was fitful. In medical school she had trained herself to sleep almost anywhere, anytime. Medical school had been tedious and rigorous training. Ruth learned to catch her rest when she could without regard for the place or the clock. Often her sleep patterns were different from the world's. If exams kept her up all night, she could do it without coffee or drugs. It was not difficult for her to collapse and sleep through a whole day after the tests were over. She trained herself to swing along on a time schedule that was her own. This had served her well as an intern and then again as a resident doctor. Thirty-six hours on, then twelve off! Most students had been so exhausted and wound up that they had somatic difficulties. But not Ruth. She was capable of turning it on and off at will. She had done this as a child when her parents punished her; she did it as an adult when it suited her life-style. But now she tried, and sleep, deep abandonment, would not come.

The ringing of the phone shook Ruth from a fitful doze.

"Hello," she answered in a somber voice.

"Hello, beautiful," came the response.

"Who is this?" she asked as if she were not quite awake.

"Ruth, it's Larry. Were you sleeping?"

She sat up in her bed and rubbed her head. She glanced at the clock on her dresser. It was seven-thirty already! "Oh, God, Larry. I'm sorry," Ruth said apologetically. "I must have dozed and never set the alarm. Where are you?"

"I'm at the hospital, Ruth. The emergency room called a while ago. I shouldn't be too long. The radiologist is just finishing up. Wear something special tonight. I made some arrangements at the Trolley Stop."

Ruth was about to protest. She didn't feel in an elegant mood now; she'd rather hide than face an evening of forced smiles. But if she didn't go along with his plans she knew that he'd be inquisitive. That was just Larry's nature. She didn't want to share this jolt with anyone until she was sure it was a crisis. "Fine, Larry. I'll be ready." The receiver clicked.

Ruth lifted her body from the bed. She stretched and yawned. God, am I tired, she thought, as she pushed her hands slowly down her body. The breast, she wondered. "Should I touch it? Perhaps there's a mistake." Her hands rested once again on the outer quadrant of her breasts. Nothing in the right; a small lump noticeable to the touch in the left. She collapsed once again on the bed. "Shit, shit, shit! Why me?" she asked herself. Over and over again she wrestled with the problem; each time she came up with the same answer. "Because cancer doesn't know a body, a person. It just strikes

134

out, kills cells, whole organs, and leaves behind a body emaciated by its ravages! "Fuck the world and release me from this bondage," she cried out loud. "How dare you assault me? I should be immune to you, you devil!" She took notice of her image in the mirror and wanted to laugh at herself while she cried. "You damn fool. You know too much; you're running scared!" And why not. Didn't everyone?

"Yes," was the answer. She had seen it with her patients as well as in her own family. She looked at the photograph of her parents which stared at her from the dresser. There was her father. It seemed as if he was looking directly at her. But that was impossible. He was dead, and she was still grieving. Ruth knew that his death had been for the best; he had been kept alive too long by machinery. "Damn doctors!" she said, aloud. He had suffered more than a human being should have to suffer for the sake of omnipotence. But now Ruth wanted him back; she felt the urgency to be near him. Her father would understand her crisis now, and he would protect her as he had always done. She trusted him more than anyone in her life. He had loved her without reservation.

She looked at her mother standing next to him in the photograph. Mother was different. Ruth felt pangs of guilt; she found it so difficult to love the woman who had brought her into the world and nurtured her. She and her mother clashed on every account, and even as adults they had never resolved their negative feelings toward one another. "Why can't I love her?" Ruth asked herself time and time again. It seemed impossible. She finally arrived at the stage in her adult life where she ignored her mother in order to avoid confrontations and conflicts. Ruth saw her mother as a dogmatic tyrant, an adversary. But now her mother was ill, too, and Ruth felt guilty that these feelings had never been resolved. Suppose one of them was to die before the battles came to an end? Suppose she could not reach her mother before the end came for either of them? Suppose both of them were battling the same enemy, cancer? Again fear overcame her, and her body shook with the frightening thought! Her mother had shown tremendous courage in her battle against cancer a number of years ago when Ruth was a resident physician. That had been Ruth's first, and perhaps last act of love for her mother.

Her mother respected her as a doctor. Ruth attended to her mother when she was ill. She found the best physicians, the finest nursing care, and further, Ruth herself had been there round the clock to cater to her mother's every need. Illness, it seemed, was the catalyst in their relationship. When her father took fatally ill, Ruth had attended to him with the same professional expertise. But in her father's case it was done not out of duty but love. She toyed with the idea of calling her mother now, but the notion passed quickly. What could her mother do? The physical distance between them was a day's journey by car.

Ruth walked into the kitchen. She'd make herself a cup of tea and try to relax before Larry arrived. On the foyer table she eyed the folder that

Dr. Engelman had passed out at the staff meeting. It now had personal as well as professional meaning. She put the tea kettle on the stove and sat down at the table. She began to read.

There have been in the last three decades a number of scattered reports on conservative surgical treatments by a minority of surgeons who decided to explore new and rather unconventional methods. But the accepted belief in most countries that no alternative treatments to the Halsted mastectomy will ever be possible has discouraged these isolated pioneers for years, and has represented a major obstacle in the progress of knowledge for a more rational and more appropriate treatment of breast cancer.

Today there is increasing feeling that the classic Halsted mastectomy cannot be the treatment of choice for all carcinomas of the breast; though adequate in a number of cases, it seems excessively mutilating in other cases. In a small portion of patients it does not appear to be radical enough. For this reason the task of surgeons and radiotherapists for the next ten years will be to explore a wide spectrum of possible locoregional treatments in order to identify the most suitable ones to different subgroups of patients, according to the extent of the disease and its biological characteristics.

The sudden whistle of the tea kettle startled

Ruth. Quickly she ran to the stove to remove the water. She fixed the cup of tea and felt compelled to continue with her reading for just a while longer.

There are an increasing number of women with carcinoma of the breast who wish to participate in therapeutical decisions, after being informed of the different approaches and respective risk for each type of treatment. . . .

Informed! Who was *informing* patients of their options? Wasn't that the very core of the issue that she and Jim were addressing at lunch last week? "Alternatives" were synonymous with "secrets"! Physicians, biased by their own preferences, were keeping countless patients in the dark, selfishly! "Informed consent"; the biggest farce in surgical oncology today! What could a woman, in a state of anxiety and terror, say to a physician who presented her with the doom of the only "consent" form available! "Here, lady," he would say, shoving the paper in front of her terror-stricken face, "Sign away your breast and your chest. It's your only chance at survival!" Bullshit, doctor, the truth of the matter is that's the only thing you're trained to do well—scare the shit out of vulnerable women. Only special cancer centers, university hospitals, and some innovative pioneers were offering alternatives. The majority of women were still being "treated" to the Halsted mastectomy.

Ruth's body gave a shudder as she visualized the

operative procedure formulated by the surgical God of breast cancer. What would the great American surgeon think if he were alive today? Would he cling to his theory, or would he bow to those who had experimented, tested, and devised better methods of treatment? Ruth visualized the elderly physician, dead for more than fifty years, screaming to his followers: "Listen, hear me, my colleagues. This is the twentieth century, the age of modern reason. Many among your ranks are begging for your attention. Listen! Hear them! Progress *has* been made; do not ignore this because of *me!* I was not a God then; I was but a man seeking to alleviate human suffering. That was a hundred years ago. . . ."

Ruth was setting a stage, a stage for her own battle. She felt emotionally charged from her personal and her professional dilemmas, and the acting out of her theme took precedence over all. A sharp ringing of the telephone broke the play. She delayed answering, for the scene in her head had not been fully played. Three rings . . . it could be the hospital; or perhaps Larry. She ran to answer.

"Ruth, it's Mother, dear. How are you?"

"Oh, fine, Mother. How are you doing?" But Ruth knew the response before she asked the question. It was always the same.

"How could I possibly be? Without your father it's not the same, Ruth. I walk from room to room talking to him. Sometimes I think I'm going crazy!"

"You're not going crazy," Ruth told her, the same as she had for months now. "That's normal grief reaction, Mother. You miss Dad, and you're trying to communicate with him."

"But I'm not making progress, Ruth. It's such a lonely existence here." Ruth knew that was true. For the most part her mother was alone in their condominium. True, all of the older people were collectively bunched into large concrete dwellings, and they should find much in common with each other. But Ruth felt it was just a glorified old age home. Every time she went for a visit, she vowed never again. Every week brought another death. One would think it was possible to build up an immunity after some time. Such was not the case. The lives of the inhabitants became surrounded by grief, and they never experienced a relief before the next episode began. People in these situations never got over their mourning period; it was a constant battle. Ruth found the environment to be counterproductive. She had often tried to coax her mother to come back north after her father's death, but her mother refused. The only redeeming feature of life in the tropics was friends.

"Mother, you are really a woman with much to offer. We've discussed this on many occasions. You could get work at any of the colleges or universities there. You'd feel so much better if you did something challenging."

"Listen, Ruthie. Living is a challenge for me. Now I want to sit back and relax," Mrs. Simson protested.

"Then why do you complain about it, Mother? If you like that life, and you're not bored, then stick with it," Ruth advised her. It was the same conversation, repeated week after week.

"But I *am* bored, Ruthie. There's nothing like family."

"Mom, even when you come here you're bored after a few days. You know that; I know that. Amy and I can't make a life for you. You need some stimulation of your own. Someone who has done as much in their life as you can't take sitting around idle." Ruth knew that her voice was beginning to sound angry. You're guilty, Ruth. Keep quiet. Her mother was speaking again.

"My stimulation isn't up for discussion. When are you taking a vacation?"

Ruth knew what was coming next. She dreaded it. Florida, please don't take me! "Mom, I'm terribly busy now. I can't explain everything just yet, but it will be impossible for me to get away."

"Ruth, the holidays are coming in a few weeks. We should all be together, you, me, and Amy and the children. Have you spoken to your sister?"

"No, not since last week. Why?" Ruth asked.

"Some sister you are. Brian is sick with chicken pox for almost one week and you haven't called your sister?" There we go again!

"Look, Mom. I'll call Amy. Why don't you think of coming here for the holidays. You need a vacation more than I do," Ruth lied.

"Do you think it would do me some good?"

"Of course, Mother. Then you can see everyone. I'll help Amy."

"Remember when you were teenagers and you were supposed to help, Ruth? You were famous for finding things to do when there was housework. Poor Amy, she always suffered."

"Okay, Mom. That's enough. Stop. I have a date and I want to be in a good mood. Do you understand that? We'll argue about my vices and virtues another time."

"So tell me, who's the man?"

"Someone I know from the hospital, Mom."

"A doctor, Ruthie?"

"Does it matter, Mom?"

"Not at your stage of the game. Give him a chance. Do me a favor, please."

"Of course, Mother. But I have to hurry. I'll call Amy tomorrow, and she'll get back to you. Is that okay?"

"Fine, Ruthie, dear. Have a good evening."

"Sure, Mom," Ruth said as she put the phone back on the receiver. She made a note to call Amy tomorrow, and went to the bedroom to get dressed. Larry would arrive momentarily.

As Ruth slipped into her blue pumps she heard the buzzer and she picked up the intercom receiver.

"Yes, this is Dr. Simson," she answered hurriedly.

"A doctor Larry for ya, Dr. Simson. Can I send him up?" Thomas inquired.

"Yes, Thomas. And thank you!" Ruth liked Thomas. He took his security job very seriously, and Ruth was sure that was the reason why there were no violent acts or robberies committed in the building. With Thomas around, Ruth did not fear her night calls, for he was there to walk her to the car and back again to the elevator when

142

she got home.

Quickly she returned to the bedroom, grabbed her make-up and began to apply some rouge to her cheeks. Now that she wore her curly hair in a short bob, away from her face, she liked to show off her high cheekbones. She ran a comb through her hair when she heard the doorbell.

"Coming," she shouted. One more glance in the mirror told her that she looked exceedingly well. Her mood certainly was not apparent on her face. How could she possibly be ill and look so well? she asked herself. It was all too insane! She would dispense with her morbid thoughts, at least for the remainder of the evening.

"Ruth, you are ravishing," Larry exclaimed as she opened the door.

"You don't look too bad yourself, Larry. Come in." They both laughed.

"I guess that we're used to seeing each other in those lab coats. The sexes don't show under the shrouds," he remarked.

Ruth led him to the living room. "Have a seat, Larry. I just want to change my handbag." Ruth walked back to the bedroom.

"I like your apartment, Ruth. Where did you get all the pictures? I'm a real bug on original art. Do you shop the galleries?" he asked.

"Oh, no," Ruth called from the bedroom. "My older sister is, or rather was, an artist. She used to live in the Village before she got married. Those paintings are from her days at the Art Students' League. Whatever she didn't have room for in her place I took."

"I'd like to see her studio," Larry commented as Ruth entered the living room.

"She turned that in a long time ago, Larry. I told you, she's married now and has six children. Amy doesn't have time to breathe, no less be creative! I'm ready."

"Great. We'll just make our reservations."

Chapter 10

The restaurant Larry had chosen was elegant. Ruth was impressed when the maître d' arrived to escort them to a window table.

"Good evening, doctor," the maître d' greeted Larry. "Your table is ready and the wine is chilling. If you will follow me, please. . . ." Larry put his arm around Ruth's waist and directed her to the table.

If Larry meant to impress her, he succeeded. The table had been exquisitely set, fresh flowers at the center, and cocktails were waiting. Ruth wondered how many times Larry had been there before, and with whom? Was she jealous? Perhaps she was, she thought, as he sat down opposite her. He looked so handsome to her now. Ruth smiled at him as he began to talk.

"You know, Ruth, I've been trying to get you to dinner for a long time now. I consider this evening a landmark in my life."

So do I, Ruth thought to herself. She was

beginning to reexperience the fears that had surfaced only a few hours ago at home. She tried desperately to suppress them.

"I'll bet you say that to every woman you invite here, Larry. How do you rate this service?" She did not mind that she sounded very curious.

"To be perfectly honest, Ruth, the owner's daughter happens to be a patient; she has been for years. They extended a carte blanche invitation, and every now and then I come for special occasions. Very nice family. I wish I could say that about all my patients."

"The benefits of the primary care physician," Ruth exclaimed.

"Hey, hold on there. You were at a wedding just this afternoon. Janet Doyle was a patient, too," Larry reminded her.

"You're right. But that was totally different. I was a support system for Janet and the man she remarried."

"Was Mark at the wedding?"

"No, he didn't come. But I think that Mark is working with them quite intensely now, which has been very positive for the marriage. Mark is from that old school of social disengagement from his patients. I do see his point."

"I think it must be rather difficult for the psychiatrist, upon whom all the 'transference' falls, to make patients into friends. They're all too aware of the relationships and the various roles they play," Larry remarked.

"That's very true, Larry. I've noticed that many of my patients who have had psychotherapy become very involved with the therapist. He becomes, as in Mark's case, the person who 'understands all.' So it's logical that he replaces someone for the patient. For a while there I thought that Janet was going to place her love in Mark!''

"The human mind," Larry said, "a hell of a complex mechanism."

"Agreed. I don't think that I could work with all those emotions so easily, Larry. Especially in cases like the Doyles'. I just didn't want to get too involved in that aspect of their therapy. They had so much anger and guilt, and as in all of medicine, a specialist was needed."

"Out of medicine and into another specialty. I liked the paintings in your apartment. Perhaps I could see some of your sister's work someday?"

"Amy hasn't really worked at painting for years. I hope that some day she escapes from the nursery to the studio again. She is a very talented woman."

"Does she exhibit talent at motherhood?" Larry asked.

"Exemplary! I adore her children, and Amy has done a marvelous job. Her husband, Joe, also spends a lot of time with them. It shows."

"Didn't you ever want to take the time out to be a mother too, Ruth? You must have had plenty of opportunities."

Ruth felt ill at ease. She didn't want to discuss her affairs with him. They were private matters to her, and she respected his personal wanderings too. She tried to be objective and impersonal.

"First there would have to be a marriage

prospect I could live with, Larry. Then there would have to be an agreement as regards my career."

"Sounds as if you're after a documented contract, Ruth. What frightens you?"

"I've had opportunities, Larry, and I still have a social life. But I also have goals and ambitions and I can't allow commitments to stand in my way."

"Marriage doesn't have to stand in your way, Ruth. Some marriages are positive experiences."

"I realize that, Larry, but it takes special people to accomplish that. I've wanted to be a doctor ever since I can remember. Amy was always the talented and favored child in my mother's eyes. Amy . . . Amy . . . Amy . . . I spend a good deal of my life competing with Amy."

"But you don't have to anymore. Amy is talented, you're talented. Both in different ways," Larry stated.

"It's more complex than you think. Do you know what it's like to follow a beautiful, talented, and favored sister?"

"I have to admit that I don't, Ruth. But you've made your point, and you've reached success."

"I suppose you're probably right, Larry. When I talk about it now it does seem rather absurd that I keep competing with Amy. Somehow I never lost many of the childhood feelings. They were so ingrained. I would look for my mother's support, help, guidance. She was busy with Amy. My father replaced her in those areas. He was aware of my problems with mother but he was helpless to do very much except love me. I miss him . . . I really do.''

"I know the feeling, Ruth. Perhaps not so deeply as you do, but I know the feeling. Girls seem to set many expectations based upon their father images."

"That's what the shrinks say. Maybe no one ever lived up to my father."

There was a lull in the conversation. Larry sensed that Ruth was uncomfortable with the conversation about marriage and a family. She was skirting his questions. He motioned to the waiter. In a few seconds a delicious shell of coquille was served.

"I hope you don't mind, Ruth. I did the ordering this afternoon. I wanted you to taste the best of the house. The chef promised an excellent meal, for an exceptional young lady!"

Larry lifted his wine glass and proposed a toast. "To us, Ruth. And I mean that most sincerely."

"Thank you. I'll drink to that."

When the meal was finished he asked if she would like a liqueur. "Oh, Larry," Ruth exclaimed, sitting back in the plush seat, "if I put one more ounce of nourishment in my body, I'm afraid it will burst at the seams! The meal was delightful in every way."

"How would you like to go dancing for a while? I know a nifty place, good music, not ear-blasting rock."

"Larry, I hate to be a killjoy but my feet ache and I'm rather tired. Could I take a rain check?" Ruth tried to be as polite as possible, but she did want to be truthful. She just wasn't up to lights, music, and dancing.

"I'll take the rain check if you'll consent to a stroll in the park. The riverside is beautiful on spring evenings."

"Sounds good," she responded. The thought of a quiet walk made Ruth feel less anxious and threatened.

They walked hand in hand along the river bank, watching the barges make their way to the ocean. The lights from the skyscrapers glistened on the water. Every now and then they passed a couple making love on a park bench. New York is for lovers, Ruth thought, lovers of every kind.

Suddenly Larry stopped walking and Ruth was pulled back toward him. As she spun around, he held her tightly. Their lips met in a warm and tender embrace. At first Ruth felt inclined to pull away from him, but his body was strong and reassuring. She let go.

It was difficult for them to part that evening. Larry asked her to spend the day with him on Saturday; he had plans to take her to a new show at the Museum of Modern Art, and then to dinner. "Yes," Ruth answered; that would be wonderful.

Ruth thought that she would sleep like a baby after all that she had drunk at dinner. Such was not the case. She tossed in bed restlessly, her thoughts once again returning to the terrorizing possibility of illness. At three a.m. she got out of bed and went into the bathroom. In the medicine cabinet she found the vial of sleeping pills she had saved for her mother's visits. Her mother had developed insomnia since her father had become ill, and it was usually necessary to sedate her for sleep. Now Ruth needed the sedative; she knew that she could not face the next day without rest, some rest. It came almost instantly.

The phone awakened her from a dead sleep. She looked at the clock. It was nine-thirty! *Saturday, April 2, 1975*.

"Ruth, this is Jim," the voice said. "I'm at the hospital. Did I wake you?"

"That's all right, Jim. I had to get up anyhow," she responded sitting up in her bed. Ruth felt deep throbbing in her head, and she held it while she tried to awaken herself.

Jim went on speaking. She tried to listen carefully. "I'd like to have a talk with you, Ruth. Do you think we could get together some time today?"

"Sure, Jim. I'm free this morning. When should I meet you?" Hopefully three aspirin would solve the headache problem.

"I'd prefer that we talked outside the hospital. Do you think eleven would be all right?"

"That's fine. Where?"

"At the cafeteria across the street from the emergency room would be fine."

"I'll see you there. And Jim, there's something I want to talk to you about," Ruth added.

"I'm all yours until noon. I have an OR schedule this afternoon." The receiver clicked. Ruth sat on the side of the bed. She was glad that Jim had called her, for she certainly would not have bothered him on the weekend.

Ruth ran the bath water, and began to tidy up the apartment while she waited. She hated the housework; it seemed so mundane, a waste of her valuable time. That was why she employed Sophie at least once a week. Sophie needed the money; Ruth needed to be free from household chores. But Sophie wouldn't be at the apartment until Monday, and Larry would be there this afternoon! Things would have to be presentable.

She took a warm bath and dressed in a spring suit. Before leaving the apartment, Ruth swallowed three aspirin with her morning coffee. Her stomach, angry at the assault, growled back.

Ruth met Jim Hayes at eleven. They took a table at the back of the seedy cafeteria. It was practically empty on Saturdays. Jim ordered coffee for both of them. Then he turned to her. "Now, Ruth, what did you want to see me about?"

"Your work first, Jim," she offered graciously.

"No. Let's get your problem squared away. Is it personal?"

Ruth's throat felt dry. She sipped some coffee trying to loosen up, but that was impossible.

"Yes, Jim. Unfortunately it's personal," she heard herself say.

"Well, come on now . . ." he coaxed her.

"Jim . . . I don't want to sound like a panicky patient. As a doctor I'm aware of the fact that what I'm going to tell you could be any number of things . . . but it's me, Jim. This time it's me. It's a totally different experience . . ." Ruth's voice was low, and it was breaking. Jim was staring at her

152

peculiarly. She hadn't told him anything, really, yet she must have conveyed her fear. She tried to go on as he gazed at her with a puzzled look. "I found a lump . . . in my breast, Jim. It's on the outer quadrant. God, I am so afraid I could scream." Ruth shivered. She dared not pick up the coffee cup for fear of spilling it.

"I understand your concern and fears, Ruth," Jim was saying, but she did not hear him. Now she had to pour it all out. What had been hiding within her mind for the past number of hours had to come out.

"Working with cancer every day of my life, Jim, I know what it's like. Yet there have been moments in the past eighteen hours when I completely denied that it could happen to me. It must be a cyst; I'm too young to have cancer . . . or am I?"

"Ruth, if I told you that you were too young to have cancer both of us would know that I was lying. You would never trust me again. And if a biopsy were not done immediately, you would be walking around in a state of denial. I would be an accessory to that crime, Ruth. You understand, don't you?"

"Yes, I understand," Ruth responded like a child being admonished. Cancer was flirting with death, and denial would get her nowhere. Ruth went on to tell him of the family history of the disease, which seemed to make Jim all the more uneasy.

"Ruth, the hospital is directly across the street," he reminded her. "Let me have a look at that lump. If it's a cyst I can aspirate in my office and the reign

153

of psychic terror will be over."

"That's very thoughtful of you, Jim. But I feel guilty that you asked to speak with me, and here I am pouring out my own problems. I feel terribly selfish," she told him.

"This is far more important; it needs immediate attention. We can talk about other issues another time. Come on, let's go," he said, coaxing her out of her seat.

Ruth's legs felt weak as they crossed the street to the hospital. She was going to have a diagnosis, now, right now. . . . And she wasn't prepared to assume the responsibility for what might lie ahead. She began to perspire.

Within minutes she was undressed and on the examining table. She felt cold and clammy all over. Jim tried to make her relax with some small talk, but she only caught bits and pieces of the conversation.

Jim completed the exam. Ruth apologized for her sweaty armpits—it was uncontrollable.

"All patients sweat on this table, Ruth. My nurses and I are convinced that nothing short of super-glue would work in these situations. You're human; give in, Ruth."

She asked him the verdict as if she were facing a jail sentence. She hadn't liked the look on his face throughout the exam.

"I wish I could say that I was not impressed, Ruth. But, I am. It's a movable mass, which is good. It's not attached to the chest wall. I'd like to try a needle aspiration, if you don't mind."

"I'm okay," she reassured him. "Go ahead."

Ruth could not watch the procedure. It was painless physically, but psychologically it was terrifying. The anesthesia that he had rubbed on her skin had done nothing for her mind. Swirling, stormy thoughts ran a constant stream of unpleasant visions. Suppose there was no fluid to be withdrawn? Ruth knew what the next step would be, and it was not a pleasant one. Within minutes Jim stood before her with an empty syringe.

"Ruth, I can't get anything out. It must be a solid mass, as I suspected. Get dressed and come into the office," he directed.

Ruth stared out the window. The day was sunny and warm, unlike the cold and bitter feelings that were overwhelming her. She found it difficult to focus on things that Jim was saying to her. She heard only fragments of their conversation. Fright seemed insurmountable. Were her patients feeling the same way when she spoke to them? Was that the reason why she had to repeat things over and over again? Were there, in fact, times in one's life when acceptance of the here and now was impossible?

"I'm going to suggest that you think about this for a few days, Ruth," Jim was saying. "You need strength and a better perspective on the situation. I can understand that you're shocked, and you need time to react to the jolt on your system. But you know that eight out of ten of these things are benign. . . . Ruth, do you hear me?" he demanded.

"Yes, I hear you. I'm just too frightened to think, feel or react! Damnit, Jim, why me?" Ruth cried in anger. "I can't live with thoughts of mutilating surgery, Jim." Feelings were beginning to surface for the first time; she was emerging from her pathetic shell.

"Ruth, please don't come to hasty conclusions. We haven't even taken a mammogram yet! I'm going to call down to x-ray now and you're going to take the films before you leave the hospital today. We have to do things with logic."

"I know you're right, Jim. I'm probably acting more like a med student than a full-fledged doctor. In medical school I imagined I was dying from every disease I studied." Ruth seemed more composed now after the explosion. Jim went on talking to her to keep her mind occupied.

"Ah, those mind-blowing years; I remember it all too well. I was one who used to play pranks for kicks, Ruth. I remember one, and my wife doesn't let me forget it. A few guys and I decided to go out for Chinese food one night after exams. We had some lobster and I saved the claws. When we got back to the dorm I planted the penis from my cadaver in the claw and injected the shriveled organ with some saline fluid. We went into the girls' room; they were out for the evening. I attached a string to the door, tied the implanted organ to the string, and clipped it to the overhead light switch. We kept our door open to listen. The lights went on about half an hour later, and the screams bordered on hysterics. One of those students was my wife!" Jim laughed.

"Oh, Jim, what a morbid sense of humor!" Ruth exclaimed.

"That's exactly Karen's feeling. And whenever

one of the kids plays a prank, she reminds me that they take after their father."

Suddenly Ruth was aware of the time. She had better get moving if she needed to take an x-ray before one o'clock. "Jim, you're a dear for taking so much time with me. I must go now, and you have surgery soon. Can we discuss your problem tomorrow? I'll be glad to work on Sunday," she offered.

"Sundays are out for me, Ruth. It's my only family day. The kids have to know they have a father, and my practice keeps me going six days a week. How about Monday, after work? I should have the mammogram back by then and we can discuss both things."

"That would be fine with me. Is it the protocol that you wanted to go over?" she asked.

"Yes, and it would be an especially good idea for you to read through that material. I think that you'll be interested now from a personal perspective as well as a professional one. Now go and take the films and I'll see you on Monday."

"Thanks again, Jim. And please, don't let anyone know about this. If something should be wrong I don't want pity and sloppy sentiments from the staff," she told him.

"I respect that, Ruth. You have my word."

When she arrived at the apartment it was well after one. It had taken Ruth what seemed like light years to get a mammogram. It was Saturday, and as usual the hospital was understaffed. One technician worked the unit. Ruth felt sorry for patients in the emergency rooms. Larry was waiting at the door for her. He was engaged in a conversation with Thomas.

"Thank you, Thomas, for keeping my guest company," she said cheerfully.

"Oh, I'm sorry, doctor. I woulda opened the door if I seen ya comin'," Thomas apologized.

Ruth turned to Larry. "I'm sorry I'm late, but I was at the hospital." They walked into the elevator.

"Double trouble," Larry muttered under his breath.

Ruth did not speak until they were in the apartment. She hadn't decided how she was going to tell Larry the news. Doctors aren't tactful, she decided, and she was no exception. But she wanted to share her fright, her upset, and possibly her dilemma with him. If they were ever going to have a trusting relationship, it would have to begin at the beginning. She didn't want Larry to hear this from anyone but herself.

"How about something to eat? A sandwich and some coffee?" she asked.

"I was going to take you out to lunch, honey. This is our day off!" he reminded her.

Ruth went about the kitchen attempting to look efficient, but it was difficult to concentrate. "Look, Larry, I was just in Jim Hayes's office."

"Want to talk about it?" he asked, thinking it was a professional meeting.

"Yes, I do. But I don't know how to say it. . . . Larry, I've got a lump in my breast!" she cried, putting the knife down on the counter. She began to sob. Larry looked distant to her, but she kept speaking to him. "He tried to aspirate it but nothing came out." Ruth broke. She collapsed in the chair next to him. He put his arm around her shoulder and squeezed tightly. Neither of them could speak for the moment.

Finally, Larry broke the silence. "Come on, let's sit in the living room. I want to hold you a little closer."

Ruth laid her head on his chest and cried. He heard every sob with pain, every teardrop left a sting on his skin. As a physician he could understand why she was crying—she could be facing a life-death situation. As a man he realized how much he cared for the woman who was being assaulted. Larry felt cheated too. After all of these years without love he had finally found a woman he cared deeply for, and the thought that she might be taken from him left him stone frozen. And finally, he realized that as a physician he could not offer her any help. Ruth knew more about cancer than he did, and unfortunately that was not enough. He pulled her closer and held her shaking body as if it were a gift from heaven, perhaps a gift that could be taken away.

Ruth finally assumed an upright position and looked into his eyes. Patches of mascara left blotches of dark color on her cheeks. Larry wanted to laugh, but the situation would not permit this, and Ruth would not understand why he was laughing.

"Do you want to go home now, Larry?" she asked him.

"And leave you alone, now? Never, honey. You

need to talk. I'm here," he assured her.

"Can we skip the museum today, Larry? I feel so teary. I don't want to go out; not just yet."

"Let's talk about you, then, Ruth. What are you going to do?" he asked.

Ruth went on to explain the morning's events in logical sequence. She felt more in control of her feelings and soon the sobbing ceased; she became Dr. Simson. She spoke about Jim and their professional meeting on Monday.

"I think I know why Jim rushed you with that meeting this morning, Ruth. He's decided to join the protocol in any case. He's not waiting for Donovan or any of the others. Jim is disgusted after the Tumor Board meeting. So far, not one surgeon has come forward in favor of the simple mastectomy, and he's pissed. He had to discharge Sarah Roget from Memorial. There was nothing more he could offer."

"Then what Jim wanted to discuss was my possible participation. He has to have the cooperation of the radiation therapy department in order to have a cancer team here at Memorial."

"I guess so," Larry said, with some hesitation in his voice. "But I'll tell you firsthand that Donovan disapproves of what Jim is doing and he can make things rough for him."

"I guess you're implying that it would be the same for me if I joined Engelman."

"I'd give it some careful thought, Ruth. You know I'm a conservative physician. Not that I'm opposed to change. That's not true. But sometimes I think that many doctors make too many waves at the wrong time which leaves the patient at a disadvantage."

"And what advantage did Sarah Roget or Janet Doyle have, Larry? Aren't they suffering from our factions? Where are these patients to be treated? Or do we just say that they go untreated?" Ruth asked impatiently.

"Okay, lady. I give up. Go get the literature!" For the first time that day he saw a smile cross her face. She ran to her bedroom and emerged with the folder and some medical journals. Larry knew he was in for a lecture, and Ruth could lecture on medicine for hours! But he knew that this would be beneficial to her now; she had to find her own way, too.

Ruth put the stacks of papers down on the cocktail table and began handing them to him one by one as she spoke. "Look here. This is a study from Canada on the value of limited surgery in early carcinoma of the breast. The trial is going on now for almost forty years. Look at the statistics— the same for partial removal of the breast as for Halsted mastectomy. And here," she cried again, "are the same promising results from Italy, England, and the Scandinavian countries."

"Wait a minute, Ruth. I can't see the words for all the papers you're pushing at me. Hold on." He scrutinized the data carefully. If they were correct, then what she and Jim had been telling him was true. Extensive surgery for early breast cancers was not the answer. Women who had excisional biopsies plus radiation therapy were doing as well, and in some instances better than those who had mastectomies. Ruth went on with her lecture.

"You see what they are getting at here in these multimodality therapies, Larry. Most breast cancers are systemic at the time of diagnosis. That's the reason why the Halsted only cures a small number of patients. And you can't chase these micrometastases with a knife; there's no telling where they might go. So, a combination of radiation therapy and chemotherapy is added to the initial surgery to get at these cells." Ruth was beginning to get agitated as Larry slowly plowed through the material. He had to be convinced.

"Let's look at some of those chemo trials. That's a difficult therapy, and it would have to be very promising to ask a woman to put up with it, Ruth. Especially if there were another possible course of action."

"Larry, are you crazy? If we could preserve a breast, that would be far more important. Amputation is the worst side of the treatment," she cried, pounding her fists on the table. "The treatment should be dependent upon the staging, Larry!"

"Then Engelman proposes to separate the biopsy from the surgery, correct?"

"Exactly. That will give him a chance to find out more about the specific tumor, and it also gives a woman time to adjust and think about her feelings. There seems to be an indication now that there are certain tumor characteristics which can predict which subsets of women are at greatest risk. If a woman does not show any of these characteristics then she's considered to be at low risk. In that case a lumpectomy or a partial mastectomy would be sufficient to cure her disease."

"And then it follows that a woman presenting all of the risk factors would have more extensive surgery, and probably adjuvant therapies," Larry added.

"Exactly. And Dr. Engelman will divide his patients into two randomized groups. Half will be treated with radiation therapy following surgery; the others will not have radiation. In that way he can assess the worth of x-ray therapy for breast cancers. Those women who have positive node involvement will also have chemo, and here he proposes a two-year period of treatment."

"Where does radiation therapy as a primary therapy fall into this scheme?" Larry asked.

"It doesn't. Not yet. But I'm going to speak with Dr. Engelman about the possibility. First I want to take the course in interstitial implants before I make any decisions. But the role of radiation therapy combined with a simple mastectomy down to the conservative lumpectomy is still tremendous progress, Larry."

Larry still looked puzzled.

"What's wrong?" Ruth asked.

"There's still one thing that bothers me. Most of the surgeons in our hospital are not convinced of the value of radiation therapy. I'm not saying they're right; I'm making an honest statement. If they aren't convinced of the worth of this treatment, how can they ask their patients to participate in the trials?"

Ruth lost her composure. Now Larry was

attacking her philosophy of medicine! "How can you sit there and say that, Larry? You know damn well that radiation therapy has been tested in many trials for more than ten years. And women have the right to be informed of alternative treatments. For those who choose to bear the risk of radiation and preserve the breast where possible this is an acceptable alternative!"

"Ruth, I'm not arguing with you. I'm trying to show you the pitfalls so you know what you're up against. It's not logical to go into a battle unarmed. And how many hospitals in this country, or any country for that matter, have the sophisticated machinery and medical know-how to perform these procedures?" he asked.

"I'm thinking, Larry. I'm thinking hard. I'm beginning to see that you're a little shortsighted. Everything has to begin somewhere, right? And that place can be Memorial Hospital. We have the know-how, or did you forget that radiation therapy is *my* department?"

Ruth rose from the sofa in anger. She was agitated from Larry's questioning as well as his responses. Medicine was becoming a gulf between them.

"Why are you putting the papers away?" he asked.

"Because obviously you're on the other side," she stated sharply.

"Ruth, listen to me. There are no real sides, just differences. We all want to see our patients cured. The goals are the same. You can't be in medicine and have tunnel vision!" he responded, his voice getting more emotional. They were both angry; neither realized that their anger was at the common enemy: cancer. It was misdirected anger, being let out at each other.

"How dare you say that to me," she raised her voice. "I may be the next woman treated to a radical mastectomy, and you sit there and tell me I have tunnel vision! You are a shortsighted male chauvinist pig!"

"You may be risking a woman's life, perhaps your own, for cosmetic values, Ruth! That's another big issue in the picture," he retorted.

"You bet your sweet life it is, Larry. I'm thirty-two years old, and I haven't been married or had children yet. My breasts mean a lot to me. The hell with what you think. I wouldn't take that treatment myself, and I'm a doctor! Put that in your pipe and smoke it!"

"Ruth, I would take you with one breast, two breasts, or no breasts. This isn't a personal fight, it's a professional difference." Larry knew that she was lost—there could be no rational thinking today. There might never be a rational argument for Ruth until she resolved her own problem. He had tried to stop the stones from rolling, but now that she was agitated she would see it to the end. Perhaps it would be therapeutic. He listened to her. Her tears were falling now.

"Maybe you could take me, Larry, but I couldn't take myself. Do you know that! I COULD NOT LIVE WITH MYSELF!" With that Ruth ran to the bedroom, slammed the door and threw herself on the bed. If you won't stand by me, Larry, she thought, then fuck you, too. She sobbed alone for a while. It took time for her to unwind from the confrontation. She tossed and tried to lull herself to sleep. She had almost drifted off when she heard the apartment door close. Larry was gone. Ruth slept.

Chapter 11

Sarah and Paul Roget cleared the china and crystal from the table. Their "last supper" had gone beautifully. Everything beautiful that they had acquired in their many years of marriage had been brought out for the occasion. Paul had bought a case of Moet and Chandron. They drank it like water, finishing all but four bottles. These would be kept for later in the evening.

Sarah noticed her eldest daughter, who had come for the occasion, looking at the beautifully carved box which was laid out in the middle of the living room. Sarah had carved each and every notch by hand. It had taken her three years to complete. Paul had brought it from her studio yesterday.

"It's beautiful, Mother," her daughter said sadly. "I wish I could understand all this symbolism. I guess there are segments of your life which I really don't know about." Her eyes looked glassy, but Sarah chose to ignore this. The decision was made; her daughter had known that for years.

"You'll understand all of it once the book is published, dear. It tells all." The manuscript was neatly typed and put into a folder with directions for the publisher on the cover of the folder.

"I like the title, Mother. It certainly speaks directly . . . *Beyond Life's Door: Toward a Philosophy of Self-Termination*. I guess that you've accomplished what you wanted to do. Everything is superbly organized. When do I deliver the book?" she asked.

"Anytime next week would be fine. By then all of my farewell addresses will be received by my friends. I wrote almost a hundred of them. And the obituary notice must be into the newspapers before the book goes to the publisher. Take it all in proper order, Patti," Sarah advised her. "I've taken too many years of planning for anything to go wrong. Your father has all the directions."

Patti looked at her father. Her feelings of compassion lay with him, for she realized how great his loss was going to be. But he had stood beside his wife in her philosophy, being a philosopher himself. He respected his wife, and he was an outspoken proponent of individual differences.

"Why don't you go on with what you have to finish up, Sarah," her husband called from the kitchen. "Patti and I will clear everything."

"I'm just going to take a shower and get dressed, Paul. I'll be with you in a few minutes," she called to him. Sarah went off to her bedroom. On the bed, laid out neatly, was her silk print dress, her finest undergarments, and the gold wedding band that she and Paul had been married with. It had been many years since she had worn a wedding band; it had always made her feel bondage, something she was opposed to in life. But Sarah had promised him that she would take it with her, and now she wanted to wear it. Would Paul marry again? It didn't matter; the years that they'd had together had been extremely productive ones. If he chose to marry again, that was his business.

She showered and dressed.

"Are you ready, Sarah?" Paul called from the living room. "I'll put some more champagne on and darken the lights for the film. You do want to see it again, don't you?" he asked.

"Yes, of course. I'm coming." Sarah went into the bathroom and opened the medicine cabinet. There she saw the two vials of seconal which she had saved from her prescriptions. The doctors had given them to her after that first hospitalization when she had claimed insomnia. But she had never touched them. She had planned it that way. She fingered the vials. Quickly she put them into the pocket of her dress. Sarah walked back into the bedroom. Everything was in order. Her living will, signed by her attorney, was on the dresser. Alongside that was the obituary notice, and directions for Paul and Patti. Sarah worried that in their frenzy they might forget the precise instructions she had given them. Okay, she said to herself, everything is as it should be. She entered the living room.

"Ready, Mama?" Paul asked.

"Ready," Sarah replied. She lifted her body into the carved box. Paul set the projector into focus, and the film began to roll. Patti continued to serve the chilled champagne as the three viewed together, for the last time, Sarah's documentary on self-termination.

"Have you all had enough to eat and drink?" Sarah asked, when the film was over.

"Patti and I are ready, Sarah. Are you pleased with the film? Do you want any cuts?" he asked.

"It's perfect Paul. I want it shown as it is. No changes," she stressed. "Now, put on that wonderful record that I love so well, and let's have a toast!"

"My speech is written," Paul announced.

Sarah reached into her pocket and pulled out the vials of seconal. "It's time."

Patti and Paul sat on the sofa, looking directly at her. Sarah knew that her philosophy, her meaning, would live on from their very presence on earth. She felt confident that her theories would be perpetuated by them, that her ideas would not die with her. The idea of the right to self-termination as a dignified exit from a life which was no longer acceptable would hopefully become a respected and meaningful option.

Sarah watched them as she began to swallow the pills, two at a time, with her champagne. Drowsiness . . . light-headed, floating . . . it was coming. "Go to sleep; let's all sleep. . . ." she whispered. But they did not leave her side until she was asleep. They never abandoned her in the end.

Sarah's head was spinning, and she felt as if the anesthesia was working. She lay down, spilling the last drop of champagne.

Paul and Patti sat there motionless until her breathing ceased. They were united in thought by Sarah's presence. There was nothing to say; she had said it all. When five-thirty a.m. came, and Paul knew that Sarah was officially dead, he followed directions.

"This is Paul Roget," he said into the phone. "May I speak with the chief of police?"

Chapter 12

Larry Stein left Ruth Simson's apartment late that afternoon facing himself for the first time in many years. He was experiencing painful anxiety, sadness and loneliness were running like blood through his veins. Helplessness, hopelessness; the old He-Ho complex, he thought. Depression was setting in, slowly, as he began to experience emotions that he would have rather left dormant for eternity.

He had tried to play physician with Ruth, the assured, convinced, and godlike figure. But in this respect he knew that his reactions had not been honest. Where were his "gut" responses? Why the hell did he hide from them?

Larry knew that he hid from many realities, although he always found justification for doing so. With his terminally ill patients his justification was professional. In medical school he had been trained to be aloof, to stay above painful situations. It was called "survival." The medical survival game meant toning the mind to be hard-core, lest one fall apart with the crisis of each patient experience. But Larry had known then, and he knew now, that something was lost in this approach, that the human element went by the wayside. Where was the delicate balance? Where could the physician be honest and at the same time preserve himself from the emotional drain of constant illness? That was a course never included in medical training. It might threaten the omnipotence of the physician. Gods were supposed to come from another place, weren't they?

Larry entered his apartment feeling totally alone. He threw the Sunday paper on the dining room table, and poured himself a bourbon and water. "Saturday night," he thought. "Date night U.S.A." He wondered whether he should call Ruth now. Maybe she shouldn't be alone; perhaps she needed him. But then again, she had made herself perfectly clear when she'd slammed the bedroom door. She wanted to be alone. She didn't want to hear his professional advice; perhaps in that respect he had lost her. He should have reacted differently. But there again his own defenses were working. Larry was preserving himself from pain. Since Cristina's death, ten years ago, his love life had been in limbo. He poured himself another bourbon and water. Distance . . . keep distance and don't get hurt!

"Oh, fuck the world," he said out loud. Another slug of whiskey would ease the pain. "Pain from what?" he asked himself.

"Pain from another goddamn loss!"

He thought about Cristina now. He hadn't faced that grieving in a long time. He remembered their love now as if it were yesterday. He had been on furlough . . . in Paris for a month for a long awaited rest. It was a beautiful day in the old city, and he had walked around the streets enthralled with the ancient buildings, magnificent gardens, and inspiring museums. He felt himself in another time and place, and the transformation gave him renewed zest for living. He experienced immense relief at being far from the duties of war, which were so painful, far from the barely human existence he'd rather forget.

He had bought himself a flask of wine, some bread and cheese, and then he'd mounted the steps to the Sacre Coeur, looking back every now and then at the view of Paris. He climbed to the highest level, sat down on a step, and began to eat, sipping the wine slowly, allowing it to take effect. Fear, anxiety, and depression began to lift, to be replaced by the exhilaration of the here and now. He began to connect with himself; it was something he had not been able to do for nearly five months. He noticed a young woman on the bench not far from him. She was busily sketching, but every now and then she looked up from her work and their eyes met. Larry thought she was beautiful. Within a few minutes she got up from the bench and approached him. He was delighted. How long had it been since he'd enjoyed female company?

"Hello," she said. Larry was shocked. He hadn't heard much English spoken in Paris. "I knew that

174

you had to be American."

"Does it really show?" Larry asked.

"I guessed by your haircut," she explained. The accent was French, but her English was perfect.

He touched his head. That's right, he realized. Who but an American G.I. wore a crew cut in the Sixties?

"Are you on leave now?" she asked.

"Yes, I am," he told her. "Where did you learn to speak English so well?"

"I have been to school in England. My father is British. He met my mother here during the war; she is French. When I was old enough to go to school they insisted that I attend a proper British boarding school. So, I can speak English. Can you speak French?"

"Not very well," he told her, pulling a dictionary from his hip pocket. "But I manage to get by with this and a little sign language!" They laughed. She understood his frustration with a foreign language.

That had been the beginning for them. Larry was free to be with her and love her for two weeks. She was intelligent, kind, carefree, and responsive; all of the things that he needed in a woman. The time came for their parting. She promised to write; he promised to return. They both kept their promises.

Their reunion came six months later when Larry was separated from the Army. He needed a vacation before going home, and he decided to take it with Cristina. Their love had weathered the months of separation and it grew stronger as the days and weeks passed. But Larry knew that he'd have to go home—sometime. The sometime didn't come for months. He had written home to his mother in response to her pleading letters for him to return to America. He begged her to take a vacation in Paris; to join him and meet Cristina.

"A *shiksa!*" she wrote to him. "Where did your father and I go wrong, Larry?" she asked over and over again in her letters. "What will your life come to? What can you offer children with religious factions in the home? Come back to your life and your work; and for heaven's sake find a nice Jewish girl!"

But Larry didn't want anyone but Cristina, and finally his mother came for the visit. Her separation from her son had been difficult for her, and a wise mother realized that she needed more ammunition to wage this kind of war. Mrs. Stein had no intentions of coming out second best.

The visit had been a disaster. Cristina felt the pushing and pulling that Mrs. Stein exerted upon her son. It caused them to argue constantly, embarrassing Cristina, who knew that she was the reason for their dissensions. Mrs. Stein was uncomfortable among Christians; to her they were "the other people."

"Larry," Cristina told him one night when they were alone, "your mother does not approve of me. I can understand her feelings. You are her only son and she thinks I am stealing you from her."

"She needs time, Cris. Please, give her time."

"Time will not solve these problems, Larry. I will always be Christian, and I will always love

Paris," she told him.

"But all of the other experiences she is having now are adding to the burden. The foreign language, the strangeness of the experience. Remember, my parents left Europe many years ago and she just can't see why I would want to stay here."

"I do understand that, Larry, but she stares at my cross all the time. I stand for other things she cannot adjust to. Religious beliefs are not easily changed."

"You are so sensible, Cris. I guess that it's because it's my mother that I'm so upset."

"Don't you realize that it is just the same for my parents? They are not happy that I love someone who is not Christian, who may take me off to the United States one day!"

"I know, Cris, but at least they have been civil to me."

"The European hospitality is different. We are not so straightforward, Larry. In their hearts they are not so happy. What will become of you and your work now that you have finished fighting?"

"They can't make me go back, Cris. I've served my active duty. There are others to take over. My life is my own now."

"You sound resentful," she commented.

"About the war?" he asked, and went on, "For me, the only good thing that has come from Vietnam is that I saved up enough leave to visit Paris."

"In a way, that's a struggle, too . . . isn't it Larry?" she asked.

Larry returned to the United States shortly after his mother's visit. Both he and Cristina realized that it was necessary for him to complete his educational training programs before they could pursue a future together. He promised to send her tickets for Christmas. They would spend it together, in the United States, where she would give New York a chance.

"Yes," she told him. "I will give your American way of life a chance, Larry. But I can't say more. I need time. Paris is in my blood, in my soul."

"But there are alternatives, Cristina," he begged. "We could live in the United States, and live well. I will make a lot of money someday. And I promise, we'll spend our vacations here. I love Paris almost as much as you do."

That was the compromise. Larry went home feeling some sense of hope about the situation. He began his residency training in neurology at Memorial Hospital in July. Cristina's letters came like clockwork.

Larry did not like living with his mother; it was a temporary arrangement he needed in order to build up a reserve. His mother got to the mail first, and she prodded him with questions each time a letter from Cristina arrived.

"Still she writes, Larry. Can't you try to forget this? She's not helping you by writing," Mrs. Stein would carry on.

"But Mother, I told you that Cristina will be here for Christmas. . . ."

"Christmas! Larry, you shock me. There's no Christmas for us. What are you saying?"

"Mother, you have your set of values, I have mine. Let's not battle more than we have to."

"What did I do wrong that you should be swayed by this *shiksa?*"

When he had saved enough money, Larry took an apartment of his own in the city. It was close to the hospital, and far away from his mother's eyes. He loved her, he understood her, he felt for her. But she could never understand his love for Cristina.

In early December, Larry sent her plane tickets. He would meet her at the airport, and he had arranged to take a car trip with her for a week. He wanted her to see the United States. He wanted her to fall in love with living here. Two weeks passed. Larry began to grow worried when she did not respond to his last letter. Finally he directed a letter to her parents. Was Cristina away? he asked. He explained that he had sent the tickets to her apartment, and had no response. Was anything wrong?

When the news arrived Larry was alone. It was a plain white envelope addressed to him with a return address in Paris. The handwriting was foreign. Quickly he opened the envelope. The newspaper clipping fell to the floor. He picked it up, and the headline spelled out its own nightmare: "Skiing Accident Takes The Life of One Young Woman and Three Students." Cristina, who was so alive, so vibrant in his mind, was, in reality, dead. He searched madly inside the envelope looking for a letter, a personal word, a touch of humanness. But nothing accompanied the clipping. He knew that he and Cristina had stood alone in their love for one another. In solitude, he had cried.

Larry took another gulp of liquor. The glass was empty. Absent-mindedly he went to the bar and poured another drink. His thoughts again turned to Ruth, Ruth whose life might be threatened. It was she whom he was beginning to love, she was his chance now for happiness again. "God, no!" he cried to himself, as he leaned against the barstool for stability. Some part of Larry's universe was shattering.

"Compose yourself, doctor," he said aloud. But there was no one to hear the admonishment but himself. His mind responded to the command, and in a few moments he felt calmer, more steady. He picked up the papers from the table, deciding that some reading would put him in a lighter frame of mind; perhaps the world's problems would be easier to cope with than his own.

He sat down in the corner of the living room where there was a clear view of the harbor from the glass doors. He felt more comfortable. As he flipped through sections of the paper, a headline caught his attention:

"Woman Cites Right To Self-Termination in Suicide Note." Christ! he thought; why the hell did people still resort to copping out when the medical profession could offer almighty help and hope. Behold its powers to relieve pain with soothing analgesics, to restore circulation to devitalized limbs, to assuage the misery of insomnia and tension, to control convulsive seizures,

180 -

to remove unsightly scars, to reattach severed limbs, and even to replace diseased hearts.

The grandiose achievements of the enthroned physician in his lofty status in society was at times precarious, but that was to be expected. The godhead, the physician, had been chosen by society in its quest for an omnipotent figure, and the physician had lived up to this expectation, had he not? At least most of the time? And when he did not, society had sought to level him a bit; hence the era of malpractice suits, the wrath of the disillusioned patients who felt that they'd been let down!

Larry had never experienced a malpractice suit; and he hoped that such a crisis would never occur in his practice. He had seen the devastation caused by these legal battles with colleagues. Professionally the doctor was dragged through the muck; his family suffered in some cases. Then, even if the physician was fortunate enough to win the case, his insurance soared to astronomical rates. In the end, for the greatest part, the public paid for these displays in higher fees, but the physician paid with his reputation. Larry thought only lawyers, perpetrators, gained. Larry frowned at the article as if he expected it to jump out and speak to him. Suicide angered him; it was a threat to the physician's omnipotence. It compelled him to read on:

A New York artist took her life after long and deliberate preparations . . . Sarah Roget, wife of a prominent psychologist. . . .

Larry's mouth suddenly became dry, but his body broke into a cold sweat. His muscles tensed, and the throbbing in his head seemed uncontrollable. Sarah Roget! She was the woman who had been a patient at Memorial Hospital just recently. The same woman who had etched the scene hanging in his foyer! She was Jim Hayes's cancer patient! He thought of Jim; he thought of the hospital. The reputation of both could well be at stake from the suicide. Questions . . . undoubtedly there would be questions. Suicide was a dangerous and suspicious crisis for doctors and hospitals. By tomorrow morning the administration would be down on every physician who had seen Sarah Roget. Another leveling threat to omnipotence—the government of the hospital Board of Trustees.

Mrs. Roget had long planned to terminate her life at age seventy-two, feeling that suicide was both a rational and artistic option. However, she ended her life twenty-five years before she had intended to. Mrs. Roget's husband offered an explanation. He told the press that his wife had discovered that she was a victim of breast cancer. Her first physician offered to perform a radical mastectomy, followed by radiation therapy. His wife, a sculptor working with large and heavy materials, had refused the treatment because she could not live with radical amputation on her dominant side. Mrs. Roget had done extensive medical research and had concluded that this procedure would anyway not enhance her ability to survive more than five years. She decided not to submit to treatment.

Some months later, when her husband insisted that she go for a second opinion, Mrs. Roget was admitted to Memorial Hospital for a complete work-up. The second biopsy, too, revealed a malignancy. The second opinion physician was hoping to perform only a simple mastectomy and hoped to get Mrs. Roget to agree to treatment, although he could not promise her that such an operation could be performed immediately, due to hospital operating policy. While the decision was pending, Mrs. Roget checked herself out of the hospital. When asked to comment on the possibility that his wife might have considered this alternative treatment, Mr. Roget stated: "I don't feel that Sarah would have accepted surgery. She was also opposed to radiation therapy. But what difference does this make now? Her decision was based upon her personal research, and there was little we could do to convince her to live our way. Sarah was her own person; she was very well connected. And her first physician offered her very little hope for cure. I think this never left her mind."

Thus far none of Mrs. Roget's physicians have been available for comment.

"Unavailable for comment," Larry thought. Had Jim been contacted already? Had he refused a "comment"? To Larry it seemed unlikely that Jim Hayes would have nothing to say. This was an issue that Jim could use for ammunition in his battle for patients' rights in cancer treatment. It was a loaded case. Larry concluded that the newspapers, like all of the mass media, were sometimes perpetrators of misunderstandings and dissension. And there was no doubt that they particularly enjoyed attacking the medical profession.

The decade of the Seventies had begun an open season on physicians. The government was putting restrictive legislation and regulation on medical practice; the press was publishing articles on physicians' salaries; malpractice suits were awarding enormous sums of money, putting many physicians out of practice. The dynamics of the situation began to form a clearer picture for Larry; he knew that it was indeed impossible for the medical profession to satisfy the demands of the public for omnipotence. "But the goddamn public asked for this," he said aloud. It was the patient who insisted that the healer could do all. And the healer, fool that he was, bought right into the theory, placed himself in the godhead position, and assumed the authority granted to him by his "people." And then, when there was failure, his "people" have to put the fuckin' blame somewhere. Now they were coming to realize that so much power should not be assigned to any mortal. The frustration of these unrealistic expectations was erupting into unbridled hostility.

Could the omnipotent physician ever humble

himself to the point where he could say to his patient, "I don't know the answer"? What would this do to the physician's sense of personal self-worth?

"How can I tell you, patient, that I don't know the answer to your problem, when you insist that I do?" Wasn't that attitude perpetuated by the public? There must be a panacea for all ills! "Give me a pill, perform some surgery, then I will know that you are doing something for me!" the public cries.

"Yes, I have something," the physician says. "I have something to offer you." After hearing these cries for help day after day, week after week, month after month, "I will do anything to get you off my back," says the physician. "I will surgerize you even when I know it is not necessary, addict you to pain-killers when there is no reason for it. I will do anything to satisfy my inflated image of *myself!* After all, it is *you*, patient, who have made *me* God."

And in his restless nights the physician with conscience begins to hate himself, and the image that he has brought into being. He begins to drown his pain; his real self is tortured. He must perform aggressively in order to relieve himself of the wrath of the angry public. He drinks his alcohol, experiments with his pain-killers. Soon he is torn apart, and he functions on a level which satisfies his public, but that gives him no sense of self-worth. More drugs, more alcohol. Larry knew many such physicians. He wondered how many of them had been driven to this state from such conflicts over their own "omnipotence."

"Screw the community," he said out loud, looking at the half-empty whiskey glass in his hand. "Am I going to be the next bastard to go down?" he asked himself. Attitudes were patterned by physicians. They were supposed to be the health-care leaders in the community. But their egos were excessively inflated, and they failed badly in the social aspects of caring for patients. Where was the physician who was willing to admit that he did not know, that he did not have a cure, who recognized individual differences, who was willing to learn? Who would stand up and say, "Yes, there are differences among us, women of the world! You have the right to know that we don't know the answer. We are not saints, but we refuse to be sinners."

But we *are* sinners, Larry thought. He took another gulp of the whiskey. Ease the pain, Larry. Why should you be any different from the mainstream? he asked himself. He got up from the comfortable sofa and walked to the window. The glistening of the lights on the river water made dazzling patterns. Larry felt annoyed with the world, his own conscience obliterated the beauty of the scene from his mind. Health-care attitudes in the whole miserable community of man were in the wrong, and what's more, he, Larry Stein, was part of it. He felt sick, and not without reason, for he *was* a party to the illness of his own profession. Now, with the possibility of Ruth's malignancy, he was touched on all bases.

Ruth, who might be facing breast cancer, who

had tried to persuade him to join the group of progressive physicians, who urged him to fight for medical and social change. It was not Ruth who was naive, as he had once accused her, it was he, Larry Stein, who was smug and adverse to making waves.

He stared out the windows again. The words raced in his mind: *riverside, suicide;* the lights played tricks with his eyes. He turned his back to the view of the harbor, hoping to restore his composure. The alcohol was bad, he knew that. He put the glass down on the table, went into the kitchen and found a pair of scissors. With resolutions made, he clipped the suicide article from the paper and put it into his wallet. If and when Ruth was prepared to confront Dr. Donovan and the administration, he would be there with her. The art of good medicine was to consider everything, lest medicine remain among the stagnating sciences of the twentieth century. The patient had rights, too. We were living in an era of informed consent. Physicians were no longer dealing with an idolizing public. Sarah Roget should have had the right to live *her* way. Leveling threats to the physician's omnipotence were closing in on all levels.

Chapter 13

Jim and Karen Hayes spent their Sunday evenings at home, reading the papers and discussing family issues. They enjoyed the relaxation and leisure after the children had been put to bed. Jim was usually exhausted after playing hard with four kids. He relished the one day a week that he devoted to his family. Problems of patients were put aside. Now he had three residents who were capable of handling surgical emergencies at Memorial Hospital.

He flopped down on the family room sofa at eight p.m. He picked up the newspapers to look through the store ads first. Tommy had asked for a new bicycle; he had outgrown the one handed down from his older sister. Then there was the new lawnmower he had promised himself. Karen needed a dishwasher. Sunday nights, shopping at home.

"Hey, honey," he called to Karen who was busy in the kitchen. "Why don't you come in here for a little while and go over these ads with me?"

"In just a few minutes, Jim. I have to prepare lunches for tomorrow. What do you want me to fix for you?"

"I'll get something at the cafeteria," he called back.

"No, you won't. Every time you do that you have indigestion. Anyhow, I have to make the children's lunches so I might as well make something good for you."

"I'll take whatever you give them, honey."

One thing about Jim, Karen thought, he was easy to please. There was no doubt in her mind that she could put two pieces of bread together and slam them between saran wrap, and he would be content. But then again, Jim was never spoiled. His mother had not pampered him, and Karen had not mothered him after they were married. They had been in medical school together and they had both learned to share the chores. There was no such thing as your chores and my chores, it was always "our" work. Karen found a great deal of happiness and satisfaction in her marriage. She and Jim had planned their family around her training program. When the kids were all in school she would be able to glide easily into a practice. In the meanwhile she was thoroughly enjoying the pleasures of motherhood.

A feeling of well-being always came to her on Sundays. She hummed a tune to herself as she went about cleaning up the kitchen. Her solitude was abruptly interrupted by Jim's voice.

"Karen," he yelled. "Karen, come here!"

She was startled. Jim never raised his voice unless he was terribly angry.

"What's the matter," she called back to him.

"Just drop whatever you're doing and come here," he demanded.

Karen dropped everything including an apple which she had taken from the fridge for Tommy's lunch. It rolled under the table.

"Damn," she said to herself as she crawled after it. "I'm always letting the kids have it for being clumsy, and look at me!"

"What did you say, Karen?"

"Nothing, Jim. I was just talking to myself," she told him as she entered the den.

Jim was sprawled on the sofa with the paper in his hands. His face looked drained. She wondered if he had been reading the obituary pages again. When he had reached his thirty-fifth birthday last year he had suddenly become addicted to that section of the papers. Karen wondered whether the "passage" would hit her the same way.

"What upset you?" she asked as she sat down next to him.

"Look at this article. It's about that breast cancer patient I presented at Tumor Board."

One look at the headline told Karen the story. She didn't read beyond the bold print. She knew how upset Jim must be, and rightly so.

"But she wasn't your patient anymore, Jim. She checked out of Memorial Hospital without asking you. You can't feel responsible for her!" Karen tried to assure him.

190

"The hell I'm not," he cried. "I'm responsible, the faculty is responsible, and the hospital is responsible. And we can take it a step further, Karen; the whole goddamn medical community who think they have almighty wisdom is responsible!"

"Shush," Karen admonished him. "I know you're upset, Jim. But please don't wake the kids."

"Okay . . . okay. I didn't mean to lecture you, Karen."

"Jim, I understand why you feel for this woman, but her suicide is not directed at you. It says here that she wanted to take her life; she believed in self-termination."

"Read the whole story and then tell me what you think."

Karen proceeded to the follow-up page and read the story. She felt her body getting cold despite the warm breeze that was coming through the screen door. She felt movement in her guts, pulsing in her chest. God! Jim was right. Sarah Roget had taken her life prematurely because she feared a life with cancer, and she rejected the radical mastectomy and therapies. She could relate to her husband's feelings of guilt and failure now, but she also felt that he was being unjustly hard on himself. There was nothing more he could have done for her in the situation.

"I see what you mean, Jim. She had no alternatives according to what some surgeons call proven medical pratice. But that does not mean that medicine put the death knell on this woman's life," Karen stated firmly. "Her husband says she wouldn't have accepted any surgery."

"I'm not pretending to assume all the responsibility for her death, Karen. What I am experiencing now is a gut hatred for the profession I'm in! How long do you think this shit can go on? Tell me truthfully? Don't you see what's happening?"

"Of course I do, Jim. But you can't educate without help. You knew that when you left the university. That's why you have to join their protocol. You need established proof; the public won't take less, and the ineducable physicians are die-hards. They'll follow in the next century! Sure, you'll suffer setbacks, a little leveling, but if you believe in it, Jim, you don't give up!"

"And in the protocol both the public and the profession will have their hand at leveling me, Karen. Right? You know where we stand on this issue now? On a pile of shit!"

"Sure it's shit, and you're going to eat plenty of it before you prove anything. That's the real problem in medicine. There are small little study groups all over the world without any unifying force. Each group pursues its preferences without sharing for the common good," she said empathetically.

"You got it, baby. The factions that are dividing us from the public, to whom we should be responsible, lie within the medical community. The omnipotent physician."

"You almost make me hope that my career will

continue at home, Jim," she said despondently. Karen felt licked. When it came to politics she took the position that she was inept. She had no experience in this arena of medical practice. Now she hated what she saw and she realized that she was not prepared to buck the "omnipotent" group.

Jim put the newspaper down on the table and moved closer to her. He knew that he had unfairly dumped all his medical problems on her. Karen always bore the brunt. Now he was engaging her in his own feelings of guilt, inadequacy, and general depression. It wasn't fair to her, especially on Sunday. It was a terrible note on which to end a perfectly wonderful day.

"I'm sorry, honey," he said, putting his arms around her. "Sometimes I get carried away with myself. Let's try to forget this for a while. Tomorrow is soon enough to face what's coming. This should be our evening. I guess I resent the intrusion."

The phone rang at that moment.

"Sit here, honey. I'll get it," Jim said running to the phone.

Karen picked up the papers and looked at the advertisements. She had a lot of shopping to do this week. She took a pencil and a piece of paper and began to write down the bargains of the week. She tried to be a wise shopper; she had learned the art in their poverty days.

Jim's voice made her look up from the paper. He was shouting.

"No, sir. I'll tell you for the last time, I have no comment. No, nothing to add . . . no, I didn't know the woman's plans. . . . Yes, I'm sure the hospital will have something to say soon . . . no, I'm not covering my own ass nor anyone else's. . . . Listen, I told you that's it. And you can quote me!" Silence.

The phone went down with a thud. Karen already foresaw the next crisis. The newspapers were asking Jim to comment on the suicide, and she knew that he would not do it until he had conferred with the administration.

Jim entered the room, his anger still apparent.

"You know what that goddamn bastard asked me, Karen?"

"No, Jim, I haven't any idea." She wanted him to play it out, here, with her, at home.

"Hey, doc, don't you do psychiatric work-ups on all your patients? Can you imagine the audacity of that son of a bitch?"

Karen broke out in laughter. "That's the funniest thing I've heard in a long time!"

Jim looked slightly bewildered. "And what's comical about that?"

"Look, the general complaint is that you put your patients through too many diagnostic procedures; but before surgery you do have to be relatively sure of what you're working with. And still everyone complains that the profits from these diagnostic tests are outrageous and unnecessary. Now they're asking why you don't have psychiatrists diagnose all your patients. What a crossroads of conflicts! When all the testing is negative, they accuse you of spending money and time needlessly. When the patient goes down the tubes they accuse you of not doing enough. Jim, the whole thing is comical!"

"Let's go to bed," he suggested before Karen had a chance to gain her composure.

"What will that solve?" she asked.

"Absolutely nothing in the medical issues, but it will do me a world of good!" Jim told her with a sudden smile.

She closed the papers, and walked toward him. "Away we go!" She threw her arms around his neck. "I don't need any more coaxing."

"That's what I like about you, honey; you never needed coaxing."

"Hey, that's an insult! What do you think I am, an easy lay?"

"Absolutely! And that's one reason why I love you, Karen," he responded, pinching her ass all the way to the bedroom.

Jim was usually able to fall asleep easily after intense lovemaking. Karen was as delicious to him today as she had been when he met her twelve years ago. Karen had no fears of flying sexually, and Jim enjoyed the freedom of her expression. But now he lay in bed, after almost an hour of deep thought. He couldn't put his mind to rest. He rolled toward Karen, rubbing his leg next to hers. If she was still awake, he knew she would respond.

"Yes . . ." she said softly.

"You're awake?" he asked. What a ridiculous

question; of course she was awake!

"Uh huh," she responded, rolling her body over to his for warmth.

"How come?" he asked. "You're the one who sleeps like the dead."

"I'm just thinking about tomorrow at the hospital, the questions you'll have to answer. The whole affair disturbs me."

It never ceased to amaze Jim how in touch he and Karen truly were. He had often marveled at his choice of a wife, at how fortunate he was to have a woman who seemed to possess every fine quality. He rarely found a fault in Karen.

Jim once overheard her speaking to his mother on the telephone. He had picked up the extension, thinking the call was for him. The two women were gossiping. He hung on to the line. Karen and his mother were good for a laugh. It was his mother speaking:

"Karen, I spoke to Mrs. Bundy, that night nurse yesterday. You remember her? Well, no matter, she remembers you well. And, I found out you were right. That anesthesiologist, we'll forget names, *is* having an affair with that snip of a nurse on three west. You were right. That's probably why his wife is so depressed."

"Mom, I knew it, I just knew it! She was prompting me for information at the hospital dance. She thought that because he operates with Jim, I would know the truth."

"Did you tell her anything, Karen?" his mother asked tactfully.

"Good heavens, Mother. Everyone knows that

196

all the doctors in the hospital screw around every now and then. It's the mode these days, it always has been, and it probably always will be! Proximity, Mom. Togetherness breeds."

"Now Karen, that can't all be true. Why look at Jim. He idolizes you. He'd never look at another woman!" she declared.

"Mother, do you know why? I'm convinced that Jim is too dumb!"

Jim's ears were burning at the other end of the phone, but his invasion of their privacy had been his choice, and he therefore was not at liberty to comment. They would have to know that he had purposely left the receiver off the hook. But later that night he got even with her. If she really thought he was too dumb to have an affair, he'd show her that he was dumb enough to let on. That would scare the hell out of her. But he didn't worry; he was perfectly innocent.

"Karen, I don't think I'll be home tomorrow for dinner," he remarked casually.

"Oh, what's up? Am I included?" He usually took her to every hospital function. It was as much her business as it was his. She would soon be on staff again.

"No, dear, just a spur-of-the-minute thing the guys and I cooked up together. I won't be too late."

Karen was curious. She was also angry because he wouldn't tell her anything. But she kept her composure and continued to live by the rules. And the rules in their house had always been honesty and truth. If she openly doubted him now, she would be telling him that she had no faith in their vows. She kept her seething silence. All the following day she tried to concentrate on things, but found it impossible. When she called the office he wasn't in, even at lunchtime. Finally, at five, his secretary told her that he had gone to dinner with Dr. Stein. "Oh, great," she thought. "Now his best friend is getting him dates!" By nine-thirty, she had taken a bath and gotten into bed with a novel for company. She would wait until he came home. But her thoughts zoomed nonstop through her mind and she constantly read her own pulse. "He's having an affair; I know it. I can feel it. They all screw around and Jim is probably no exception." At nine-fifty, the doorbell rang. She was almost afraid to answer without Jim home. She threw her gown and robe on and went to the door. Through the panes she saw Larry.

"Well," she said opening the door. "What brings you here at this hour, Larry?"

He walked into the foyer trying to look as if he had had too much to drink. "Put on your jacket, Karen. I have someone out in the car and I need help."

"Oh, my God," she shrieked. "What's happened to Jim?"

"Nothing that a little rest and black coffee won't cure," he told her. His speech was slurring. Karen grew frantic.

Larry opened the screen door for her and they both descended the walk to the driveway. Karen, half scared to death, screamed with delight as Larry shone a lantern on their brand new station wagon.

"So that's where you two monsters have been!" she cried.

Jim got out and joined them. "Where the hell did you think we were?" knowing the answer all too well.

"It's gorgeous, Jim! I love both of you."

"Hey, none of that Karen," Jim admonished. "We don't believe in hanky-panky in this house!"

Karen felt guilty about that for months, and it wasn't till a year later, when the anesthesiologist and his wife were separated that she told him her own fears.

"From now on don't announce to my mother or anyone else that I'm too dumb to have an affair. Why don't you tell them the truth?" he asked.

"And what's that?"

"Simply that I married you because you were the best lay in the hospital!" She was still the best lay, a most intelligent woman, an excellent doctor, and a terrific mother. Jim often wondered how long his luck would last. He was suddenly back in the moment.

"What disturbs you about tomorrow, honey? My head won't be in a block. I'll be home," he assured her.

"I know Jim; but I also want you to know that I'm behind you in whatever you decide to do. If you can't take the shit at Memorial anymore, than you should move on. Don't fear for money. We'll all fair well. We can both work and earn good incomes. . . ."

"Hold on, honey. That's not what's keeping me awake. I'm not concerned about my job position. I was totally caught off guard, thrown, by Sarah Roget's suicide. But that doesn't stand in my way. I'll go down fighting. You know that."

"Then why are you still tossing, Jim?"

"Would you do me a favor in the morning, after you get the kids off to school, and Cindy is in for a nap. Call Ruth Simson. She should still be at home. I doubt that she'll be concerned about the Tumor Board meeting."

"Why not? She's one of the big people in that group," Karen said.

"Because she's got her own medical battle now, and I've advised her to do a little homework before we get together tonight."

"And where, my dear husband, are you going with a single woman tonight?"

"Old suspicions?" he asked with a smile.

"New concerns! I'm jealous!" she confessed, crossing her heart with her hands.

"Well, there's a lot to be concerned about." Jim told her the story of Ruth's visit.

"Shit," Karen said. "What can I say to her?"

"Whatever you think would be comforting. But I want you to remind her that we have a meeting at five. I also feel that this will be our opportune time to introduce another procedure. Ruth is the best radiotherapist I know here in the city. Women like Sarah Roget need options."

"I smell the medical wheels burning rubber," she told him. "What's the radical approach this time?"

"Hardly radical, my love. The interstitial implant is a very conservative treatment. It's most suitable and promising for women refusing any surgery."

"Let the bombs fly and the best men win!" Karen told him. "Now if we don't get some sleep, Jim, you'll have lost the fight to battle fatigue." She kissed his forehead, rolled over and made her body comfortable against the small of his back.

Chapter 14

Ruth awoke on Monday experiencing that peculiar feeling one has after sleeping off jet lag. Where was she? How long had she slept? Had the calendar flown full speed, while she lost days?

She lay on her bed, staring at the wrinkled dress that was twisted around her small body. She looked at the surroundings. "Yes," she assured herself. It was her room, there was the clock on the dresser. It was seven-thirty. The sun shone through the curtains, so she knew it was early morning. She rubbed her eyes, trying to wash away the sleepy feeling. It didn't help. She lay her head back on the pillow and stared at the ceiling. Ruth had slept off the day of emotional turbulence which had now left her completely lifeless and drained. Generally she felt better after these tantrums; usually a better perspective came to her from rages in which she vented her anger. But this morning she did not feel the relief. She pushed her head deep into the pillow, as if she could escape from the day. She hadn't the energy to face it. Why the hell had she let loose on Larry? When was she going to learn to cope in a more adult way with her frustrations? She felt only disgust with herself. She had responded to him like the Ruth of her childhood, not the mature person she had hoped she had become.

"Lift yourself out of bed Ruth," she said. "It's Monday, remember? Sophie is coming and you should be working. The world shouldn't fall apart because you're living through a crisis!" she admonished herself. Monday was Tumor Board. Shit, she would miss it, but she didn't care. Sam would go if she didn't get there on time. He would take some of the residents. At least the department was in good hands. A morning off would do all of them good; she couldn't contribute much, feeling the way she did. They would function better without her company.

Ruth removed her tatty dress and threw it in the cleaning basket. When she realized it was full to the brim, she made a mental note to stop at the cleaners on the way to the hospital. In the kitchen she made a full pot of steaming hot coffee. She sat at the table looking out the window, wondering in which direction to go. She didn't want to stay in the apartment while Sophie cleaned. Sophie loved to talk nonstop, and Ruth didn't feel much like listening. The phone rang. She was tempted not to answer. On the fourth ring she thought it could be important.

"Hello," she said in her cheerful voice. It was Larry. How could he call her after the way she had behaved the night before? Was he a glutton for punishment? Or was she overreacting?

"Good morning, beautiful. Are you feeling any better today?" he asked. He acted as if she had done nothing wrong. Why was she waiting for him to chew her out? Because her mother had always done so the morning after her tantrums?

"Hanging in, Larry. Trying to find out why I was such an ass on Saturday when you were only trying to help me."

"Don't worry, Ruth. You were right in being agitated. I should have given you a chance to do your thing without throwing all the obstacles in your path. But I'm glad I was the available person. It could have been worse; it could have been your mother!" he joked.

"Thanks for showing understanding, Larry. It makes me feel a little more comfortable."

"Listen, honey, I'm taking the morning off. I slept off a mild hangover. What are you doing for the morning?" he asked.

"Nothing. I already missed Tumor Board. Sam will handle everything until I get there. Why the hangover, Larry? If I remember correctly it wasn't late when you left here and we didn't even drink." She realized after the fact that she shouldn't have asked. Perhaps he had a date on Sunday. Worse than that, perhaps he was drinking because she had made him so miserable!

"I spent my weekend getting stoned and watching the boats in the harbor. I was alone, Ruth. I just couldn't get my mind off you. And it's still on you. Will you have breakfast with me this morning?"

"I'd love to, Larry. Where shall we meet?"

"At my apartment. Say an hour? I'll do my jogging and then prepare something special. How does that sound?"

"Like the best offer I've had since Friday!" They laughed together for the first time in two days.

Ruth was searching her closet for something presentable to wear when the phone rang again. This time she ran to answer. Perhaps it was Larry again; had he changed his mind?

"Ruth?" the woman asked. "This is Karen Hayes. How are you?"

"Oh, fine, Karen. Thank you."

"I'll make this quick. I know how busy you are. Jim asked me to call and remind you about your meeting with him this evening. Five."

"Of course, Karen. But I wouldn't have missed the appointment. Did Jim think I would forget?" No, that wasn't the answer; Ruth knew that. Something must be wrong. But she knew it would be wrong to question Karen; Karen wasn't involved, and she shouldn't be made to feel uncomfortable.

"I'm sure he didn't, but you know Jim. Punctuality, responsibility. He has certain fetishes!"

Ruth tried to be sociable. Jim and Larry had been good, strong friends for years, and she knew that Karen was part of the "group." And Karen could be a friend to her on many counts. They did have much in common. "Thanks for calling, Karen. I hear so much about you and the children. I feel as if I know all of you."

"That's Jim bragging. But we all ought to get together some evening for dinner. I hear a lot about you, too, Ruth. But let's make it without the kids; it's impossible to concentrate with them around. You'll meet them soon enough."

"Sounds wonderful to me. And if you speak to Jim, tell him I'll be in his office promptly." She hung the receiver back on its cradle and went about dressing. But somehow she didn't feel at all comfortable. Karen had been pleasant, there had been nothing upsetting said. But still Ruth felt uneasy after the conversation. She dressed in her blue suit with a bright floral blouse. "There you go," she said to the mirror image. "You look spring-y, Ruth. Now, smile for the people!" Oh, hell, she thought. Life was a shit sandwich, you take another bite each day! It was true; she felt threats and crises closing in on every side.

Before leaving the apartment she placed a call to Amy. Her mother would have her usual cryptic remarks to make if she didn't take care of the holiday plans.

"Amy, it's me, Ruth. How are you doing?"

"Not too badly considering the chicken pox," Amy responded. Poor Amy, Ruth thought. She had the worst luck with those kids when sickness was in the air. Perhaps it was because Amy had so *many* kids. They passed germs around like a football.

"Well, my dear sister. Just think, Brian will give

206

it to Paula; Paula will pass it to Jeffrey and so on down the line. Then you'll be finished with the chicken pox for life!"

"Ruth, there's nothing wonderful about receiving a certificate in 'chicken pox.' But that will be my grand contribution for the spring!" Amy assured her.

"Amy, when your family is over it, the epidemic will cease!"

"When are you going to stop teasing me about the size of my family, sister? Enough is enough. I'm taking care of your share while you make some contribution to society!"

"Thanks. I'll remember that when I get to thinking about a family," Ruth offered sarcastically.

"Don't tell me . . . I want to guess!" Amy howled. "You're getting married. That's why you called."

"Oh, Amy, for God's sake. Where are your senses. Me, married?"

"I guess not, Ruth," Amy responded, a little let down. "It's not your style, is it?"

"I'm toying with the idea, but if you let on to mother, Amy, I'll never forgive you! Promise?"

"I promise. Now, tell me about him."

Ruth told her about Larry. How their professional association was taking on new color, how interesting he was, and surprisingly, how much she enjoyed his company. "You'll love him, Amy. He's an art freak, and he really likes your work. If you ever get all those kids out of your hair some year you should really get back with it."

"I hear that from Joe all the time. He always tells me I'd feel better if I did something for myself for a change. But until the little ones are in school it's impossible."

"I'd better get down to some business with you, Amy. I really must get to work today. Mother called. She was her usual depressed self. She wanted me to come for the holidays. She knew that you and Joe would never make it with all the kids sick. But I made the suggestion that she come here. . . ."

"Oh, God, Ruth. You didn't!"

"Listen, Amy, I promise I'll have her stay with me. I know you're cramped for space and with the kids sick you don't need company. But I can't have dinner here. You'll never be able to bring the kids out anyway. But I'll be out there to cook with you. It'll be nice to have a family seder after all these years. When Pop was sick we never made plans."

"Okay. I give up. When is Mother coming?"

"I'll call the airlines and get her ticket. A week from today will be fine. That will give her a few days before the holiday." It would also give her some time to recover from whatever surgery was going to take place. But she did not tell Amy. Amy was now in a vulnerable position. She would be surrounded with cancer, threatened on all sides. There was no need to get her sister all psyched up when there was no diagnosis. Amy might tend to make some irrational decisions, and now with her kids sick, Amy had enough immediate problems.

"I'll call Mother, Ruth. Brian left half his summer wardrobe there on our last visit. He'll need it for camp."

"That would be great. Spare me the call and the inquisition."

"Oh, Ruth. This guy you're dating. Are you considering bringing him here for the holidays?" Amy asked cautiously.

"I'm thinking about it, Amy. I'll let you know . . . a lot can happen in a few weeks," Ruth replied.

"The best thing that could happen is that we get the chicken pox out of this house!"

"Don't wish too hard, Amy. Mom will stay with you! Bye, love."

Ruth drove up to the luxury apartment on Riverside Drive. Number 108 was a new and imposing building with a magnificent view. She was greeted by a valet who promptly relieved her of the car. A doorman stood waiting.

"Please tell Dr. Stein that Dr. Simson is here," she requested.

"Yes, ma'am," he replied. Ruth wondered just how much of the local color and gossip these doormen absorbed. No doubt some of them could make fine authors, never at a loss for good material.

She rode the elevator, alone, to Larry's sixth-floor apartment. The aroma of good cooking filled her nostrils. Another plus, she thought. He can cook!

"I'm here," she called as she entered the foyer. The door had been left ajar.

"Come into the kitchen. I can't let the eggs burn," Larry answered.

Ruth followed the sound of his voice, walking slowly in order to absorb the full beauty of his apartment. She wanted to feel how he lived. The foyer was carpeted in pale green. The walls were filled with etchings, lithographs, and wall hangings. She wondered which one was Sarah Roget's. A small table with a lone piece of sculpture caught her eye. It was a bronze of a man and a woman embracing in a very sexual position. It was placed so that its reflection was caught by the mirror on the wall. She found herself entwined by the piece. Ruth entered the large living room which faced the view of the river. The decor was modern, but not the sort of modern that was cold. It was inviting, comfortable, and elegant all at the same time.

"Where are you?" he called to her.

"In the living room; it's beautiful," she replied, spinning around at the sound of his voice. He was standing on the threshold of the room. He was wearing a blue jogging suit and worn tennis shoes. His hair hung over his blue eyes. All this gave him the rugged appearance of an athlete, which to Ruth was terribly appealing. Her heart began to race.

"Sorry about the outfit," he apologized. "I haven't had a chance to shower. I decided to do a couple of miles this morning. I was afraid I'd be late. Here, let me take your briefcase."

"Thanks," she said. "Can I help you in the kitchen?"

"All ready, beautiful woman. Let's eat!"

She followed him into the kitchen. The table

was set with green and yellow linens, and yellow and white stoneware. Everything was tastefully done, carefully chosen. "Your place is lovely, Larry. You really took time with it."

"I can't take the credit. I have a good friend whose wife is a decorator. She knows me well, and all I did was approve her selections. Some things I do the easy way."

Ruth made a decision to call Amy about her own apartment. It was really a hodge-podge of everyone's leftovers; family donations. She really should take the time to redo some pieces, add some life to the surroundings. Amy would help her; she had the knack necessary to make something out of nothing.

"Help yourself," Larry offered.

"I haven't seen a breakfast like this in years, Larry."

"It's my favorite meal, so I take pride in cooking it. I'm rarely available for lunch. I'm running between the office and the hospital at noon. This suffices me until dinner."

Larry noticed that while he ate with gusto, Ruth merely picked at her food. "Is it that bad?" he asked.

"No, of course not, Larry. I was just thinking about something that happened this morning. My mind just seems to look on the bleak side of things these days. It's foolish. . . ."

"Well, shoot. I'm all ears," he said, continuing to eat.

Ruth put down her fork. "Karen Hayes called this morning, right after we hung up. She said that

Jim asked her to remind me of my appointment this evening. I thought that was strange, don't you?"

Larry thought he knew the reason for the call, but now was not the time to share it with Ruth. She'd know soon enough. Besides, he wanted to be totally selfish, and that was in Ruth's best interests, too. They deserved some time together without the intrusion of crisis. He would laugh it off.

"I'm sure that the only reason he had Karen call to remind you is because he hates being late for dinner. He probably thought that if you were top heavy on patients later in the day it would be a good idea for you to ask Sam to cover. That's probably the only reason she called."

"I guess you're right, Larry. Today is just not one of my better days. Since I got up this morning I can't shake that doomsday feeling."

Larry changed the subject quickly. "Have you ever met Karen Hayes?"

"No, but I told her that we'd get together sometime."

"She is good looking, charming, and bright. I give them a lot of credit, Ruth. Their life has been a struggle. Jim is first starting to make some money now. Surgery is a long haul, and everything depends upon referrals."

"He's well on his way now, Larry. He's even operating on Saturdays."

"Well, he's got a large family to feed. Those kids are adorable. I remember all of their births as if it were yesterday. I'm the 'godfather' for the baby."

Ruth's thoughts turned to family and children. Larry was programming her now, feeding her with ideas that presented conflicts in her life. Marriage and a family were wonderful, for other people, Ruth concluded. She didn't think she could handle all that responsibility and make the union work. She was too devoted to keeping her position; strengthening her credibility as a radio-therapist. If she married, how would her husband take that? Would there be jealous fights over whose career came first? If there were children, who would care for them? A housekeeper? A nanny? No, that was not the right way. But the right way, the way in which she would want to do her best as mother and wife, eliminated her goals in a medical career. "Karen must be an extremely flexible and well-adjusted woman, Larry. I give her credit," was all Ruth could offer.

"Do you think you could do it, Ruth?" he asked gently.

"Was that a proposition or a proposal?' she asked with a quivering voice.

"Both," he told her as he took her hands in his. Their eyes were locked together in thought. Larry got up from his seat and put his arms around her. She stood up to feel the full strength of his body. She lay her head on his chest; the tears from her eyes dropped onto his shirt. Conflict . . . conflict, Ruth thought. I think I love him. I'm afraid to love him. God, give me the answer.

Larry bent his head down to her hair. The smell was fresh and youthful. He kissed the top of her head. "You know, honey, I love you."

Ruth wanted to respond, say something. But she couldn't. The emotional aspects of their involvement were too much for her to cope with now.

Breakfast was left, unfinished plates on the table. For the rest of the morning they gave in to their desires for each other and filled the hours with intense lovemaking. They lay, side by side, silently, until Ruth kissed his sweaty forehead and laughed.

"What's so funny?" he asked.

"Nothing is funny. I just like your salty body. It tastes good."

His arms began to run over her body again. She relaxed. He wanted her again; she would respond, he knew that. His fingers caressed her small breasts. The nipples stood out, and he continued to play. He felt the tiny lump and experienced pangs of pain. He almost felt like crying: "God, not this woman. This beautiful woman I adore. Don't rob me of this love." But he kept silent. Again, they made love.

Ruth knew that he was feeling her breasts, testing the little intrusion in their happiness. She was frightened, but she understood his feelings. Would he want to be in this same bed with her tomorrow if she were bandaged from shoulder to waist, breastless? She would be self-conscious, stripped of her sexuality, and he would be repelled! She cried silently.

Finally Larry lifted his body and propped himself on his elbow. He looked longingly into her eyes. "Are you happy, Ruth?"

"Yes," she replied. "Very."

"I want you to do me a favor, lovely one. And before I ask I'm telling you the answer I want to hear: 'yes.' It's really very important to me."

"Anything," she told him seriously.

"On Wednesday I usually have dinner with my mother. Since my sister and brother-in-law moved out of the city, she depends upon me for family companionship. Will you have dinner with us on Wednesday?"

Ruth thought for a moment. This was more serious than any previous involvement. This time she deeply cared. She looked at Larry. Larry who loved her in crisis, Larry, who was strong, intelligent, and giving. He was going on with his plans as if nothing was wrong! Perhaps she was in the midst of the cancer crisis? Why would he want to sacrifice his life and love for a sick woman? Conflicting thoughts were coursing through her mind! And he had made such a simple request: "Have dinner with me and my mother." Ruth felt foolish. From this simple request she had already imagined she had one foot in the grave!

"I'd love to have dinner with you and your mother on Wednesday," she heard herself say.

"Fine. I'll call her this afternoon and let her know. She loves to cook, especially if she has company."

"Larry, don't put her to any trouble. I always eat simple meals," Ruth assured him.

"Are you kidding! My lovely Jewish mother measures her love in food intake. She'll fill you up with love, Ruth. I know it. Let her feel good."

His arms were around her again. He was hard

and ready to love her. She felt the tingle of his legs, the brush of his arms, the warmth of his kiss. Again they were lost in each other.

Ruth arose with a start. It took her moments to orient herself. She rolled her head toward Larry. He smiled and blinked.

"I was watching you sleep," he said. "You know, you're beautiful when you're sleeping?"

"What time is it, Larry?" she asked, getting excited for the moment.

"Eleven-thirty."

"God, Larry it's late," she cried as she slid out from under his arm. "We both have to work today."

"I have an hour," he told her.

"But I have to be finished by five, remember?" she reminded him.

"Okay, but first let's take a shower. Then we'll get to serious matters," Larry told her.

"You mean all of this wasn't serious?" Ruth said, with a bit of chagrin.

"You're pretty even when you're angry. Listen, Ruth, there are two distinctly different sides of Larry Stein, rolled up into one great personality. When he loves, it's very serious. But it's not business! We have medical business to discuss, and that's aside from my love for you, Ruth."

Bath time ran through lunchtime. Larry was serious but slow at getting down to business. Ruth was both touched and delighted. She felt more love for him with each encounter. She had been sexually fulfilled with Larry. Other men had not known how to make love with her, only to her. She wanted it to go on, never end, so that she might never lose touch with herself or with him. She was falling deeply in love.

Larry made both of them lunch while Ruth dressed and put on some make-up. She thought that she would not make it to the hospital in time to see Donovan today. That would have to wait. She was also too involved with her own problems, and Donovan, unknowingly, could hurt her. She was vulnerable. Yes, she thought, cancer was in part a state of mind.

Larry was sitting at the table when she came into the kitchen. He had cleared the breakfast dishes and prepared some sandwiches.

"That's quite a lunch for someone who never eats lunch," she told him.

"I usually have quiet mornings, honey, but today I'm starving."

Ruth blushed. They both ate with good appetites.

Larry went into the bedroom to finish dressing. Ruth cleared the table and began washing the dishes.

"Forget the dishes, honey. Come in here and keep me company. I won't see you until tonight. That's a long way off!" he called to her.

She stopped running the water, walked into the bedroom and watched him knot his tie. He finished, put on his suit jacket, and kissed her. "Come on into the living room, honey. There's something I have to show you before we get to the hospital." They went into the living room. The sun was pouring into space which was filled with happiness. Larry felt sorrow that he had to botch up a perfectly beautiful morning. But he would have to be the "bad news bear" now. If Ruth found out in the hospital, where she was unable to react, it could be worse for her. He took the article from his wallet and gave it to her.

He watched Ruth's eyes as they moved across the paper. He thought he saw her wince when she read the words "breast cancer." He realized her anger at Sarah's doctor, who had offered her no hope for "cure." He saw her lips curl, and her eyes fill when she read the account of the entire suicide act. Ruth finally lifted her eyes from the paper, and fixed her eyes on his face. He could feel her anger and rage; he knew that the tirade was about to begin.

"Can you see the light now?" she asked.

"Yes, Ruth, that's one reason why I wanted to be with you today. That's why I had the hangover this morning. I just sat here late into the night, drinking bourbon, trying to figure this whole thing out for myself. The more I drank, the angrier I became. I gave many things a lot of thought. It was not just Sarah Roget's death; that was only one incident, obviously. But the deeper reasons for my own depression came with my realizing my own attitude about the whole health-care system."

"I'm sorry that you had to drink alone, Larry. I guess that it would have been more comforting for us to have had each other. But I was luckier than you. I slept off my anger," she said.

"But I had a chance to think alone. And that was beneficial for me. I don't quite understand the reasons for my blindness, but perhaps they're totally personal. There's a disease that lies within our profession. I think I caught some of it in medical school. Part of that was reinforced when I had to be a field surgeon in the Army. One tends to harden, work without feeling, in order not to give way to that hurting human element. After a while, one becomes immune to the suffering. I guess that's why my most intelligent patients seem to pose problems. They want to know; they want to assume responsibility for themselves. And, of course, then I would have to become engaged in their feelings, give up some of my rights as their 'God.' It takes a strong and noble person to do that, Ruth. In our profession there aren't too many of those. We're too busy trying to keep our distance, above and beyond the lay person. But we're not really there, are we?" he finally asked.

"No, Larry, we aren't there. But those who have chosen to remain there have lost their touch with people. That's why they don't practice good medicine. And here we are with a suicide on hand, an act which *might* have been prevented. But who yet has made a study on the correlates of suicide and cancer? I personally don't know of any. But here's a woman who has made a public spectacle of her feelings. I'm sure there are many more cases in which this has happened silently. The silence of suicide, the silence of the physicians who refuse their patients any human right. The oath of Hippocrates turns many doctors into hypocrites. The silence is loud, Larry; once you begin to think about it for a while the sound becomes deafening!"

Larry took the newspaper clipping from her lap

and put it back into his wallet. "I think that this is why Jim had Karen call you this morning. I'm sure he realizes that this incident will put Donovan in a compromising position. He has a lot of answering to do."

Ruth's eyes were fiery. Something else was on her mind, and as she began to lecture to him again he realized that her battle was not only against the omnipotent physician, but that it was directed at *male* surgeons in particular. The feminist in her was showing her distaste for male-oriented, male-formulated morals and attitudes. Beyond God the Father there was also a Ruth, the Mother. Her philosophy—that women should develop rather than adapt to a male viewpoint—was apparent.

"The Halsted radical mastectomy was formulated by a male surgeon," Ruth said emphatically. "In his time the biology and treatment of breast cancer was very much in the thick of the forest. But today there are some excellent alternatives. Tell me why male surgeons are not accepting this? Suppose the female surgeons of the world were in the majority; suppose these same female physicians felt that the 'en bloc dissection' of the testicles and penis was necessary to cure cancer in men? Suppose we female practitioners decided it was best to refuse men their sexual pleasures in life because we believed it was their only chance for cure? Tell me how many of these men would refuse treatment before they would lose their balls? And how many of them would adjust so well emotionally? Most of these bastards are half-men to begin with, Larry, and you damn well know it. Take away their balls, and you know what's left? Nothing! Absolutely nothing!"

"I hope you don't plan on using that reasoning with Donovan, Ruth. I don't disagree with you; I just don't think the point will be well taken," he advised. They laughed.

"Oh, Larry, I know this. But don't you realize how much of this is a sexist war? If men were subjected to the same injustice as women are, they would slaughter us. Withholding information is a serious crime. And that's what we are accessories to. Sure we all have preferences. Our training and backgrounds are so diverse that it's inevitable. But the knowledge of trial and study; the obligation to disseminate information, is the same for all of us. How dare we take the rights of another person away? How dare we set ourselves up in this position? Goddamnit, no one will do this to me!"

"Ruth, let's keep it a medical and social problem, not a feminist movement. I know you don't like me to say that, but you have to fight this on the proper ground," he advised her again.

"Larry, when I was training I tried to keep track of all the prominent women physicians. I wanted to see them rise above men, become heroines, the same way in which male physicians who made enormous contributions became heroes. But you know what I found? That there were *no* women who were chiefs of staff in hospitals; there were no women who became deans of medical schools; there were very few female physicians who could make a contribution even though they were competitive. And it's because they've been kept in their place, under the thumbs of men whose watchful eyes kept saying, 'Beware woman, you'll be thought mad if you oppose the majority.' From the beginning of time men have used this excuse to limit the possibilities for women's intelligence and creative and original impulses. 'Too bad, she's probably crazy.'"

Ruth went on and on, delivering her sermon. Larry listened; she didn't offend him. He was connecting with her feelings and attitudes. Women had suffered at the hands of men. He was learning about the woman he was hoping to marry. Surely there would never be a dull moment in their lives. She was too intelligent, too insightful, too filled with emotion and feeling, for there to be anything less than a soul-stirring marriage.

". . . and probably one of the foremost women physicians. She is a radiotherapist by the way, practicing in Canada. Her study is one which spans almost thirty-five years, Larry. Remarkable! She studied the partial mastectomy, with and without radiation as an adjunct therapy; the studies are matched against two groups receiving the radical mastectomy. And . . . she concludes after all these years that the survival rate was the highest for that group receiving the partial mastectomy alone!"

"Okay," he cried. "I give up, I give in. You don't need to convince *me* anymore. I'm convinced, Ruth. But from here on in I want you to promise me one thing . . . only one."

"What's that?"

"That medicine never comes between us. Love is not based on a diagnosis; it's built on treatment. Final?" he asked.

"Final," she answered, lovingly. They left the apartment.

Chapter 15

Ruth and Larry parted in the parking garage. He reminded her to be punctual for their appointment with Jim Hayes.

"I'll be there unless I decide to do some late-afternoon shopping," she said smiling.

He thought he knew what she was up to, but he wasn't going to allow her to get away with it; not this time. "Save it for another day, honey. Denial won't work in this situation. We've been over this enough times. You be there or I'll embarrass you by calling the police with a missing persons code! Understood?"

"Yes," she laughed as she waved good-bye from the stairway of the hospital garage. It was easier to run the one flight of steps to the sub-basement than to wait for an elevator. As she opened the fire-door, she bumped into Sam.

"Wow, am I glad to see you, Ruth!" he said, with a sigh of relief.

Ruth was surprised. "Is something wrong?"

"I'm not referring to our department. Everything's fine there. But this goddamn place is in a rumble since the news of Sarah Roget's suicide!" Sam waved his hands as he spoke.

"I heard just a little while ago, Sam."

"There's one redeeming feature," Sam stated. Ruth thought that to be a peculiar comment.

"What can be redeeming about a suicide?" she asked.

"Only that Donovan is locked in the office. Hopefully, this will give him some fuel to begin working."

Sam was learning the ropes fast, Ruth realized. He had only been at Memorial with her for two years. He was an astute person, a good mixer, and he knew what was going on in most arenas. Sam was attempting to show her the "plays" of the morning. He enjoyed acting.

Ruth leaned her elbow against the wall and watched him. "Okay, let's have the blow by blow of the action, Sam."

Sam quickly positioned himself for the scene, pushing his arms directly in front of his body, using them to gesture effectively. The smile on Ruth's face only made him put more drama into his acting.

"There were the usual set-ups, see . . . everyone was on their morning coffee break by eight a.m. That's always a good indicator that there's something amiss. Too early. Donovan, Davis, and Thompson had the *Wall Street Journal* there on the table, same as every day. Only today the paper was closed . . . no delighted looks . . . no angry looks . . . get it?"

"Yes, Sam. I've heard that they're all heavy investors. What's the market like these days?"

"Not good. But I passed their table, on my way to meet Jim and the others. They weren't discussing the market, Ruth!"

"Oh, really. What could be the reason for that, Sam?" she asked with a smile.

"You know why, Chief. They're all a little concerned about what Donovan is going to say when the administration puts the pressure on . . . and we all know that's coming. They're darn scared about this suicide, Ruth. It casts a dark shadow on their strong bias for the radical mastectomy."

Ruth motioned to Sam. "Let's walk back to the department. I'd rather we spoke closer to home." As they walked she continued to speak, her tone subdued, almost a whisper. "But I agree with you, Sam. There will no doubt be a lot for them to answer to. Whatever Donovan says will be influenced by his bias, too."

"We know he's not in our favor. That's been evident for a while. But he's a sharp mediator; don't underestimate the man. He may not be a hell of an educator or surgeon, but he can manipulate people. And if he's made to see our side of the coin I think we'll have a foot in the door now."

Sam closed the office door and they sat down. He felt tired after being up late last night with company, and again tonight he would have to face his wife's routine of physical exercise on the tennis courts in mixed doubles.

Ruth opened the pamphlet she had received from Dr. Hillman and showed it to Sam who stretched it across the desk.

"I'm going to take the course, Sam."

"Well, now's as good a time as any to begin working on it. The Roget suicide will certainly help your efforts in that direction," he agreed.

"Sympathy is on our side now."

"Who's she?" Sam asked laughing.

"Come on, Sam," she begged. "Can't we have a serious conversation?"

"Absolutely not, chief. I'm married!"

"Sam, you're insubordinate!"

"My wife tells me that sometimes. Okay. I believe in it, Ruth. It is a logical move for us to make now. It's probably the best alternative for women who are refusing any surgery. But you know that we're not going to elicit any sympathy from the surgical people. They are going to fight this thing to the end."

"Suppose we take this to the protocol breast project, Sam?"

"Have you spoken with Engelman about it?" he asked.

"No, not yet. But I'm hoping to get an audience with the man himself this week."

"Good. Do you want company, or do you want to go at this alone?"

Remembering the dual purpose of her mission, Ruth decided not to have Sam with her. "I'll take this alone, Sam. You run the department well. We'll be shorthanded if you're not here. Tom will be taking his vacation any day now, and without him the residents are absolutely lost. How's his wife?'' she asked.

"Fine. So Tom tells me. But she's overdue with this baby and I guess that's getting to him. You know his mother-in-law came to stay. Now she'll overstay. That doesn't suit Tom!"

"Babies are family affairs, Sam!" Ruth cried.

"I wouldn't know. If I ever pin my wife down long enough, maybe I'll have the experience!"

"Any new cases coming in this afternoon?" Ruth asked. Her mind was getting back to work.

"Yes, one. It's a pediatric, Ruth. You'll probably want to handle this one yourself. A patient of John Davis."

"What a way to begin a day! That should take time, Sam. I only wish some of these general surgeons would spend some time explaining radiotherapy to their patients. Most don't have the slightest notion as to what we're doing."

"Ruth, you can accomplish that with more empathy, more hope and greater sympathy than most of the other physicians. They take such little time with their cancer patients, especially when they feel the person is terminal! And this hospital atmosphere, Ruth! It does nothing for the patient. Everything is so depersonalized, ritualized, timed, schemed! There's no warmth or close contact."

"You're beginning to sound like me!"

"Well, damnit, Ruth. I have learned from you! People with fatal diseases need to vent their anger, and they can't do it here. We just don't allow it! And they need to bargain, something else they can't do here. We don't permit people to indulge in these very human needs."

"Sam, things are beginning to change . . . Mark Fenster has made progress with many of our patients."

"Yes, but the patient has to come here first. That's the problem. Some of them never get to radiation. We never see them. And the general surgeon, all too busy with his cutting and sewing, doesn't take time for psychological needs. Besides, I think that's a very real threat to many of them."

"Of course it is! When a physician has to admit that he or she doesn't know something it's a threat to their omnipotence. So they go on pretending that there's nothing wrong, lest they lose some control. Now we're back to the starting post."

"What's that?"

"The problem of cancer education and personal bias. Those are the very reasons why surgeons like Davis and Thompson won't give an inch. It's a threat to their omnipotence," she concluded.

"I'm going to make rounds. I'll see you later, Ruth," Sam said, rising from the comfortable chair.

"Who's my pede patient?"

"Oh, I almost forgot. I prepared the papers . . . Suzie Thomas, age nine; Wilm's tumor. We've got to shrink it to operable size. Good luck!"

Everything in the department changed when a child came for therapy. Ruth visualized the changes in personality that were taking place beyond the door of her office. The usually tired faces were assuming bright and cheerful looks. The language among the technicians was cleaner.

Jars of candies would be opened and put out on the desk. And, of course, the child would not have to wait in the room more than a few minutes. The idea was to personalize, as pleasantly as possible, to treat as quickly as possible, and to allow the patient to leave the unit with speed. Why? Why? Rush asked herself over and over again. Why the hell was it so difficult to face childhood cancers? Why did physicians avoid direct contact with parents of fatally ill children? Ruth knew why; it just made little sense to her. She would spend time with her pede patients, their mothers and fathers. She would give them what they needed most— some part of herself!

Ruth walked into the hallway to greet Suzie Thomas.

"Well, Suzie, I'm delighted to meet you!" she said, hoping that her deep concern did not show. "I'm Dr. Ruth Simson."

Suzie extended her hand. "I'm happy to meet you."

"Well, I'm certainly glad to hear that because we are going to spend a good deal of time together for the next few weeks." Ruth extended her hand to the woman who accompanied Suzie. "Mrs. Thomas, I assume. You and Suzie look very much alike."

"I'm glad to meet you, doctor," the woman answered. Ruth felt the woman's cold and clammy hands. She looked frightened, fearful of the unknown. It was time for a talk.

"Won't you both come into my office? We need to discuss radiation a bit. I know that you have some questions, and I'd like to help you to find the answers. Okay?" Ruth asked.

Suzie looked up at her mother, who nodded affirmatively. They followed Ruth.

The three sat down, Ruth behind her desk. Under the fluorescent lighting Ruth noticed the dark rings under Mrs. Thomas's eyes. How difficult it was for parents to cope with the crises of their children, with the helpless state that they were quickly reduced to when they had to rely upon others. And the guilt, a problem so delicate to handle. Why my child? Have I done this to her? God, why do you choose to punish the innocent? Children were the innocents; their parents the transgressors. Is this the way in which you choose to punish me, God? By taking my child? Again a search for meaning, more bargaining, and finally, hopefully, a resolution. Ruth wanted her patients to reach their resolutions quickly. She was upset at the thought that people expended emotional energy on meaningless questions. It was nonproductive. But there was no getting around it, patients had their rights, and those rights meant that they had to express *all* their real emotions. It was a useful process when guided by skilled hands. So she led these patients to Mark Fenster, the physician who she knew could assist her patients with that expertise.

"Would you like a piece of candy, Suzie?" Ruth asked extending the jar.

"Yes, thank you very much."

"Now, tell me exactly what Dr. Davis told you about me?" Ruth wanted her explanations to be in line with what Davis had said, if he had said anything. The patient needed continuity, not confusion.

Mrs. Thomas spoke. "Well, he told me that Suzie's tumor would have to be shrunk to an operable size. And that you could accomplish that with x-ray treatments. Is that true, doctor?" Mrs. Thomas asked.

"Yes, quite true. We are seeing very good results with x-ray therapy for Suzie's type of tumor."

"Will that hurt me?" Suzie began to cry. Mrs. Thomas was visibly upset. Ruth urged her to allow Suzie to express her feelings. Only in that way could Ruth really know what was bothering the child and hopefully allay her fears. Mrs. Thomas wiped Suzie's eyes with her handkerchief. Ruth left her desk and sat down next to Suzie. "No, sweetheart," she told her, extending her hand. "You won't feel anything. And I don't usually make absolute promises, Suzie, but this one is true." She rubbed the child's cold hands. Suzie began to show signs of relief, the wrinkles in her forehead relaxed. "Now, Suzie, tell me, what do you like best to eat?" Suzie thought for a moment. Then her face lit up.

"Chocolate ice cream!" she answered quickly.

"Fine. I'll see that you can have that as many times a day as you like. But there's a reason for that, dear. Sometimes your little tummy is going to feel upset. But there's nothing to worry about; it will pass over. Perhaps you won't feel like eating spinach or meat."

"Oh, I hate spinach!" Suzie made a face. Her

mother shot her a reprimanding glance. Suzie apologized.

"That's all right, Suzie. Between you and me, I don't like it either." Mrs. Thomas relaxed. There was something distinctly different and refreshing about Dr. Simson. "Well, now, we have the treats squared away, Suzie. I'm going to tell you a few things about my business here. First, and most important, I want you to get well real soon. We are going to go into the treatment room very soon. In there you'll see a large machine which is suspended from the ceiling. It's something like a robot." Suzie looked excited. "It even speaks in 'blurps.' One of my girls will help you onto the table. Now here's the important part of *your* act, Suzie. You must stay perfectly still for the few minutes that you're on this table. Do you think you can do this?"

"Sinchy! Sure I can!" Suzie let Ruth know.

"Wonderful!" Ruth told her. They had their act together. All except the mother. Ruth knew that she would have to take some time alone with Mrs. Thomas. Ruth took her marker out of the desk drawer. She would have to explain this to the child. The scarlet "indicators"; the symbol of cancer. "Suzie, I'm going to make a little red rectangle on your belly. But don't worry, it will wash off easily; but I don't want it to come off until we are finished with the treatments."

"Oh, we use them with the play lady all the time. But she told us never to put them on anything but the paper!" Suzie told Ruth.

"Yes, she's right. But this is for another reason.

233

It would take a lot of time for us to keep measuring the area for the machine every day. That would mean that you would have to take more time away from your play and schoolwork. You wouldn't want to do that would you, Suzie?" Ruth asked.

"Oh, no. I miss my time in the play room. I have a good friend there and we like to play checkers. I'm really good, doctor. But my teacher says I can only play when I finish my schoolwork, so I like to have a lot of time."

"You can't avoid that schoolwork, Suzie. Soon you'll be back in your own school and you don't want to be behind! Now I'm going to call Debbie in. She'll take you around the room. You can ask her lots of questions. Debbie loves to talk. And may I have a few minutes with your lovely mother?" Ruth asked.

"Oh, yeah! That's fine with me."

Debbie popped into the room at the sound of Ruth's buzzer and whisked the child off for a house tour. When they were safely away from the office, Mrs. Thomas broke. Ruth was prepared, from her years of experience with parents of sick children. Ruth handed her a box of tissues.

"I'm sorry, doctor. . . ." Mrs. Thomas sobbed. "It isn't right for me to make you watch this . . . but there's so much for us to cope with now, and I don't know how we're going to manage. . . ."

"I understand, Mrs. Thomas. I can imagine how difficult it is for you to see your child sick," she said to the woman, putting her hand on her shoulder. The woman responded.

"Thank you, doctor, for treating Suzie and me

so kindly."

"Mrs. Thomas, can you tell me a little more about yourself and the family. I would like to know how things are going, who Suzie's relatives are, etc. It would help me in handling her, and perhaps we can do something for you, as well."

"It's just the four of us . . . my husband is home now with the baby. Suzie has a sister. But this has taken so much out of us, my husband and me. One of us is always here with Suzie, and one stays home with the baby. We're torn; we don't speak to each other . . . it's terrible, doctor."

"Mrs. Thomas, you look as if you haven't rested in a long while. Is that true?" Ruth asked.

"I can't sleep, doctor. I try, but there's always that same gnawing in my mind. Why? Why did this happen? Will it happen to our other child, too . . . will Suzie be all right?"

"Suzie will be fine here, Mrs. Thomas. And I think we should have a good response to therapy. But you and your husband need to live together. You need to gather strength from each other."

"How, doctor? We are both so afraid to talk, afraid to hurt the other."

"Mrs. Thomas, we have a wonderful psychiatrist here on the staff. He has been able to accomplish many good things for families in these crises. Would you and your husband like to meet with him?"

She looked up at Ruth and stared, with disbelieving eyes. "Do you think there is something wrong with us, doctor?"

"No, of course not, Mrs. Thomas. I think that

for what you're living through you are having a perfectly normal reaction. But sometimes people need intervention by a professional to help them see how to cope with a situation. Dr. Fenster can accomplish this.''

''Then, of course. I'm sure I can persuade my husband to come.''

''Would you like me to arrange to have him call you, at home?''

''That would be best. I go home at dinnertime for a while, before my husband comes here.''

''Good. Now, let's talk about the therapy a little. I want you to go over this informed consent sheet with me, Mrs. Thomas. With the children it is difficult and unnecessary to explain everything. . . .'' Mrs. Thomas had many questions. Ruth answered them. After their conversation, Mrs. Thomas signed the form. Ruth thought she saw a ray of hope glisten in the young woman's eyes. Perhaps she had accomplished something constructive today . . . even in the throes of her own crisis.

Suzie was at the TV screen. Debbie was telling her jokes while they watched the robot move about.

''Hey, Mom,'' Suzie called to Mrs. Thomas. ''This is better than *Space Command* on TV!''

Mrs. Thomas turned to Ruth. ''Oh, God,'' she said. ''If only I could adjust the way she does!''

''You will, Mrs. Thomas. I'm sure that things will begin to look up as Suzie begins to respond, and you have some time for yourself. Let's see how the treatment goes.''

"Can I stay?" she asked, rather surprised.

"Yes, you can. But only outside the therapy room, with me. Suzie is going to be alone," Ruth explained.

Ruth approached Suzie. "Now young lady, we're going to get serious for a few minutes. I'm going to help you up on the table this time. And when I put you in position I want you to stay perfectly still. Remember?"

"Got ya!"

"Good, because I'm going to watch you on television!" Ruth told her.

"Can my daddy and my sister see me too?" Suzie asked excitedly.

"No, not on this screen. But you will have an audience, and your mother will be there." Suzie fixed her hair. Ruth loved to watch the children. They were so innocent, so believing, so lovely. They needed special care. "There you go. Now everything is in place. Mother and I will watch you on the screen. We're all going out of the room. Okay, dear? You're on the stage!"

Mrs. Thomas took a seat next to Ruth and watched as the machine began to descend toward Suzie's body. Instantly the woman covered her face, as if she expected that the machine would crush her child. Ruth put her arm around the woman. "It's all right, Mrs. Thomas. The machine will not touch Suzie. I promise you that."

The screen was turned off when the machine completed the therapy. Ruth and Mrs. Thomas accompanied Debbie into the room.

"Hey, Dr. Simson, Suzie's shivering. I can't get

this air conditioner regulated. I called down this morning. So did Dr. Ray. Nobody's come," Debbie said.

"That's absurd. They have to send someone up. We can't freeze out patients. Deb, get them on the phone again and see what they say when you tell them *I'll* be down to the office to report it."

"That'll scare them a little, doctor," Debbie replied. "They need to know you'll take the matter into your own hands. That's when they come." She walked out of the room to the phone.

"Well, Suzie, we didn't intend to freeze you. Next time tell me when you're cold."

"But, Dr. Simson, you told me not to move! I would have had to use my mouth to tell you!"

"Suzie, you're the absolute end!" Ruth exclaimed. She lifted her down from the table and the three walked from the therapy room.

"Should I come back tomorrow, Dr. Simson?" Suzie asked.

"Yes, of course. The nurse will tell you exactly the time. Now how would you like to have that chocolate ice cream?" Ruth asked.

"Before my school lesson?"

"You bet. And I'll order some for your little friend. Then you can have a party! And Suzie, I asked Mother to go home for a while. Don't you think she needs a rest? Maybe some time with daddy?"

"Oh sure, Dr. Simson. I have a party to make and all my schoolwork to do. I won't have too much time to spend with her, anyhow!" Mrs.

Thomas gave Ruth a grateful and knowing glance.

"Thank you, doctor. For everything, for all of us!" the woman replied.

"If you need me, both of you, please call. If I'm not here, Dr. Ray or Dr. Kresh will be here."

"But I like you!" Suzie cried.

"And I like you, too!" Ruth told her. "But wait until you meet those two dashing young princes, Suzie. You may forget *me!*" The three laughed. Ruth walked them down the corridor until her office door. They said fond good-byes. She hoped that they felt as good as she did at that moment.

Chapter 16

"Dr. Simson," Debbie called. "It's for you on line one." Ruth was startled for the moment. She had heard the ring but was too submerged in thought to answer.

"I'll take it in a minute, Debbie. Put the call on hold."

Ruth placed Suzie Thomas's folder into the "active" files and pressed the button on line one.

"Dr. Simson, this is Dr. Donovan. How are you today?" he asked in a pleasant tone. Ruth was confused. After her talk with Sam this morning she had assumed that the chief was less than happy.

"Fine, Dr. Donovan." She normally would have asked, "And yourself?" but she contained the question. She knew the answer.

"I have here in my hand the letter from your review board. They have given us three alternate dates for their visit. . . ."

"I'm prepared, and I'm delighted. I'd like to get

this program more well-rounded, Dr. Donovan," Ruth tried to add tactfully. He would know what she meant.

"Well, I think we should concentrate on putting our efforts into the program that exists, Dr. Simson. This is not the best time for changes," Donovan stated rather meekly.

"I agree, Dr. Donovan. We should present a program that is well-established. That is necessary. However, I feel that it is also important for a teaching hospital to serve the interests of research. We can't remain in the stagnant position with radiotherapy. We are an up-and-coming unit here," she said firmly.

"Yes, you're right, Dr. Simson. But we need to have some time together beforehand to review the presentation. . . . There are aspects of your teaching program that I haven't looked into sufficiently. You know I'm trying to keep up with as much as possible."

"Yes, Dr. Donovan. I'm sure that's a particularly difficult task with as many disciplines as we have here. I mean, keeping abreast of new data, changes. But I'm sure I can help you, and myself. We'll be going in the right direction."

"That's fine, and very efficient, Dr. Simson. When can we have our conference?" he asked.

"This week is hectic for me. Many new patients. How about early next week, before the holidays?"

"Good, I'll have Mary set aside the time for our meeting. She'll send you a memo."

"Thank you for calling, Dr. Donovan."

"And thank you for being so well-prepared. It

gives me confidence."

Whew! Ruth sighed with relief. Perhaps Sam, for all his play, was right about Donovan's administrative strategies. He was certainly looking for her good side, and perhaps she had a chance of convincing him of the worth of a more expanded radiotherapy program. For once in all the times that she had need for direct contact with Donovan she was glad that she had contained herself. He would be more pliable, easier to work with, if she could convince him rather than cross him. And he was probably relieved himself; he had the here-and-now problems of the politics of the hospital to contend with. Ruth felt confident that he was in a compromising position.

Ruth began to sift through her patient folders. She compiled the papers on her lectures for Ann to type. Ruth hated "pushing papers." Too many heads of departments got caught up in this hassle. They became organizers rather than physicians and teachers. A knock on the door interrupted her train of thought. "Come in."

Debbie was standing at the threshold in her usual pose. Sexy Debbie! Ruth often thought that Debbie's circular movements in the rear end made the male patients smile in the waiting room. She'd have to remind Debbie to take it in slower motion, lest others get the impression that all was fun and games on the cancer ward.

"Dr. Simson," she said. "Janet Doyle is here and she'd like to see you for a moment."

"Send her in, Debbie." Ruth got up to greet her. Woody was there.

"Taking time out?" she asked Woody.

"Just a little. We have to see Dr. Fenster this afternoon."

"You both look wonderful. Please sit down," Ruth offered.

"We just want to thank you for coming to our wedding, Dr. Simson, and for the lovely gift. It will fit into the new decor of the house," Janet told her.

"My wife here has decided to redecorate the house, Dr. Simson. I can't keep this woman down!" Woody laughed.

"Are you feeling stronger, Janet?" Ruth asked.

"Oh, yes. What a difference being home can make! I sleep full nights, cook delicious meals, and take care of myself!"

"How's the chemotherapy going?" Ruth inquired.

"Dr. Driedan told us that everything looks clear. So I guess he feels we're still on the right track," Janet offered.

"Now you know that the whole miracle began at the wedding!" Woody said with pride.

"Well, I guess we have three doctors working on you now, Janet. Woody has made a great contribution. But seriously, I feel that the nodes look good, too. No more swelling in the axilla. So we'll finish up here in about a week's time."

"That would be marvelous!" Janet exclaimed. "Do you think I could get some time off for good behavior?"

"The reason better be good!"

"We'd like to take a short honeymoon. Is that

good enough reason?" Janet smiled.

"Good enough. Where to?" Ruth asked.

"We thought the Islands would be the place to go. Nothing too taxing, just lounging on the beach, basking in the sun." Woody was ready to plead his case when Ruth interjected.

"All right on my count with one reservation."

"What's that?" Janet asked.

"No basking in the sun without a blouse or covering on. The rays aren't too good for you now. Okay?"

"Accepted, doctor. Can we bring you anything from the islands?" Woody asked.

"Nothing but a well patient!" She walked them into the waiting room. It was still full.

Ruth walked quickly back to the office. She wanted to make a call to Mark Fenster before the next interruption.

"Mark, this is Ruth. Let me compliment you. Janet Doyle looks and feels very well. You've done a great deal for them."

"It was nothing, dear. Just a few magic tricks I keep up my sleeve for emergencies!"

"Roll up the sleeves, Mark, I have another crisis intervention case," Ruth said seriously.

"I think you need a full-time cancer shrink, Ruth."

"I do, I really do. But until the day comes when we free you of all those other mundane duties, Mark, I'll settle for half-time. Look, this is a pede case. The little girl has Wilms tumor. I began treatments today. It is a hopeful case. But the parents are in the throes of guilt and personal crisis. The mother looked so worn that I sent her home. They need someone to help them through this, Mark. They just can't communicate."

"What's the name and number?" he asked immediately.

"Suzie Thomas, age nine . . . and Mark, you're a love!" Ruth told him.

"So are you, my dear! I'll stop in and see Suzie myself as long as I'm in the hospital today," he offered.

"That would be great. And Mark, have you gotten any news of what's going on with the Roget suicide?"

"Nothing good, if that's what you mean. Jim and I talked at lunch today. Some reporter on one of the papers called him at home last night. Wanted to know why the woman hadn't been seen by a shrink. Can you imagine the bastard asking why we don't do psychiatric work-ups on *all* our patients!"

"Wow," Ruth responded. "What did Jim offer?"

"Nothing. He didn't want to say anything until the hospital made some comment. And he knew I had seen her. My personal feeling was that this crisis had nothing at all to do with the fact that she committed suicide. This was a long-planned act, Ruth. The cancer crisis only pushed it up a few years. I was convinced of that the first time I went to see the woman. She was extremely hostile and angry, not so much about the cancer as at our intervention, Ruth. She wrote her own script. It was a self-fulfilling prophecy. And I might add that it was the first time in all my years practicing psychiatry that I was unable to find some level of communication. She was closed on every count. Perhaps if we had a longer period of time to work with her, but, of course that was impossible. You can't keep a patient cooped up in a hospital against his or her will."

"And you really don't feel we could have offered her an alternative treatment, Mark?"

"I know what you're after, honey. And because I believe so much in what you're trying to accomplish, I'll leave myself open on that answer. It will serve a bigger and greater purpose. But, just between us, no, I don't think it would have made a difference."

"I understand, Mark. Thanks."

"No thank you's please. But Ruth, I do have some interesting material that supports my belief."

"And what's that?"

"Some new studies of the correlates of suicide and cancer. Very few patients with cancer actually commit this act, especially not when hope and treatment are offered. There are suicide ideations, but I believe that's normal with any terminal illness. Perhaps cancer patients are very strong people. Most cope quite well, with guidance and a strong support system."

"Like the Doyles. Mark, I can't believe how well they both seem. I saw them today and they advised me that they are going to take a honeymoon!"

"Now there's an unusual couple. Both of them had an abundance of problems to resolve. They're working well, and hard, together and individually. The man loves her; there's no doubt in my mind. But I wasn't sure he could deal with that deep anger. Human beings don't take well to abandonment, and he was abandoned!"

"But I think she had regrets about leaving that marriage in the first place, Mark. And she was finally seeing the light on her choice of careers. She didn't get what she thought she would from those girlie magazines."

"Janet was directing her anger and bitterness at him because she didn't feel the 'total woman.' I guess all females have that reproductive desire some time in their lives. Janet felt unwomanly in not fulfilling that role," Mark told her.

"So she chose another feminine role—girlie magazines. And in the end those people didn't want to know her, Mark!"

"It's no wonder, Ruth. They were party people. When she became ineligible for the game, they quit."

"Now there's a woman who would have been a candidate for a conservative therapy, Mark."

"There you go again, Ruth. 'If Grandma had wheels she'd have been a trolley car!' We can't look back and say 'if.' But yes, I think you're right. She'd have taken *anything* that didn't upset her feminine image."

"I'm glad I have you on my side, Mark. Somehow you lend me a powerful weapon."

"Now if I really possessed all that power, Ruth, you and Jim and all of the others involved here wouldn't be in the jam you're in. But don't fret, I think we've devised an act to keep Donovan over the barrel."

"Saved by the shrink! Tell me."

"Jim will, soon enough. He's got the dirty work to do. See you later." The phone clicked.

The light on line two flickered. It was for her again. No breathing spell. "Hello, this is Dr. Simson."

"Dr. Engelman here, Dr. Simson. I have a message that you called."

"Yes, Dr. Engelman. It's good to hear from you."

"What can I do for you? Personal or professional?" he asked.

"A little of both," she said with a feeling of swelling in her throat. Ruth, don't panic, remain professional, she calmed herself. "I found a lump in my breast, Dr. Engelman. I saw Jim Hayes. He couldn't aspirate it. I did take mammograms. He wanted you to give an opinion." Wow, I'm through that one, she thought. I've said it without emotion, no crying, no anger.

"How would Wednesday afternoon suit you, dear?" he asked quickly.

God, he thought it was urgent!

"That's fine, Dr. Engelman. And thank you. But I also want to discuss the breast protocol with you. Will you have time?"

"Surely. There's always time for research and new researchers."

"Fine. I'll be there at one. Is it the Chatham Building?"

"Yes, dear. Ninth floor."

Thank God that's out of the way. Now perhaps I can concentrate, Ruth thought as she put down the receiver.

At five, Ruth pushed her notes and journals into her briefcase. She'd review them tonight in peace. The office was too busy for her to get any extra work accomplished. Tomorrow morning she would have teaching rounds with her residents. She needed to address the emotional aspects of the cancer crisis. Somehow this often neglected aspect of cancer care was the most vital issue for the patient and the family. Why the hell weren't the medical schools teaching it? She wrote a quick note for Ann to type and post:

To All Residents in Radiotherapy:
Grand rounds tomorrow morning at 8:00 sharp! Discussion: Emotional problems of the patient undergoing cancer therapy.
Dr. Simson

"Ann, I'll be in the hospital for about an hour. If you need me I'll be in Dr. Hayes's office."

"Fine, Dr. Simson. Have a good evening."

"Oh, and Ann, will you type and post this for the residents?"

"Surely, Dr. Simson," Ann replied, as Ruth rushed to the door.

The elevator was on her level. She got in and pressed her button. As the car rose she began to wonder why she hadn't taken a few minutes to look in the dress shop across the street. But how could she think about clothes now? she asked herself. It was easy, she concluded: denial works wonders!

Ruth entered Jim's office with a lively step. Larry was there. The two men were engaged in conversation when she arrived; this ceased when they both became aware of her presence. Frantically, she glanced from one to the other, trying to read something from the expressions on their faces. Nothing connected.

"Busy afternoon?" Larry asked as he rose to pull up a chair for her. For a moment she relaxed.

"Busy isn't the word for it. The phone didn't stop for a minute, the department was full of patients and requests. . . ." Her voice trailed off. Somehow Ruth became aware that something wasn't right. Her mouth was sputtering words, empty words. She had come here to confer about a crisis, and now she was engaged in small talk. It was a preamble . . . or was it?

"Okay, gentlemen, what's the verdict?" she heard herself ask.

Jim spoke. "None, Ruth." He turned his back to her and put the mammogram into the view box. "The radiologist and I agree, it's inconclusive."

Ruth jumped up from her seat. Surely the mammogram was a good diagnostic tool. It must reveal *something*. Perhaps they didn't want her to know just yet. She leaned over the desk to see the film. Her legs felt weak and numb.

Jim went on talking about the picture before him. "You see, here is the lump. It's small, not infiltrating. No indication of dimpling. However, these small areas in here concern me, Ruth. Calcification is a possibility; then we have a trouble spot. The only rational move to make now is a biopsy."

Ruth felt Larry's hand clasp hers. It felt warm by comparison to hers. "So I'm the patient now? Is that what you're trying to tell me, Jim?" Her voice was quivering with the words. She wanted to run, far, and be alone. Isolated where no one would touch or feel her pain, but her inner self knew better. She turned to Larry. "Where do I go from here?" She was asking for help, direction. She was letting him know that she could not manage this herself; she needed him. But it was Jim who began to talk.

"Ruth, Larry and I were doing some talking about this before you came in. In view of what's going on, and on the other hand what's *not* going on here at Memorial, we both felt that it would be best to get you to Engelman at the University. If this was Karen, that's what I'd want for her."

Ruth was so caught up in her own fears that she hardly heard Jim speak. His voice seemed distant, as if the sound waves were bouncing through the water and were simply distorted mumblings. "Suspicious." That was the word that the radiologist had used in the report. The few days of psychic relief that she had somehow managed for herself over the past weekend seemed like a fleeting moment. Her powers of denial in those few days had allowed her to change the priorities of her whole life. She had learned to love a man more than she loved medicine. Now this seemed to slip through her fingers with the threat to her life. Her head throbbed from the temples to the back of her neck.

"Jim," Larry was saying, "I'm going to take Ruth home now. I'll speak to you in the morning. She's too shocked to do any talking now."

"That's probably for the best. I'll call Engelman, or better than that I'll see him tomorrow," Jim told him.

When Ruth heard the name Engelman, she told them that she had spoken to him herself this afternoon. Yes, she had an appointment. Did they hear her?

"Larry, do you think you ought to call her family? Perhaps they should be with her now."

"No, no," Ruth shouted. "Not my family. Please don't let them know. My mother isn't well and my sister is not equipped to handle this. Larry, please tell Jim that's unnecessary!" she pleaded.

"She's right, Jim. It would make matters worse for all of them. There may be no reason for concern, and Ruth's family is very spread apart. I'll take care of everything."

Larry rose and Ruth held on to his arm. She felt secure with him, and he gave her all his strength.

"Listen, Larry, if you need me, call the house. Karen and I can be there quickly. The babysitter's only next door."

"Thanks, buddy. I appreciate that." He turned to Ruth. "Are you all right, honey, or should Jim come down to the car with us?"

"No. Please. I'll be fine. I just need a little rest and some time. Thanks, Jim. Really, I appreciate how difficult this is for you."

Larry kept his arm securely around her waist. When they arrived at the parking lot Ruth began to make a fuss about leaving her car there. "You can't drive now, honey. Just get in. I'll tell the attendant that you're leaving it overnight. Nothing's going to happen." He locked her door and hopped in on his side. She immediately began to speak in a frenzy.

"Larry, I have so much work to do. Sam and I are going to do a grand rounds course in the morning . . . Donovan called to say that he wants to meet with me next week . . . Tom Kresh's wife is having a baby and we'll be. . . ."

"Ruth, get ahold of yourself. None of those damn things matter now. Do you understand that? Everything can wait for a more appropriate time, except for Tom's wife's baby; and perhaps she'll hold off!"

They laughed. A bit of humor always broke the terror, and gave some psychic relief. Larry knew that she was trying to clean house, a normal response for a woman like Ruth facing a crisis. But he had to do the thinking now and assume the responsibility for a while. He might have to shake her some for a while. He hated to do that, but in the end it would be for her own good. Denial, one of the human being's most powerful means of coping, would have to come to an abrupt end.

Chapter 17

John Davis and Bruce Thompson had agreed to meet for coffee after five. They shared concern for Alvin Donovan's change in attitude. They had seen that during their midday meal. Al, a long-standing colleague and friend, had pretty well shown his cards. He was confused, upset, and wavering. It didn't look good for the future. They were sure he would crack under the pressures of the radical group and the problems of the suicide. Neither of them noticed Ruth Simson and Larry Stein alight from the elevator at the main floor. Together they walked toward the cafeteria. It was unusually empty, but then again visitors were not due for a while, and most of the hospital staff had gone home. John spoke.

"Market's bad this week, Bruce. I've got too much into those blue chips. They're going nowhere."

"I'm in the same position. Thought they were safe. God, if I tried to sell now I'd lose a bundle!"

"Don't," was the advice offered.

John Davis turned to the counterman. "Two cups of coffee, black."

"I'll take a booth in the back, John."

"Listen Bruce," John said, giving him one of the cups, "I'm really concerned about Al. Our policies here are conservative. And as far as we have all been concerned for years, this has served the best interests of our patients.

"I'm afraid that we're going to enter a period where cancer surgery is going to be compromised, adversely affecting some of our patients."

"You mean the breast patients, of course."

"Well, those are the objects of criticism just now. But I'm afraid this will extend to all cancer surgery.

"Diagnosing the severity of cancer in a patient is still an imprecise art, and until doctors have better ways of diagnosing cancer, some patients will have to be overtreated in order to get the maximum results."

"I agree, John. We've got to retain the Halsted Radical rather than compromise the principles we have developed over a number of years."

"You know, my personal feeling is that too much emotion has entered into this field of breast cancer surgery. I've never encountered a woman who'd rather lose her life than her breast!"

"It's this Roget case. It's a real stickler. What came first? The suicide plans or the cancer?"

"Unfortunately, we'll never know."

"Well, I can say this, and with firm conviction; I am not going to compromise my patients for the likes of other therapies. I was trained with the knife, and for cancer that's the first line of defense," Bruce stated with conviction.

"We can only hope that Al is not easily swayed by these radicals. And it also concerns me that a university surgeon like Engelman is compromising in his field."

"We can't stop it, but I agree that under no circumstances will I join them," Bruce assured his friend. "Now, let's get on with this investment program I wanted to talk about. . . ."

Alvin Donovan's light was still lit in the office when the cleaning service arrived at nine p.m. Papers were stacked high on the desk. He tried to concentrate on the meeting and the presentation he was going to make the following morning. He posted the notice for the entire staff. He had pissed away the whole day on the telephone. "Goddamn blasted machine!" he said as he glanced at it. It was a conspirator, no doubt! Calls were incoming all day from the media, the staff, the hospital administrator, and the goddamn Board of Trustees. New York was bigger than he'd realized. Everyone in the whole damn town wanted something from him about the suicide. Over and over again he heard himself repeat the same phrases. They rang like his wife's dinner chimes.

"No. We do not have the situation sorted out yet . . . I will have a statement for you when I meet with my staff . . . no, sir, not until Tuesday morning . . . no, we haven't changed any policy."

By three o'clock he was so incensed that he told

Mary, his secretary, to hold all calls. He would not speak with another living soul about this problem until *he*, Alvin Donovan, had found some solution. The only calls he took were from his wife, Claire. He might be president in the hospital, but he took the position of vice president at home. Claire would be furious if she were put off by a secretary. That would fuck up his home life. And he needed peace there at any cost.

Over and over again he skimmed the papers written on the biology and treatment of breast cancer. Still he could not find the answer; perhaps he expected it to fall from the sky, to arrive like a great dawning. But that wasn't the means by which humans were educated. Finally, in a state of disgust, he called in the chief on the opposing team. He had to have answers, and despite the fact that he didn't agree with Jim on these matters, he knew that he was the man to get the answers from—the right ones. Not that he was open to changing sides; he didn't think that was possible. There were too many variables in these new theories. What really bothered him was something he hated to admit. He didn't know enough!

"Mary, get me Jim Hayes's office, will you please?"

"Certainly, Dr. Donovan."

Within ten minutes, Jim was on the phone.

"Hayes, I need to have a talk with you. These goddamn inquisitions are going to drive me mad. Tomorrow I have to call a staff meeting. The newspapers will have their sneaky reporters roaming the halls. The whole place is going to come down. The reputation of the hospital is at stake."

"Yes, I'm aware of that, Dr. Donovan. But don't get yourself high blood pressure over it. Your ass is covered. Nothing went wrong here at the hospital."

"Now, Hayes, don't get snippy. It's a very real problem. The world outside is going to be screaming that we didn't do anything for this poor woman, and inadvertently caused her to kill herself."

"Listen, Donovan. I feel as guilty about this woman's death as you do. And perhaps more, because I should have been able to offer her more. My hands were tied in this hospital. You know that, don't you?" Jim began to let his wrath flow. He hated the bastard, and there was little reason for him not to suffer the consequences for his poor judgment. Donovan knew damn well what was going on, and if he chose to avoid these issues, let him swim in his own blood.

"I need your help, Hayes," Donovan told him in a somber tone. "Can we meet in my office? I'll have some dinner sent up."

Jim sat back in his reclining chair. He puffed on the pipe, allowing the smoke to pass through his nostrils. The sweet sound of defeat was in Donovan's voice. Jim knew that he had him in the position he wanted him now. Check—just like Mark had told him. Keep the man quietly in check. Offer him nothing. When he comes in, lost, wanting and ready to talk, use every man, every tool you have, to justify your claim. Mark was right.

"Fine, Donovan. I'll be there. But after five-thirty. I have one more surgery, then a consult."

Jim packed his briefcase at five-forty-five p.m. It was stuffed on each side, brimming over with literature. This will stone the old man! Charts, statistics, and research papers that would take him months to study. Jim felt more like an attorney than a physician. He was going to the medical tribunal.

He glanced at the mammogram on his desk. Somehow it made him feel incompetent, which, in turn, made him feel uneasy. Giving a "doomsday" report to another physician was difficult; even more so when it was a good friend and colleague. He had wanted to spend more time with Ruth, but that was not possible. She had reacted in the same way that all other patients reacted. Physicians were not entirely different; they only knew too much! He could help Ruth, and more women like her; perhaps the meeting with Donovan could do more than soothing words. He could win the case for humanity, the right to choose intelligently, the right to assume some control over a seemingly uncontrollable circumstance.

At six o'clock the hospital was more quiet. Most patients were resting after the evening meal; shifts were not changing; visitors were not due until seven. The hustle and bustle of the day's routine was over. Jim enjoyed the hour between five and six. He walked slowly toward Donovan's office and let himself in. Mary had already gone home. He went immediately to the inner door.

259

Donovan was sitting in his large leather chair. The lines in his face seemed tight, giving him the appearance of being older than his years. His eyes were puffy and the circles were deeply colored. He looked as if he had lost a lot of sleep over the issues at hand. Jim didn't blame him. He would not have wanted to be in Donovan's position.

"Good evening, Dr. Donovan," Jim said, breaking the older man's gaze.

"Oh, Hayes. I'm glad you're here. Have something to eat," he suggested, handing Jim the tray of sandwiches. "Hardly the best but it beats the cafeteria!"

"Thanks," Jim responded, helping himself. "I am hungry. Now let's get down to the business."

"I hope we're not interrupted, Hayes. I had to let Mary go home. She's been handling the calls all day, and this has been one of the worst days in my life."

"I sympathize with you, Donovan. I'll try to be of some help," Jim offered graciously. He was soliciting the old man, but then again that was the politics of hospital work. One favor deserves another, one referral deserves another, and so on down the line. That was the way medicine worked and there was no escaping the politics; it was the world of compromises. Jim was prepared to compromise on some issues *if* Donovan was; it was as simple as that. But he would hold back his trump cards for a while, using them sparingly and wisely.

"Now, Hayes, tell me just what happened with this Roget woman. You had the most contact with her, so you could probably assess the case better than anyone."

Jim gave him the story as clearly and concisely as possible, including Mark Fenster's visit. He wanted Donovan to be sure to let the press know that a psychiatrist had seen Mrs. Roget, and that many of the physicians on the staff at Memorial considered this to be routine for their cancer patients. It would be a valuable comment.

"Yes, a shrink did see this woman." It had been Mark's feeling that Mrs. Roget would not have chosen the alternative treatment, but Jim was not offering that additional information. Mark would say, "It was difficult to determine"; a very open-ended statement.

"The only treatment we could have offered her, of course, not at Memorial, was a lumpectomy. For this I could have sent her to the Cancer Center. The other alternative was an interstitial implant, which Dr. Simson could have possibly handled. Both of these avoided extensive surgery and preserved the breast."

"Thanks, Hayes. I hope I have a clearer picture for the press."

"Dr. Donovan, I'd like to take the liberty of discussing our whole approach to this dilemma. The real issue is not Sarah Roget's death; the real issue underlying all this commotion is patients' rights. And we are withholding their right to *know* here at Memorial. That's the real problem. That's where the trouble is going to come in. I understand your personal preference for the Halsted Radical, but you must face the reality of the matter. There have been too many reputable studies which indicate that the biology and treatment of cancer must be explored along other avenues. The media have already begun to address these issues. Women are informed, but not by those professionals who can help them."

"What do you mean, Hayes?"

"I mean that every surgeon in this hospital has the duty to inform every potential breast cancer patient of the alternative treatments which are medically acceptable, Donovan. He may not be willing to deliver that particular service, but he is obliged to *inform*. We, the physicians, are the leaders of health care in the community. If we don't inform then the press will exert pressures on us, and then the patients. Now, who do you want to have the upper hand? Do you want the leadership to change hands, or do you want to keep it in our ball park where it belongs?" Jim asked sternly.

"Hayes, I realize what you're saying, but personally I don't agree with this lesser surgery. We're allowing women to play on our emotions. Those adjuvant therapies are also too risky."

"Listen, Donovan, what's your cure rate? Come on, be honest? Eighty percent? Sixty percent? Or is it more like twenty-five percent?" Jim needled him.

"Well, we don't have a 'cure' yet, Hayes. I know we don't salvage a hell of a lot of lives. But damnit, those other treatments may be potential killers, too!" The old man continued to argue his case.

"After all these years of study and trial you're

still unwilling to take another risk to possibly cure? Donovan, you don't make any sense. For Christ sake, do you expect to chase cancer cells with a knife?"

"No . . . no . . ." Donovan said, pensively. "Let me see some of the protocol data, Hayes." Jim emptied his briefcase onto the desk. The old man looked weary, confused, and shaken. Perhaps he would break at some point. Jim sat back and ate his sandwich and sipped a Pepsi. He watched as Donovan tried to sort the papers and make some sense out of what he was reading. "At least I am forcing him to read the studies," Jim thought. He knew that many of the surgeons ignored them. They were still a strong camp and as a group they presented a large obstacle, resistance to change. But perhaps Sarah Roget's death though an isolated suicide, might be the catalyst. When Jim saw the old man's eyes rest, he began to speak.

"If you perceive the biology of cancer as being systemic, then the first obligation you have to a patient is to remove the large tumor cell burden. Regardless of the procedure, Donovan. And we won't argue procedure; it has been established that there are *many* procedures. Okay?" Jim asked.

"All right, Hayes. There are other ways; put it that way."

"Good, you're learning. Now to node dissections. These should be done to establish as nearly as possible the stage of a particular breast cancer. We also know that about forty percent of the node negative patients become treatment failures. Perhaps the cancer cells are bypassing the regional

263

lymph nodes?" Jim posed the question and continued. "If these nodes acted as an effective barrier, then it should follow that all women who had histologically negative nodes should be cured by surgery alone. Correct?"

"Of course, Hayes. What are you proposing now?"

"I'm proposing that breast cancer is a systemic disease for most women at the time of surgery, Donovan. Those cancer cells have escaped the lymph nodes or they have been blood-borne. But that the cancers are for the most part systemic, even in stage one, is becoming more and more apparent. Of course we have to start with the high-risk group. That has always been established medical procedure. We can't employ experimental drugs and radiation on the group we are most likely to cure by surgery alone."

"I'm bending a bit. The high-risk patients is the place to begin," Donovan consented.

"Chemotherapy trials are extremely promising, as you can see from Engelman's data. The high-risk group deserves the opportunity to elect this therapy."

"What I don't like about all these trials and choices is that women think they are at liberty to pick and choose, Hayes. They don't take medical advice."

"Granted. Some women will do that. But if you consider that you are open to everything that is established within the medical community, not only one lousy procedure, then your patient also knows you can offer more. In that way, Donovan, your opinion is respected. You can make a judgment; we all do. There will be cases where a simple lumpectomy seems to be an adequate cure. And, of course, there are cases where the disease is so progressive that even the Halsted won't help."

"But as I see it, Hayes, within the limits of the protocol there won't be any choices. Is that correct?" Donovan asked.

"Yes, that's right. But in the protocol you're testing and studying. Patients must be randomized, otherwise the results are worthless. You know that. But every woman who elects to join the study will be given full information about alternatives, with all the supporting data. Nothing will be overlooked. These women will know all there is to know. It's our obligation."

Donovan sat quietly at his desk now. He thought, and thought some more. He rehashed and churned the data in his head. It seemed overwhelming. Had he been a fool to ignore this problem? Was it inevitable that it would blow sky high one day over a suicide? Was he really man enough to admit to himself that he had been a barrier to progress? Would his "camp" ostracize him?

"Hayes, I'll tell you the truth. I never did accept the younger, more radical faction here. I guess at times I felt that they were a threat to me, my education, my personal concepts about the practice of medicine. That's a confidential statement; don't repeat it."

"You have my word."

"Unfortunately, I know that there are other less

important issues that are going to mask this problem. Some very outspoken radicals have at times done medicine a great disservice by making medical treatment an issue for public debate. Patients think that surgeons count the dollars by the number of stitches they sew. This may be true of some of them, Hayes, but they are in the minority."

"What percent of the physician population at this hospital do you think is educable?" Jim asked.

"A good number. And I think that with support we can begin to make some changes, Hayes. I just have to plan the strategy well. I don't want to be influenced by women refusing radical surgery, women refusing to live with cancer, anymore than I want to be influenced by the dollar aspects of surgery. The decisions must be based upon sound medical practice."

"I grant you that, Dr. Donovan. I'm sure you'll make the right choices. You'll realize your position of leadership, I'm sure." That was a peaceful note on which to end, Jim thought. There was little more he could say, and he wanted to get home. "Now, I must get home to Karen and the kids. And thanks for the snack." Donovan had been waxed and polished.

"Oh, Hayes. What do I tell the media about the Roget woman?"

"Tell them you offered her alternatives. She refused." Jim let the old man off the hook, but it was honest.

"Thanks, Hayes. I appreciate that. And best regards to the wife. She was a good intern. I remember her."

Now it was late. Donovan sat back in his chair again. No doubt he should call Claire, perhaps meet her for dinner. She always liked that. The speech would come to him. He was always good with words. He'd placate both sides. The only theme that came to his mind was that of individual differences. That was what the world was about, individual differences. Respect. Let each man take what he must. He could not be more decisive than that. It was his nature.

He picked up the phone, and dialed his home.

"Donovan's residence," he heard.

"Oh, Charlotte. Is Mrs. Donovan there, please?"

"I'm sorry sir, but she's at a meeting tonight. Your dinner is warming."

Damn, he thought. She's never home when I need her!

"Oh, thank you, Charlotte. I'll be home shortly."

Chapter 18

Larry was in the kitchen when the phone rang. He raced to answer the call before the ringing woke Ruth. He dropped the onion into the skillet and burned a finger when the hot oil spat back at him. "Damn," he muttered as he quickly dashed for the sink. Cold water should keep the skin from scarring.

"Hello," he said into the phone, as he cradled it on his shoulder.

"Who is this?" the voice asked.

"Hey, Jim, it's you!"

"Has Ruth calmed down some?"

"She's resting in the bedroom. I'm trying to prepare something for dinner."

"Why the hell aren't you in the bedroom with her?"

"Because I burned my finger when the damn phone rang!"

"I hope I didn't interrupt your plays, Larry," Jim teased.

"No plays now. She's trying to rest; bring herself around to the talking stage. She needs a better perspective. She's still in shock."

"That's to be expected. You and I would not be any different," he reminded Larry. "The reason why I'm calling is twofold. I wanted to let Ruth know that I had a meeting with Donovan. He's in a hot seat between the media and the administration."

"That's not all bad, Jim. It might start his thought process in our direction—or rather, your and Ruth's direction."

"I think it did. We may have reached a compromise. I offered to take responsibility for answering to Sarah Roget's death. He wants to get off the hook on that one."

"What are you getting out of the deal?" Larry asked. He knew Jim well enough to realize that comparable gains would have to be made in each camp.

"The old man is going to let us practice medicine, Larry. Our medicine, the kind of stuff we were taught to do."

"You don't really mean that, Buddy, do you?" Larry asked.

"Absolutely. Now I'm not saying that he's been reformed. He'll be neutral. But that's where he needs to be. However, for our purposes that's a tremendous gain. He won't stand in the way, and he'll buck any flak from the administration."

"I'll tell Ruth the good news. She could use some cheering tonight."

"Do you want Karen and me to come over for a

269

while? We'll certainly be glad to help," Jim offered.

"No, but thanks. I'm sure we'll hit the sack early tonight. Ruth has a big day ahead of her tomorrow, and she needs sleep."

"I've got ya. Enjoy yourselves!"

Larry went back to his cooking. The sauce was just about ready; he'd have to awaken her. He turned the burner down to simmer and walked toward the bedroom. As soon as he entered, she looked up from the pillow. "Who was on the phone?"

"It was Jim. I thought you were asleep, honey."

"I'll bet he got a big thrill out of your being here at this hour."

"He did," Larry admitted. "But he knows about our relationship. There's nothing to hide."

"How does he know?" she asked.

"Because I told him."

"You told him what, Larry? That we were sleeping together?" Now she was nearly in tears.

"Ruth, for God sake, no! I told him I was going to marry you."

"You're what?" she asked in amazement.

"I'm going to marry you!"

"You haven't asked me yet, and you told Jim?" She was both angry and delighted with him.

"I'm asking you now . . . Ruth, will you marry me?" He bowed. His head bent down to the covers. She leaned over and kissed him.

"I can't answer you yet, Larry. For many reasons I just can't commit myself. Will you wait?" she asked lovingly.

"Do you love me, Ruth?"

"With all my heart, Larry. That's why I can't give you the answer now. I've got to feel well and whole when I give you an answer. I've waited a long time for marriage, and I can't make the choice, for either of us, when my mind is so cluttered with questions." It was an honest statement, one which came from her heart and her soul. She was in the midst of a life-threatening crisis; could she realistically make plans for tomorrows?

"I'll wait," Larry responded. "I'll be out there in the field when you want me." He reached out to hold her, for just at that moment he needed to feel the warmth of her body. But she recoiled from his advance and rolled up in a fetal position on the side of the bed.

"Ruth, please come here," he begged. "I love you and I need you!"

She responded. He held her shaking body. "What the hell is wrong with my loving you?"

"Larry, I can't . . . I just can't. Please leave me!" she cried.

"I'm never leaving again. Now get over here!"

"How can you love me when I may be a cancer victim? I may be breastless soon, unable to bear children, unable to cope with myself, and you want to marry me? Are you a glutton for punishment?" she demanded.

"So that's it," he said, pulling slightly away from her. Now they were face to face. "You have some ridiculous notion that the course of an illness will make me run away from you? You idiot! I love you unconditionally! That's the way it should be, Ruth."

"Do you want a life with a sick woman? A maimed woman? And what will your family think, Larry? God, Larry, be sensible. Your mother will never accept me!" Ruth sobbed.

"You're wrong, Ruth. She's going to love you. You're all that she could want in a daughter-in-law."

"And what's that?"

"You're a Jewish doctor!" They had a good laugh. The Jewish-doctor dream fulfilled on both sides of the family. Mrs. Stein, Mrs. Simson, both gloating!

"Larry," she said, brushing tears from her eyes. "That's rather comical, you know. My mother and I have disagreed on almost every count since I was a child. If I marry you that will please her no end, I'm sure." Ruth suddenly thought that she might subconsciously have avoided intimate relationships simply because it would have pleased her mother! How adolescent.

"Beautiful, my sauce will be burned. How about some nourishment?"

"Larry, that was a big plus for you from the very beginning. You can cook!"

"Come," he urged. "I'm starved."

"For me, or for dinner?" she spoke coyly.

"The sooner we get dinner out of the way, the faster I can have you."

"Will you stay?"

"I'm not leaving. I need you, Ruth," he said, kissing her warm lips. She was very receptive.

As he carried her to the kitchen she smelled the rich, full aroma of the dinner. "Umm," she whispered. "That's delicious. What are we eating?"

"My Italian cooking at it's best. Both rich and fattening!" He lowered her into the chair, and poured her a glass of wine. "Eat, my lady, before it gets cold!"

Ruth ate well, and when she scraped her plate clean he went to fill it again. She put her hand up in an effort to stop him. "I'm going to burst, Larry. Not another thing!"

"You don't mind if I scrape the pot myself?" he asked.

"Go right ahead . . . now, tell me what Jim had to say?"

"He and Karen offered to come over tonight, but I told him that I could handle the situation myself," he said confidently.

"Oh, did you tell him that?"

"Of course I did, and he understood. Jim and I have been friends for years, honey. We don't play games."

"What else did he say?" she asked.

"How did you know there was something else?"

"Because you were on the phone an awfully long time."

"Business," he told her casually.

"What business?"

"A surprise for you."

"Well, am I supposed to guess?" she asked.

"No, my love. I tell it like it is," he said teasingly. "Jim had a powwow with the chief of the Indians tonight. They worked out a peace treaty. The agreement says that Memorial Hospital has the right to participate in the Breast Project.''

There was a slight look of shock on Ruth's face. The shock turned to tears, then to laughter. She broke a smile. His heart felt flooded with warmth. Ruth was responding.

''Oh, God, Larry. I don't believe it. It's too good to be true. But how did he accomplish this?''

''I think that it was a little of Mark's psychology, too. They planned their strategy carefully.''

''But how is the administration going to take all this?'' she asked.

''We'll see tomorrow. Jim doesn't know how the issues will be resolved; only that Donovan is going to have to do the work. You'll see, the death knell will toll.''

''Death knell . . .'' Ruth repeated the words. ''The death knell will toll on the radical mastectomy.''

''You're too far into the future now. We've only just begun,'' Larry reminded her.

''All beginnings are difficult, remember that, Larry?''

''And there will be more to come. When you marry me, I'll complicate your life!'' he announced.

''The hell you will!'' she laughed.

''Listen, we're going to have lots of little Steins around our house. Enjoy the quiet and peace for the moment. It won't last long.''

''The change looks good! Maybe that's what I

need in my life, Larry! A few kids to drive me out of the house and back to work."

"I'm going to be a super father, Ruth. I love kids; they're my favorite patients."

"Let's see if you have the same 'patience' when the kids are your own!" she laughed.

"Honestly, honey, I never tire of kids."

"What will happen to my practice? Are you going to stay home with all of them?" she questioned.

"With my mother around we needn't worry. We'll have all the help we need," Larry reassured her.

"Did you tell her I was coming on Wednesday, Larry?"

"She started to cook today," he said as he began to clear the plates from the table.

"You know I have to see Dr. Engelman on Wednesday; God, that's the day after tomorrow!" she cried. "Larry will you meet me at the university?"

"You couldn't stop me. Should I be there for the consultation?"

"No. There's no need for that. I feel all right about it. My decisions are made now, and I believe in Dr. Engelman," she said confidently.

"Will you let me in on the decisions, Ruth?"

"Uh huh."

"I'm listening."

"If he wants a biopsy, I'm going to get that out of the way as quickly as possible. It's all the waiting that makes me nervous and edgy, Larry. Coping with the unknown is difficult."

"I know, honey, but you're doing well."

"After the biopsy, I'll wait for the pathology report. I know that Dr. Engelman will make a decision, and a wise one, based upon the tumor pathology. I'll have time to adjust to things; that is, if I have to. But for now, I'll keep my spirits up and take one thing at a time."

She had her act together, Larry was sure. Ruth had come a long way from the shock to the reality, and her decision was sensible. The medical shopping was done; the surgical decisions would be made later. She was doing it alone, independent of him. That was good, he realized. She was an independent woman, and she would always want to assume responsibility for her life.

"I love you, woman," he told her when she finished. "Can we go to bed now?"

"And who's going to do the dishes?"

"We'll let them soak. I'll rinse everything when I get up to jog."

Their lovemaking was filled with many emotions that night. Larry, filled with thoughts of taking Ruth as his wife, for better or for worse, was at peace. Ruth, feeling loved unconditionally, and being able for the first time to give in the same way, held tightly on to his strong body. She would love and need him in the days that followed.

Chapter 19

April 5, 1975

Every staff member at Memorial Hospital was greeted with a message from the office of Dr. Alvin Donovan:

A general staff meeting will take place this morning at ten o'clock sharp in the Memorial Auditorium. Your presence is requested.

Larry had left Ruth off at the main door of the hospital, with intentions of meeting her for lunch. He drove off into the traffic to get to his office for early appointments. Ruth had teaching rounds to make. When she arrived in the office she saw the note on her desk. "Oh, Christ!" she thought. "How could anyone upset plans the way this man does?" Although she was anxious to hear what Donovan had to say, her first responsibility was to her resident staff and her patients. Didn't Donovan realize that grand rounds always took place in the mornings? She picked up the interoffice phone and dialed Sam's number.

"Sam, we've got to get those rounds in early this morning. The chief called a meeting for ten."

"I got the note. It's right here. Do you know what he's going to say?"

"I'm sure that it will sound like an inaugural address. He's got some explaining to do about the suicide case."

"It's about time. I think we've had reporters here snooping around for the past two days."

"That's why Donovan's closeted in his office. Listen, Sam, before we begin this morning I'd like to talk with you. Can you be in here, in say, ten minutes?" she asked.

"Sure." He hung up the phone quickly. Ruth pressed the button for an outside line, and dialed Larry's office.

"Dr. Stein's office. May I help you?" the voice of his secretary responded.

"This is Dr. Simson. May I speak with Dr. Stein?" she asked.

"I'm sorry. He isn't here right now. Our hours begin at nine. May I take a . . . oh wait, he just arrived, Dr. Simson. Please hold."

Within a minute she heard Larry on the line. "Hello, love."

"Larry, I got the message as soon as I arrived. Donovan is going to make his speech this morning at ten. Can you be here?"

"Sure. I'll meet you in the auditorium. It will be

short and appeasing."

"I'll see you then. And thanks, Larry."

Sam was at the door. "Come on in, Sam."

"Want to discuss patients?" he asked.

"No. It's a personal problem. I want to get this off my chest as quickly and quietly as possible, Sam. But if I break, please pick up what's left."

Sam braced himself. Ruth Simson was not usually in pieces about anything. She handled life well, especially his constant joking. What could be so serious?

"You're going to take over this department for a while, Sam. I hope it's only a short experience for both of us. But I trust. . . ."

Sam flushed; guilt gripped him. He had been hoping for the chief position someday . . . perhaps he had wished too much!

Ruth was still talking. He listened. "I'm going into the hospital for a biopsy. I hope it's sometime this week or the next. Dr. Engelman is going to do it. . . ."

"Not you!" he cried in utter disbelief. Not Ruth Simson! "Ruth, I don't know what to say."

"Don't say anything, Sam. If it's benign, I'll only be gone a few days. I'm going to call in sick. But you have to run this department, and I know you can do it. I'm just warning you in case I'm out longer than I planned."

What a hell of a way to attain a position, Sam thought. He couldn't rid himself of the guilt.

"Well, don't just sit there, Sam. You have work to do. You always wanted that position, didn't

279

you?" Ruth asked candidly.

"How did you know, Ruth?" The blood in his veins was hot, the adrenalin was shooting through his body. He felt like a child caught lighting matches!

"Sam, you're bright and ambitious. You never put me down, don't misunderstand me. I respect you, and we work very well together. I didn't mean to be so candid and tactless. I wanted you to know that I understand your feelings and ambitions for yourself."

"Thanks, Ruth. I appreciate the quality of your sentiments. But I never wanted things to happen this way."

"I want you to know that if anything does happen to me, you'll be the first asked to assume the position. You have what it takes. And then again, Sam, I may be ready for a short retirement from full-time responsibilities even if I'm well."

"What the hell are you talking about, Ruth? This department, this whole hospital, needs staff like you!"

"But I have other needs too, Sam. And they take priority."

"Over your work?"

"Some. But I want to study, Sam. Research may be where I want to direct my attentions in the future. And I'm also thinking of motherhood!"

Sam laughed heartily. "I can't believe you've found a match!"

"I have, Sam. And he's too wonderful to pass up."

"Ruth, is it Larry Stein?"

"None other, Sam. But that's not for publication yet, either. Right now I'm concerned about my health, and you have to concentrate on the department. Are we ready for grand rounds?"

Suzie Thomas was the first patient that morning. As Ruth entered the room she saw that the child was deeply engrossed in a jigsaw puzzle. The residents relaxed. "Hi, Suzie," Ruth said cheerfully. Suzie looked up from her tray.

"I'm having trouble, Dr. Simson. Can you help me find the piece to the teddy bear's tail?"

"Wow," Ruth answered as she looked at the thousand pieces spread all over the bed. "That's going to be a tough one. Do you think we can wait for a few minutes. I'd really like you to meet some of my doctor friends?"

"Oh, sure, Dr. Simson. But will you help me later?"

"Of course, dear. Now this is Dr. Ray," Ruth told her as she directed her glance at Sam. "Then there's Dr. Kresh, and Dr. Wooley. Do you mind if they stay while I examine you?"

"Not if you find the teddy bear's tail, I don't!" Ruth thought Suzie was a remarkable child. Larry had said that he liked the kids the best. It was true. They were cooperative, for the most part, when they had confidence in you. And they were always refreshing and different. It was a challenge to work with them. Suzie proudly displayed her red rectangle for the doctors. Ruth palpated the area. It was over in seconds.

"Everything's looking fine, Suzie. Now I want to talk to you for a little bit. I'm not going to be here for a few days, and these very capable 'princes' are going to treat you until I come back. What do you think?"

"Where are you going, Dr. Simson?" Suzie wanted to know. Ruth saw the expression of fear on her face; she knew she'd have to explain. Suzie might feel abandoned.

"Suzie, I must go to the hospital for a small operation, something like yours."

Suzie's face lit up, then her lips curled down, and a tear fell from her eye. "Are you going to be all right, Dr. Simson? Will you be here in this hospital?"

"No, honey. I'll be in another hospital. But I won't be away very long. We can even write each other letters," Ruth suggested. "You can give me a full report on how these guys are treating you!"

"They better treat you good, too, Dr. Simson. If they don't I'll write them a nasty letter."

"Suzie, you're adorable!"

"Thanks, Dr. Simson!"

Ruth turned to Sam and the others. "Why don't you go on without me for a while. I'll catch up. First I must help Suzie with the bear's tail."

When they left the room Suzie and Ruth started their search for the missing puzzle piece. But Ruth's mind was more on the child than on the problem of the animal's tail. How wonderful it would be for Suzie to spend time with her outside the hospital. Paula, Amy's oldest daughter, was just the same age as Suzie. And Paula, too, enjoyed puzzles. It would be nice to get them together. Ruth was developing a great attachment to her little patient.

"Suzie," Ruth asked, looking to get her attention, "have you ever had chicken pox?"

"Oh, sure," Suzie told her. "That's awful! I had them when I was in nursery school. Boy, does that itch!"

"You know I have six delightful nieces and nephews. And one of them has the chicken pox now. I was just wondering how he might be feeling."

"He's feeling terrible, Dr. Simson. I mean the one who has the pox. But you know what my Mom did when I had them?"

"No. What?"

"Well, she gave me a big bag of tootsie rolls," Suzie said, making a motion with her hands to indicate the size of the bag. "She told me that every time I had an itch I should eat a tootsie roll."

"Did you do that?" Ruth said laughingly. The thought of so many sweets made her stomach turn.

"Sure I did. And it was fun. But Mom told me when I was older that she asked me to do that so I wouldn't make pock marks on my face. I guess I couldn't understand that when I was little."

"Well, you don't have any marks, Suzie. I guess it worked!"

"You bet it did. I ate three big bags of the candy before the pox went away!"

"Maybe I should tell Brian to do that."

"Maybe I should tell him, Dr. Simson. I was the one who did it."

"That's a marvelous idea, Suzie. Should we call him?" Ruth asked.

"Uh huh!"

Ruth picked up the receiver on the phone next to Suzie's bed. "This is Dr. Simson. May I please have an outside line?" Within a few seconds Ruth had Amy on the phone.

"Amy, it's me, Ruth. How are the children?"

"Coming along well. So far only Brian has the disease, and I'm keeping my fingers crossed. Just a week until Passover."

"You might be lucky yet. I have a little friend here who would like to speak with Brian. Is he available?"

"Oh, sure. He's bored to death these past few days. You know Brian when he's not able to be active!"

"Yes, I know how difficult it must be trying to keep him down. Once the very sick feeling passes they're ready to resume normal activity."

"If only he'd stop scratching his face! I keep telling him that his rosy clear skin will resemble potholes if he doesn't keep his hands away."

"I think we have a cure for you, Amy."

"Really?"

"Sure. Put Brian on the phone and let him speak to Suzie. She's already had the experience." Ruth handed Suzie the phone. "Remember, his name is Brian."

"Brian, this is Suzie Thomas. I'm a friend of your Auntie Ruth. Actually, she's my doctor." Then there was silence. Suzie looked pensive as she listened to Brian.

"She's my doctor because I have this trouble with my kidney. She's making me well again. Where's the kidney?" Suzie put her hand over the receiver and asked Ruth, "Where is the kidney?"

Ruth wanted to laugh at the conversation. Children were so candid. "Here," she said, pointing to the area on Suzie's body. Suzie went on to explain, anatomically, to Brian.

It took several minutes before Suzie felt assured that Brian understood her. "Now you got it!"

"Tell him about the candy, Suzie," Ruth coaxed her.

"Oh, yeah, your aunt asked me to tell you about the time I had the chicken pox, Brian. You see whenever I wanted to scratch. . . ."

Ruth half-heartedly went about looking for the bear's tail. She was enjoying the conversation between Suzie and Brian. Finally, Suzie held the receiver once again and spoke to Ruth. "Brian wants to know if I can come and visit with him sometime?"

"Tell him as soon as I finish my treatments with you, I'll take you to his house."

"Will you really, Dr. Simson?" Suzie asked. Her eyes were shining with delight. She and Brian, both sick in other ways, had each found a friend in the other.

"Of course. We'll take a ride there and all of you can play together."

Suzie returned to the phone. "Your auntie says we can play together when we both get better, Brian. Okay? Enjoy your tootsie rolls. And Brian, I hope you get well soon. . . . Thanks." Suzie again turned to Ruth. "Do you want to speak?"

"Yes, thanks, dear. Ask Brian to get his mother." Ruth took the receiver. "Amy, did you hear that talk? Yes, it was darling . . . I know they want to meet . . . I guess so, she's already had the chicken pox. You don't get that twice . . . about a week or so . . . yes, we'll see. Right now I have to find a bear's tail!"

"A what? Ruth?" Amy asked, rather puzzled.

"Suzie's like Paula. She picks the jigsaws with a thousand pieces!"

"Good luck. That's hard work. And Ruth, that's motherhood too," Amy told her.

Sam Ray and Tom Kresh walked the corridors of the hospital, checking in on patients. Tom turned to Sam. "What's Ruth talking about with Suzie Thomas this morning, Sam? She didn't say anything to me about going to the hospital."

"Well, I didn't know about it until this morning myself, to tell you the truth. But she was being honest with the kid. She's got a lump in her breast and it has to be biopsied. That's all I know."

"Jesus Christ," Tom said aloud. "I can't believe it!"

"I said the same thing, Tom. You know it's funny. We work here every day with cancer. I don't know how many patients we treat a week, and yet we *can't* accept the fact that someone we know, and perhaps love, has cancer! Isn't that strange, Tom? Cancer is our daily lives, our bread and butter, and we still can't accept it?"

"I guess you hit it, Sam. We think it can happen to everyone else. We should have a built-in immunity. Maybe that's the unconscious reason we all got started in this business."

"I wish you wouldn't say anything to the others around the hospital. Ruth hates sympathy. It would make her more depressed than she already is. No fanfare, no pity."

"She gives so much of herself to this disease. You'd almost think that would be a bargaining card. I only hope they treat her well. God knows she gives enough to everyone else."

"You'll learn from being around Ruth. She's always been ahead of her time. She's ready to get started on the interstitial implants soon," Sam said confidentially.

"Do you really think it's in the wind for the near future?"

"I'll let her tell you after we attend the staff meeting this morning. Donovan should have some. . . ." They both heard the clicking of Ruth's heels as she walked hurriedly to catch up with them. Silence.

"Hey, wait," she called. They stopped.

"That was fast, Ruth," Sam said. "I thought it would take the entire morning to find the bear's tail!"

"I was saved, boys. Mark Fenster came in to see Suzie. I had turned the whole box of pieces upside down. It took him half a minute to find the right piece. Incredible!"

"That's because in his business he's used to looking for needles in a haystack," Sam remarked.

They visited with two more patients. Much time was devoted to discussing individual problems.

Mrs. Parrish was having trouble eating; her diet was not suitable for her health condition. Ruth called the dietician to explain that Mrs. Parrish must have a light diet, one more suited to her appetite. The woman in the kitchen gave Ruth a hard time. She wasn't a short order cook, she said. Ruth told her that she knew she wasn't. She reminded her that the job description had called for a more difficult type of work: human involvement, caring for sick people! The angry woman shut her mouth.

"And if they don't send the tray you request, Mrs. Parrish, please call the nurses immediately. They will let me know. I'll leave a note on your chart. Your diet is important now, and we want you to eat," Ruth instructed her.

"Thank you, Dr. Simson. I don't like to keep asking all the time. I feel like a burden to everyone."

"You're not a burden to anyone, Mrs. Parrish. You're asking for something that's rightfully yours. And if I were you I'd probably scream!"

"Good luck with your operation, Dr. Simson. Please have someone come here to tell me how you're doing," the woman requested.

Sam put in the final word. "Don't worry, Mrs. Parrish. You'll be seeing us every day. We'll keep you happy, and posted."

At nine-forty-five, Ruth and Sam left the residents in the unit to attend the staff meeting. On the way up, Sam wanted to speak to Ruth, but he couldn't find the words. His feelings were strong, but the translation into sentences was impossible.

It all sounded absurd, but he'd try.

"Ruth, do you really know how much I have learned from you? Do you realize the impact you have on the residents who are fortunate enough to pass through this program?"

"Speaking of residents, Sam, I must sidetrack for a moment. You don't mind, I hope."

"No, not at all. What's on your mind?" he asked.

"You know Tom will be finishing up with us on the thirtieth of June. His three years are up, and I have hardly had a chance to ask him about his future plans. We've been caught up in so much work and program planning that I completely forgot."

"Jesus, you're right. In a few months we'll have changes of the guards again. How I hate the month of July!"

"Has Tom spoken to you at all about wanting to join our staff?"

"Ruth, I do know one thing. Tom would stay if the program were expanded. Much in the way we want to do it. But in the past year he's been feeling the same way you have; he needs to branch out, be innovative in his work. Tom has an artistic and scientific quality in his nature that the others never had."

"That's exactly why I want him, Sam. He's good. Very good. I've watched him closely for three years, and from the day I hired him on as a resident I knew there was something distinctly different about him."

"Then you want to offer him a position?" Sam inquired.

"Well, how would you feel about working with him? You may be the next chief, Sam."

"Hey, hold on, Ruth. I don't want to hear that one!"

"Okay. But be honest. Do you think he would complement us?"

"I think he'd be great. But we have to persuade him! I hope the results of this meeting do that for us!"

They entered the auditorium. It was packed. Ruth saw faces that she hardly remembered anymore. Everyone was out from under the woodwork and the paper. Sam escorted her to a seat. Larry saw Ruth from the door and joined them. He had a chance to get in a quick hello before Donovan began to speak.

"I need not elaborate on the suicide of Sarah Roget. However, many of you have been contacted by the media in their efforts to evoke confidential information. I am glad to report that common sense dictated to those of you involved. The 'no comment' rule was used. As I am the official spokesman for this staff no one here must feel responsible for the answers. I intend to meet with the press, and Dr. Hayes, the attending physician, will give his report.

"The problem of Sarah Roget's death has brought up a far more complicated message for us to focus upon at this time. Everyone involved in cancer must begin to search for answers; and this means education, re-evaluation. It seems that newer theories of the biology of cancer need to be explored. For too many years we have turned our backs, masking the problem with less important issues. Now we must ask ourselves, 'is cancer a systemic disease, in most cases?' Is our approach failing because many of us do not recognize the systemic theory?"

Ruth turned quickly to Larry, as Donovan paused for water. "He's running through this like a fire, Larry. How can he hope to accomplish anything?"

"That's always been his tactic—style, evasive manner, honey. He's not going to attempt to educate the staff; he's just giving you the liberty to educate yourself. It will be that 'to each his own' type of thing," Larry whispered. Donovan went on.

"There are many reasons why we must look toward new horizons. Although this suicide was not a debatable medical issue, it was a social issue. I am going to make policy changes at Memorial based on both problems.

"The fact that there are two distinct camps of thought on the biology and treatment of cancer needs some consideration. For those of you who will uphold the Halsted theory, I respect your views. For those of you who feel you must move in other directions, I cannot pass judgment. You have valid reasons. Memorial will not neglect the promises or studies of either camp. I can assure you of this. Therefore I am taking steps toward condoning our participation in protocols which are evaluating the worth of limited surgery, and a multimodality approach to this disease. At the present time I have little to add to these issues. Dr.

Hayes will speak to the media as concerns Mrs. Roget's passing. I share the grief of her family. However, it was not within our powers to prevent this unfortunate incident.

"I will be accepting protocol applications at your convenience. Thank you, and may I wish you all well."

Alvin Donovan made his exit from the auditorium quickly. He didn't want to speak with staff members from either camp. He needed space from the issue, breathing time, and some rest. His would be a middle-of-the-road policy, for that's where he stood as a physician: on the line. He would always be pushing papers; they would have to find the answers.

"I guess the war is over," Ruth commented to Larry and Sam.

"I think it's just begun," Sam answered as he heard the commotion surrounding them.

John Davis and Bruce Thompson walked out of the auditorium together. It was John who spoke.

"What did you think of that speech, Bruce?"

"I thought it was really in our favor; very noncommittal. He couldn't do much more in his position. But that doesn't change my mind a bit. I'm as confident as ever that we're doing the right thing when we do the radicals. And, of course, it may mean losing a few patients. . . ."

"Something I can ill afford!"

"Listen, I heard from my brokers this morning. Got some excellent tips and I said I'd get back to them. Why don't we discuss this at lunch?"

"Fine. I'll meet you then."

"And John, let's take the heat off Al. It's over and done with. I know he still feels the way we do. But the pressures are just too great."

"Yes, I know. Only my financial pressures are getting to me now."

"Relax. I told you I have something going. . . ."

Chapter 20

April 6, 1975

"Why didn't you wake me sooner?" Ruth yelled to Larry. He was in the shower and obviously did not hear her. She yelled again. He turned the water off. "What did you say?" he called loudly.

"Why didn't you wake me earlier? I need time to get dressed and eat."

"After all we drank last night I thought you needed the rest. Come on, sleepy head, admit that you had too much!"

"You're right. But it isn't every night that you celebrate such an event!" Ruth declared, an air of victory evident in her voice.

"Don't worry about it. Karen was as loaded as you were," Larry reminded her.

"Well, the dinner was great, and the company even better. They are a delightful couple, Larry."

"I knew you'd like Karen," he said walking into the bedroom. He was drying his hair with a towel.

"You two have a lot in common. Even your inability to hold booze!"

"Are you finished with the bathroom, doctor? Remember I need to be presentable today. It's my big day!" she reminded him.

"I know, honey. But it will all work out fine. You'll see. You won the professional war, now it's on to your own fight. This will be the easy part, and remember, I'm with you."

Ruth shuddered. Easy part! How easy would it be to face her appointment with Dr. Engelman? It would be so wonderful to believe in the world according to Larry Stein! Everything was roses.

It was late by the time they finished dressing, so they ate breakfast out. Larry dropped Ruth off at the hospital and continued on his way to the office. He would meet her at Chatham, soon after one.

Ruth tried to keep her mind on the work at hand. This would be her last week around, possibly. She didn't want to leave the loose ends for Sam. With that in mind, she hurried to the office. The door was ajar, the lights were on.

"Hail to the chief," was the theme that greeted her when she pushed the door open. Sam, Tom, and the junior residents were putting candles on the cake.

"Is it someone's birthday?" Ruth wondered, thinking for a moment that she had possibly lost track of time. "What the hell is going on here?" she demanded.

"The birth of a new era, chief! And the birth of my second son!" Tom cried.

"Oh, my God, Tom. When did she deliver?" Ruth asked excitedly.

"Last night. She's always a night person. We admitted her at two and the baby was born at two-thirty. Kresh efficiency!"

Ruth kissed him on the cheek and wished him well. "I'll see Ellen and the baby as soon as I get back from the university, Tom," she promised.

Sam tried to get back to the business at hand. More than anything he wanted to give Ruth that send-off he felt she needed. "Hey, listen, Ruth. The hospital is buzzin', and everyone knows who was at the bottom of all this. The rebel and delight of the radiation therapy unit!" Sam looked at Ruth. She seemed excited, and delighted with their praise and cheers. He was carrying off the masquerade, as planned. He only hoped that she did not connect with the undertones of the event. She needed love and support, and he vowed to himself that he would offer it to her; partly because he liked her; mostly because he felt so damned guilty about his personal ambitions.

They enjoyed an hour of laughter and jokes while the unit carried on with patient therapy. When the last bits and crumbs of cake were eaten, Ruth declared with some guilt, "Okay, boys, this is the last of the goodies. It's time to get to work!"

"Work! Shit. Ruth, this is a national holiday!" Sam declared.

"The National Holiday will come when we have the answers, Sam. We've only begun to fight. . . . now who said that?" she asked.

"J.P.J.," Tom told her. "Hey, I like that

name, Ruth. John Paul Kresh. What do you think?"

"I think it's beautiful. But don't you think you should ask Ellen?"

"You're right. I'm off to the nursery. Gotta take another look at that son of mine. You know this kid has the longest, most beautiful fingers. He would make an excellent surgeon!" Tom declared as he took leave of the group.

The rest of them gazed at her. She knew the thoughts that were coursing through their minds. She had to get them out now; it was time to be alone. "Okay, boys, scatter. It's time to work!"

Ruth sat down at her desk. It was full of crumbs. She made a short attempt to tidy things up. The phone rang.

"Dr. Simson," she said.

"Ruth, it's Dan. How are you doing?"

"Just finished a few celebrations. Tom's wife delivered another son, and our 'camp' delivered a new era of medical research, I hope."

"Well, you've got a lot to celebrate. Both you and Jim are to be congratulated. You did a fine job. Jim was lit up like a light bulb this morning at the breakfast table."

"That's because he had too much to drink and too little sleep last night!"

"Listen, Ruth, I know that this is going to sound very trite to you. But I can't find any other words to express what I want very much to say. Jim was confiding in Mark and me this morning. We know what's going on in your personal life now, and we are deeply concerned. I mean with the biopsy procedure, of course. . . ." Dan was fumbling.

"And what else were you three talking about, Dan?" she asked knowingly.

"Nothing else of great importance. Now we want you to know that we're with you, dear. Our sentiments are in the right place even though we're locked up in these laboratories all day. . . ."

"I know that, Dan. And it gives me strength. . . ." Ruth replied. But she could not take much more of the conversation. She knew that she would be drawn to tears, and she tried to suppress her emotions. She changed the subject. "Speaking of labs, Dan, how are those experiments going?"

"Now that's the second reason why I called. I told you about the physician in Germany, didn't I?" he asked.

"Yes, you did. He's doing some research in the same area, isn't he?"

"Yes, and by God I was able to track him down, Ruth. It took many phone calls but I've located the man. We had a short conversation last night. He thinks he might have hit on a means of suspending the tumor cells."

Ruth's ears picked up. Suddenly she forgot her own troubles and became excited. "Why, Dan, that's probably the best news I've heard since Donovan's speech!"

"Well, my dear, we are still in the planning stages. But I think that I am going to use what time is left on this grant very wisely."

"What are you going to do?"

"I'm going to ask for a leave of absence. . . ."

Before he could finish telling her his plans she

interrupted. "Dan, you can't leave!"

"There are many other competent doctors to care for your patients in my absence. This is something that must be done, Ruth. There are time limits imposed upon this grant, and don't get me wrong; I'm still hoping for an extension. But I must use these last months to our advantage; and I think that combining knowledge is the primary source."

"Then you're planning to go to Germany?" she asked.

"Absolutely. My wife and I gave it consideration. There's nothing to hold us back now. All the children are married or away in college. And she's been delighted with the thought of travel. Now I only need to find coverage for my practice," he told her.

"Well, as you said, Dan, there are many capable physicians here. I'm sure they'll share your patient load. If there's anything I can do, please let me know."

"Just take care of yourself, honey. That's of primary concern to all of us. . . ."

"And Dan, please excuse my selfish reactions. I'm really delighted that these positive things are happening in cancer. We're moving ahead in every discipline."

"That's what we've hoped for for so long. Now the reality is here. Well, it's time I got to work, Ruth. The preparation for this journey might just take the entire six months if I don't get back to work. We'll have this damn disease licked some day."

"Cheers, Dan."

Within the next two hours Ruth worked well and feverishly to complete and transcribe the plans for the review board. She sent the tapes to Ann, who would in turn type them and pass them on to Dr. Donovan for his approval. At noon she left for the university.

Ruth found Chatham Hall and took the elevator to the ninth floor. "Surgery," the sign said, with an arrow pointing to the left. That must be the office, she thought. She entered. There were six women working at typewriters; no one looked up. Engelman wrote numerous papers and she surmised that the women were employed for the sake of the many medical journals in which his work appeared. She cleared her throat. Finally, the receptionist acknowledged her.

"I'm Dr. Ruth Simson. I have an appointment with Dr. Engelman at one o'clock."

"Oh, yes. Dr. Simson. Please have a seat. Dr. Engelman is in his lab. I'll tell him you're here."

Ruth took a seat and waited. She noticed that the walls were filled with lithographs. She had already begun to appreciate an "original" graphic. That had been Larry Stein's art lesson number one. She recalled his words. "Remember," he had told her, "in the original you'll find the artist's name signed in pencil in the right-hand corner. On the lower left you'll see a fraction. The top number tells you in order, which piece it is in the particular run. The lower number tells you the amount of the run." So much for art.

In a few minutes she saw the large form of Dr. Engelman appear. Her heart began to skip.

"Well, hello, young lady," he greeted her. "It's good to see you again!"

She was delighted that he remembered her. She felt dwarfed, like a child, in his presence. He ushered her into the office, and while she took a seat he spoke.

"Ruth," he called her, "I have to be perfectly honest with you. I saw Jim Hayes this morning. I know that he didn't confer with you about our meeting, but it was primarily in reference to the breast project. He brought your mammogram along with him. He has been disturbed about it and he wanted my opinion as quickly as possible."

Ruth felt glued to the seat. She had expected to trial and jury her own case, but everything had been settled before her arrival. She was cheated; Engelman had been forewarned.

"I know that for you this is a time of great psychic terror, Ruth, and because of that I want to get this biopsy out of the way as quickly as possible. . . ."

"Will I faint here?" Ruth asked herself. "Shall I wait until I leave this office? Will Larry be there to pick up the pieces? Why am I at such loose ends? Because, goddamnit, he's telling you it might be a malignancy!"

But what had she expected? Jim had told her the lump was suspicious on Monday. X-rays don't change! She didn't even know how she felt, *if* she felt, anymore. Obviously "denial" had been working again.

"When and what are you going to do?" she asked trying to be as calm as possible.

"Tomorrow I want you in the hospital for a complete work-up. Friday morning I'll perform the biopsy. If it's benign, you go home the following day, with my blessings."

"And if it's malignant?" she managed to say.

"Then we'll discuss the approach after the pathology is back. Okay?"

"Okay," she responded.

"Now, what is this Jim tells me about Memorial physicians joining us for the breast project?" Engelman was able to flow from one issue to another easily. Ruth found herself unable to make the transition. Her thinking was clouded; if she spoke she knew it would not be in intelligent statements.

"Dr. Engelman," she pleaded, "can we discuss the protocol another time? I just can't handle anything more now."

"Of course, dear. I'm not terribly tactful. I pressed you, and this is the wrong time for stress," he said apologetically.

"That's my problem, Dr. Engelman. You don't have to be sorry."

"It certainly is *my* problem. I have to learn myself. Let me walk you down. Is someone meeting you?"

"Yes, one of the doctors from the hospital."

"Good. Now I want you to be here tomorrow no later than noon. I need those test results before the surgery. And if you have any questions before morning, please call me. I'll be at this number all day," he assured her.

Larry's car was in view when they reached the

entrance to Chatham Hall. Ruth said good-bye to Dr. Engelman and walked slowly to the car. It was early, and she knew that Larry had skipped lunch in order to meet her. Thank God, she thought. It was better to collapse in his car than on the street.

He got out and opened the door for her. "I was almost tempted to come up . . . hey, honey, you look glum."

"Larry, I have to be in this hospital tomorrow. He's going to do the biopsy Friday morning." Larry noticed that she was aloof, almost in a trance. What a rapid transformation from this morning, he thought. All her "starch" was gone.

As soon as they arrived at Ruth's apartment he called his office. He left numbers where he could be reached for the answering service. He would not work for the remainder of the day, and possibly tomorrow.

"Honey," he called to Ruth, who was sitting on the sofa, "why don't you wash up and refresh? We'll go out for a while."

When she didn't answer, he walked into the living room. "Ruth, do you hear me? I want to go shopping for some things. Why don't you wash and change your clothes?"

"I've got to call Sam," she replied. But she didn't look at him. She continued to stare into space.

"All right. Call Sam, and then get yourself ready. We have a dinner tonight with my mother." She got up slowly and seemed to go about what she was doing without interest or intent. Larry was concerned. He would have to do the psychic work for both of them. He didn't want to remain in the apartment. That would only be morbid for her. She would sit and stare, without connecting to anything. And then they would discuss probabilities; something Larry also detested. The only feasible solution also seemed ridiculous—get out and do something, anything, but don't sit here feeling sorry for yourself. Now they had the task of living out the worst twenty-four hours of their lives.

He took her to Saks. It was her favorite store, yet nothing interested her. He would pick out an article, show it to her, and perhaps she would manage a nod. Nothing more. He bought her nightgowns and a robe, then a gift for his mother. She participated in nothing.

They walked the city streets looking in the store windows. Larry had always liked to do that as a child. But he could never afford to buy anything. Now, when he could spend the money, when he wanted to shop "therapeutically," he couldn't. Ruth didn't say anything; she never so much as smiled. By four-thirty he decided to drive to his mother's. He wanted to beat the traffic from the city.

Mrs. Stein lived in Brooklyn. She had been born there, and in spite of the fact that the neighborhood had changed drastically since he was a child, she refused to leave. She still had many of her friends there, and Larry realized that older people were more comfortable with the familiar. He respected the fact that she wanted to stay, even though he worried constantly about her safety.

"I'm a friend to all here, Larry. People like me,"

she would assure him. "Nothing will happen. I put dimes in the overdue parking meters. All the shopkeepers know me by my first name. This is where your father and I began our lives together. This is where I want to stay."

She stayed and he visited with her almost every week. None of his friends were in the neighborhood anymore, but still he experienced a thrill when he revisited the places of his childhood. He would have wanted to show Ruth all these places, to relive some of the times with her. The high school, the handball court, the BMT subway station where he used to shine shoes on Sundays. But that was before his father caught him cutting Hebrew school. He should probably eliminate that one! But Ruth was not up to anything, and how could he try to laugh through her sorrow?

He parked the car. "This is it," he told her.

"I hope your mother isn't disappointed."

"There she is. Waving to us from the window. Look up. There's Mrs. Goldberg!"

They took the old elevator to the fourth floor. Mrs. Stein was waiting at the door. Ruth sensed that others were waiting behind doors, peering at her, sizing up the girl Larry Stein was bringing home. She hoped they were pleased. Should she show her teeth for their approval?

"Welcome," Mrs. Stein cried, waving her arms at Ruth. She had a broad grin on her handsome face. It was from her that Larry got his good looks, Ruth thought.

"Come in, children," she said, leading the way to her apartment.

"Mother, take it easy," Larry reminded her. "You'll smother Ruth!"

"I intend to, Larry. Every day I hear more about her, and every day I love her more!"

"What's that?" Ruth asked.

"It's my mother divulging family secrets. She has called me every day for the past five days to ask me about you."

"And I have waited the five days like it was five years," she told Ruth. "You make Larry so happy, so I'm happy!"

Ruth handed Mrs. Stein the bud vase they had bought for her. She was delighted and once again kissed Ruth. Their meal was spent engaging in small talk. Mrs. Stein wanted to know all about Ruth's family, her job, her sister. Mrs. Stein had a knack for extracting information.

"That was a delicious meal, Mrs. Stein," Ruth said as they drank coffee.

"You don't eat enough, Ruthie."

Uh, oh, Ruth thought. She was going to be a "Ruthie" here, too. Mrs. Stein would have a lot in common with her mother!

"Oh, really, Mrs. Stein, I do my share of eating. I'm still full from last night."

"And what was last night, children?"

"Nothing more than a hospital celebration, Mom," Larry said.

"So what are you two planning for the holidays?" Mrs. Stein asked. Ruth did not know what to say. She and Larry hadn't made any plans. She only knew that her mother was coming and that Amy would expect her to help, somehow. Now the terror of planning for tomorrows hit Ruth. What could she say? This was not the time nor the place to spill the beans. She and Larry had planned to keep the families out of this matter. She looked at Larry and gave him direction to speak for both of them.

"Ruth's mother is coming up from Florida next week, Mom. I think that we all will probably go to Ruth's sister Amy's for dinner one night. But Ruth will call you on that. Okay?"

"Oh, that would be delightful, Ruthie. Then maybe we could have the families here too," she suggested.

"Of course, Mom," Larry assured her. "I know that Mrs. Simson would love that."

The dinner went well. Larry made excuses for their early departure. He wanted Ruth to be able to rest after packing her hospital baggage; and if he knew Ruth, that would take hours. She always had work along with her, and being in a hospital as a patient would not stop her from working.

"You were great tonight, honey. My mother adores you."

Ruth looked at the nightgowns that he had bought her earlier in the day. "Larry, where the hell do you think you're taking me tomorrow? To the Hilton?" she asked as she looked at the fancy nightwear.

"No, dear. But you can use them later on for our honeymoon. That was my plan. Besides, I'm going to be looking at you for the next twenty-four hours in the hospital. I want you to be gorgeous."

Chapter 21

April 7, 1975

Her room was not the Hilton. It bore little resemblance to anything she had ever seen before. At least at Memorial, and other hospitals in which she had worked, there were pictures on the walls, curtains on the windows, a small dresser in which to keep personal articles. There was nothing in this room that exhibited evidence of human inhabitance. The University Hospital might just have easily been the city morgue. Larry looked for some place in which to deposit her things. When he found nothing evident, he began rapping on the walls, hoping that a secret closet would appear. "Hurrah!" he cried. A space in the wall parted and low and behold, there was a cubby with two hangers.

"I guess they don't plan on long stays," he commented to her.

"Either that or they don't plan on letting you

out," she remarked. She was sitting on the bed watching him do the work.

"I guess it's a matter of how you view things, honey."

"Well, I plan to get out, Larry. And on my own steam!"

They both sensed a third party at the threshold.

"I'm Dr. Nilsen, Dr. Simson. I'm going to be taking your P.H. in just a few minutes then we'll begin the testing."

"All right," Ruth answered. But Dr. Nilsen continued to stand at the door. Did he expect something of her? Finally she glared back at him, and like a reprimanded child, he fled. Within a few moments a nurse appeared at the door. "Come in," Ruth said.

"I'll just take a minute, Dr. Simson. Dr. Nilsen would like to begin his work with you, but you must change your clothes."

"Listen, nurse, I want to remain in my street clothes until the tests are completed. I have some work I'd like to do, and I would feel much more comfortable in my slacks," Ruth said.

Larry noted hostility in Ruth's voice. For a moment he thought he should try to handle the situation, but it was not his affair, and Ruth would be angry.

"I'm sorry, Dr. Simson. That's our hospital policy," the nurse continued.

"Well, that's ridiculous. I don't have to be in bed, and I certainly don't have to be undressed for a P.H. And you can tell that to Dr. Nilsen!" The nurse left.

Larry turned to Ruth. Their eyes met, and in that glance he tried to tell her that she was the patient, not the doctor, this time around. She knew why she had reacted and she tried to explain to him as best she could. Ruth was experiencing "patient reaction."

"First they're stripping me of my professional status; then they're stripping me of my personal right to dress in street clothes. They want me stripped naked, Larry! Authority, Goddamn hospital authority," she cried. "Imagine, that doctor telling a nurse to have me strip myself for a P.H."

"Ruth, we do it every day. We take that all away from the patient. Unfortunately, my love, you're going to have to do the same. Here and now you're the patient, and there's no sense in getting upset. Come on," he begged.

She sat on the bed and cried. He held her hand until she was ready to realize the situation and cope with it. His empathy was with her; he probably would have had much the same feelings.

"I'm ready," she said.

"Good. Now go into the bathroom and get into one of those knock-outs I bought you. I'll go downstairs and get the paper."

"Be back in a hurry, please."

"Ten minutes," he promised.

When Larry returned to the room, Dr. Nilsen was taking the history. He sat quietly and listened. Ruth was answering the questions without sarcasm. He was afraid that she might be angry enough to play with him.

"Well, everything is in order, Dr. Simson."

"Thank you, Dr. Nilsen."

"The nurse will be in in a few minutes. You'll be in nuclear medicine for the scans for about an hour and a half."

When he left the room, Ruth turned to Larry. "Why don't you go back to the hospital for a while? I won't even be here for most of the day, Larry. You'll go stir crazy."

He was getting a little edgy himself. She was right; he could do more for his patients than he could for her this afternoon.

"All right, honey. But call me if you need me," he told her. He began to walk toward the door.

"Larry, you forgot something," she reminded him.

"Oh, my kiss," he remembered. She walked up to him and kissed him. She knew that he wanted to escape as much as she did. She almost made it to the door with him, when a nurse entered the room. Ruth changed her plans quickly. "No escape." In a moment, Larry was gone.

Hours later when her preoperative tests were completed, she was given a tray. Ruth lifted the metal cover and looked at the contents. She thought of poor Mrs. Parrish.

"No, thank you," she said to the aide who had carried the food to her bedside. "I don't feel terribly hungry tonight."

"Can I get you something else, ma'am?" the woman asked.

"Yes, please, my sleeping pill."

*   *   *

"Wake up, Dr. Simson. It's time for prep!" a voice said.

Ruth looked up with her sleep-filled eyes at the nurse with the smiling face. The smile made Ruth angry.

"What time is it?"

"Almost seven," the nurse told her. Ruth rushed to the bathroom, washed, and brushed her teeth. Larry would be there soon.

When she came out of the bathroom she saw him sitting on the bed. A nurse was posting a sign overhead. "Nothing by mouth."

"I hope that doesn't mean I can't kiss her," Larry said trying to kid around with the woman. She did have a sense of humor.

"Just one minute, sir, and I'll be out!"

He kissed Ruth and they sat back on her bed, holding hands.

Dr. Engelman walked in. "Good morning, Ruth," he said cheerfully. "How are you feeling?"

Ruth thought that perhaps he was going to a party. He was dressed in a grey pin-striped suit and a starched white shirt. He was certainly distinguished looking. "I'm hungry," she told him.

"We'll get you something light to eat after the biopsy. I'm going down to dress and scrub. I'll see you there."

They came for her almost immediately. A shot of valium was administered. Larry held her hand as they wheeled her down the hall on the stretcher. She thought that she would feel upset, angry, self-conscious and damned. But Ruth felt nothing but euphoric as the sedative put her into another world.

She was laid out on the OR table. Dr. Engelman was talking to her. Another doctor was pumping something into her I.V. Ruth felt nothing; emptiness. Their voices were like sound waves passing through water. "I don't give a damn. . . ."

She awoke in her room. Dr. Engelman was sitting and talking with Larry near the window. The sun was streaming in, and the glare made it difficult for Ruth to see. The anesthesia also impaired her sight; objects and people were turning in peculiar directions. She managed to grunt so that they were aware that she was awake.

Larry ran over to the bed. "I hurt," she whispered.

Dr. Engelman called for medication. He spoke to her softly. "Ruth, do you hear me?"

"Yes," she told him.

"The frozen section was benign, dear. You're going to be fine."

"Yes . . . yes . . ." she said. The nurse came with another injection.

When she finally awoke only Larry was in the room. The sun was setting. The orange light shone on his hair. She lay there looking at him, silently reading, waiting for her to wake up. She thought of the two of them, alone. How wonderful he was, how exciting their love was. She had waited a long time, but she felt sure of the direction in which she was going.

313

"Larry," she whispered. "Come here."

He quickly darted from the seat, dropping the newspaper on the floor.

"I had a funny dream," she said.

"About what?" he asked.

"About surviving," she answered.

"That wasn't a dream, honey. It was Dr. Engelman speaking to you. The biopsy was benign."

"I can't believe it's over, Larry. I can't believe I lived through this."

"Tomorrow it's home, angel. Do you want to eat something?"

"Yes, I'm famished."

"I'll ask the nurse at the desk to send up a tray. Dr. Engelman said you could eat after eight hours. It's long past."

On Saturday she felt more like Ruth again. The nightmare was behind her; good health was the reality. It had seemed like an infinite amount of time in her life, yet it was but one week—seven days in spring.

Dr. Engelman had come in to check her out. "Ruth, I'll call you at home on Monday. I'll have the final pathology by that time. No work, and I mean it, until I remove those few stitches on Thursday. Call the office for an appointment."

"Thank you, Dr. Engelman. I feel like a woman reborn."

"No thanks. You're a valuable and lovable woman, Ruth Simson," he said, as he walked her to the nursing station.

Larry met them as he was stepping out of the elevator.

Dr. Engelman spoke. "You've got a strong woman here, Dr. Stein. I expect great things from her. I'll probably see both of you on Thursday. Good-bye now, in good health."

When he was gone, Ruth turned to Larry. "There's something extremely lovable about that man."

"Save that stuff for me, lady. Are you ready to go home?"

"As soon as I speak with a nurse. I'm sure that there will be mail coming in and I want to be sure I have it forwarded home."

"Can I help you?" the nurse asked her.

"Yes. May I leave you an address for my mail? I expect it will arrive after I'm gone."

"Are you discharged, Dr. Simson?" she asked.

"Yes. It's in the chart."

"And what is the new address?"

Larry answered before she had the chance. "That's 108 Riverside Drive."

The day was sunny and warm. Ruth felt lightheaded and happy as she and Larry drove home. Their silence was full and rich with love; they gathered strength from each other's presence. And life would go on, though the experiences of the last seven days would undoubtedly change the course and perspective of their lives. But *now* there was a FUTURE, a very real and exciting future. The block was lifted from their shoulders and the tomorrows, the plans, could be made. How lucky she was. What a narrow escape. The emotional impact of living with cancer would shape and alter attitudes and thus enhance her life infinitely. Her goals and ambitions were focused clearly on these issues, by virtue of her personal experience; something that was not reversible.

Chapter 22

Larry had the alarm set for seven. He jumped out of bed as the buzz sounded and raced to the bureau to turn it off. He did not want to awaken Ruth. He would have just the amount of time he needed to dress, check in at the office, drive to the airport and return for their appointment with Dr. Engelman. As he quietly made his way to the bathroom, Ruth looked out from under the covers. "Trying to escape?" she asked with a grin on her face.

"From my own apartment?"

"You're right. That would seem odd. What are you doing this morning?" she asked.

Ruth had been getting bored in the house. She had become the phone doctor of the unit. She called in at least four times a day to make sure everything was going well. The only redeeming feature of her convalescence was that she had time to focus on herself and enjoy some of the delights of being a homemaker. But she was feeling perfectly well and her anxiety about getting back to the hospital was mounting daily.

"I'm going to get things squared away at the office first. Then I'll go out to the airport and pick up your mother," he replied.

"Oh, gosh," she cried. "I almost forgot! She arrives today!"

"That's right, princess. And someone has to be there. I told her when we spoke on Monday night to look for a handsome guy driving a Rolls Royce."

"You're joking, Larry! She'll never find you!"

"Wanna bet?"

"Should I go with you?" she asked.

"No, you rest. I'll get her and bring her to your apartment. It'll give me a chance to get to know her. Remember she'll be my mother-in-law in a few short weeks." He marched to the bathroom humming "Pomp and Circumstance."

"Who's graduating?" Ruth asked, following him to the bathroom.

"Me. I'm going from bachelorhood to husbandry!"

"Larry, when will you learn to use the English language?"

"I thought I was rather expressive," he replied, knowing what she was thinking. "Come here, I'll show you."

"You can't catch me!" she cried, running into the bedroom.

"Yes, I can," he answered, falling on top of her in bed.

*   *   *

Larry arrived at the airport just as Mrs. Simson's plane arrived at the gate. He felt relieved. Whenever he desired Ruth, as he had this morning, he was lost to time and place. Now he had almost missed the arrival of his mother-in-law to be. That could be considered a criminal offense in the Simson family. He spotted her directly. She was the only woman to alight from the plane looking like she had her life's belongings with her. "Jesus," he thought. "I hope she isn't planning to stay indefinitely!"

"Larry?" she asked, approaching him from the ramp.

"Mrs. Simson. I'm delighted." He bowed slightly. She laughed.

"You are as handsome as you said," she told him.

"Here let me take your packages," he offered. "I'll have to get the car after we find your luggage. The walk is long."

"Oh, I brought a few things for Ruthie, Amy, and the children. How's Ruthie?" she asked.

"Oh, she's fine, really. She'll see the doctor this afternoon."

"I don't know why she didn't tell me, Larry. I should have been here with her. But she did have you, and I'm glad."

Larry helped her grab the two suitcases from the luggage trolley, and posted her at the glass door with the parcels. "I'll be a few minutes with the car. Just wait here; and don't carry the bags. I can park for a few minutes."

Mrs. Simson was delighted by her first encounter with Larry Stein. He was handsome, well-spoken, and chivalrous. She only hoped that her daughter appreciated this man. Ruth had the habit of running away. Mrs. Simson was of a mind to complete all the wedding arrangements before her daughter could change her mind. She would need Larry's assistance in doing this. Mrs. Simson's mission was to see her younger child married, and Larry Stein seemed an excellent prospect. It was certainly the closest Ruth had come to taking the matrimonial vows. When Larry had arrived and put her baggage into the trunk of the car, she took the front seat next to him.

"So, Larry, tell me. Has your mother met my daughter?"

"Just last week. Unfortunately it was the night before I took Ruth to the hospital. She wasn't emotionally up to the meeting; but I couldn't put my mother off," he told her.

"And what does your mother think?"

"About what?" Larry asked, knowing well what Mrs. Simson was trying to find out.

"About Ruthie; what else?"

"Oh, she loved Ruth. Who wouldn't?"

Mrs. Simson had quite a few answers to that question churning in her mind. But she didn't want Larry Stein to know them now. He would find out through his own experiences how difficult her daughter could be. She was reminded of Ruth's self-willed personality, of all the troubles she'd had bringing up a determined and rebellious daughter.

Larry read her mind precisely. "You have quite

a daughter, Mrs. Simson. She wasn't easy to catch. A woman who possesses as much intelligence, charm, and beauty as Ruth is sought after by many men."

"It's a relief to me, to tell you the truth, that she's finally decided to get married. My husband and I worried about her for a long time. She was always in and out of love, but not with thoughts of marriage like the other girls."

"Ruth had a lot that she needed to accomplish. And she has done it; professionally, I mean. She's quite a little fighter!"

"Oh, is she a fighter!" Mrs. Simson agreed.

"My mother is planning a dinner for the second night of the holiday, Mrs. Simson. I think that she wants all of us to come and meet her side of the family. There are too many of us to congregate at Amy's for the first dinner. And Ruth has also invited a guest family."

"That's perfect, Larry. Yes, there is so much for Amy to do. And having the children sick and all those worries. She needs my help. I think I'm going to go out to the Island tonight instead of the weekend. Help her prepare. I just want to see Ruthie first."

He was going to tell her that he appreciated this. It would not be necessary for Ruth to go home. That had been the only imposition of his future mother-in-law's visit. He would have to live alone.

"Ruth and I can take you out to dinner and then we'll drive you to Amy's."

"Have you and Ruthie made any wedding plans yet? Or shouldn't I ask?"

"Oh, you can ask; certainly. But Ruth will have to give you the details. It's becoming quite complicated!"

"How complicated can arrangements be?" Mrs. Simson asked. "You decide on the place and date and I'll make the dinner. It's very simple. Leave it to me."

"Oh, no, Mrs. Simson. The date is not the problem. We just need to adjust our time schedules. Did Ruth tell you she's taking a leave of absence from work?" Larry asked.

Mrs. Simson flushed. No, she thought. Ruth is too sensible. She couldn't have done anything so dumb. She wasn't? Or was she? Ruth would never leave her work unless something forced her to do so. She had to ask, but tactfully. Was she prepared for the answer? Was her daughter locked into this arrangement?

"Ruth never wanted to leave work, Larry. I don't think I understand. . . ."

"She's going to be working, Mrs. Simson. But not here. She'll be taking a grant to study. We're going to be weekend mates."

Mrs. Simson was relieved. A child was not on the way. But she suspected that a weekend marriage would be a difficult thing to handle, especially during the first year.

"Why is she doing that now?"

"Because the opportunity has come her way. And because it is very important to her."

"How do you feel about this, Larry? A husband can be very lonely without his wife around."

"That's part of our planning. If Ruth starts

during the summer, I hope to take my vacation with her. She's going to be on the New England coast; ideal for a honeymoon. Don't you think?"

Mrs. Simson sat in her seat lost in personal thoughts. Yes, her daughter was different. And certainly this was exactly the kind of man she needed. They were probably very much alike. Unconventional. She would not interfere. Both of them were well-directed and obviously had worked out a marriage agreement that suited them. For the first time in her life she, too, felt resigned. But the resignation was not quite so negative as it had been in the past. At least this time Ruthie would be doing something conventional; she was finally getting married. Larry Stein was suitable.

Ruth left the apartment almost immediately after Larry. She didn't feel like resting; she was already reaching the restless stage. She would go to the hospital before returning to her own apartment to greet her mother. She was glad that Larry was with her, that the two would be acquainted before they were all together. She was sure that he would charm her mother, who would be delighted at the prospect of the union. And Larry would answer all the questions; there would be no entanglements. It was a relief.

"Good morning, Debbie," she said, as she entered the unit.

"Well, my God, if it isn't Dr. Simson! What are you doing here? We had the word not to bother you for anything until Monday."

"I wanted to get a few visits off my mind and

take a look at some of the patient charts. And I feel fine, Debbie."

"Dr. Ray is in the treatment room. Do you want me to get him?" she asked.

"Yes, please, Debbie. But wait until he's finished with the patient. And Debbie, will you post my thank you notes? I can't tell you how beautiful all those gifts were!"

"Just a small expression of our love and admiration. And by the way, Suzie. Thomas is so anxious to see you that she calls here every afternoon. 'Is Dr. Simson back yet?' You've got to see her!"

"How's she doing?"

"Fine on the treatments. Dr. Ray says the progress is remarkable."

"I'll be in the office. Just send Dr. Ray in when you see him."

Ruth sat at her desk and sifted through the mail. An envelope from Dr. Donovan's office caught her eye. She opened it quickly. Resident and staff forms for the coming year. Interviews for positions for first-year residents. July first would be upon them quickly. She would need to submit her staff roster before May fifteenth. Vacancies would have to be filled; first-year applicants interviewed. Quickly Ruth scrawled a note to Dr. Donovan advising him that interviews could be set up immediately. The new staff would be hired before she left for New England.

A quick view at the in-patient roster showed that there was little change in admissions. Most were doing well. She pulled Suzie Thomas's record:

responding to radiation therapy. Ruth looked up as the door opened. It was Sam.

"Well, you're back to work without an absence note, chief."

"I don't get one until this afternoon, Sam. But I'm going crazy staying home."

"I know what you mean," he said approaching the desk. "The kid's doing very well, Ruth," he said, as he noticed Suzie's folder.

"You know, Sam, I love that little girl. She sent me two letters while I was in the hospital. They both arrived after I was discharged."

"You know that every day since you've been gone she's asked for you. And in the afternoons she calls down here. Parents are making great progress too. Mark's seeing them."

"Yes, I know."

"The mother is looking real good; rested, and all that. I think that the little girl is so hung up on you that she's less demanding on their time."

"Parents of sick children need time away from the hospital too, Sam. Especially when they have other children at home."

"Got a little surprise for you," he said with a twinkle in his eye.

"What's that?"

"Well, I was going to leave it to Tom to tell you, but he'll be on vacation until end of next week."

"How are Ellen and the baby?" she asked.

"Both doing beautifully. And Dr. Kresh will become our Junior partner as of July one."

"Thank goodness," Ruth said, with a sigh of relief. "Now I can take my leave with confidence."

"You're going to study then?"

"I had decided to do it, Sam, but I was concerned that we'd have to hire someone from outside the hospital staff. That would have been a setback. But now with Tom, there's no problem. You can move up for a while, and Tom can fill your shoes." Ruth sat back and relaxed. All the crises of the past two weeks were coming to resolutions; all the resolutions seemed to fit into place snugly.

"I noticed that Donovan asked for next year's roster. He wants everything completed as soon as possible. You can put Tom's name in for approval; the others are staying too. Very little changes will have to be made. This year will be easy compared to all the others. Two first-year men is all we need."

"Men?" Ruth questioned.

"Sorry, chief. Two first year residents, men or women."

"That's better, love."

"No discrimination. We'll work this together. Just tell Donovan to set the interviews for the week after the holidays."

Ruth looked at the clock on her desk. There wasn't much time. She'd have to forget the mail, for the time being, and answer it tomorrow. Her mother would be angry if she were not at the apartment when Larry dropped her off. A terrible way to begin a holiday.

"Sam, I'll be in early tomorrow. Just get this envelope off to Dr. Donovan . . . Oh, and take the material for the review committee too . . . Let him see it before we go to bat next week."

"You don't foresee any difficulties, do you?"

"No, none. We have a solid program, and I was able to expand . . . in many areas. You know which ones I mean?"

"You included the plans for the implant?"

"Everything for radiation as a primary therapy, and also as an adjuvant therapy. We just need Donovan's approval; and I don't think there will be any objections. Jim is already involved. He set the pace."

"I'll look it over and then get it off. Will you be in all day tomorrow?"

"Yes, why?"

"I'll post a note for the patients. Some of them have been driving us mad for answers. So long as they see you for a short visit they'll feel better."

"I'm going up to see Suzie now. Then I must get to Dr. Engelman's. And my mother is in for the holidays."

Ruth took the elevator to the pediatric unit. She walked quickly to Suzie's room. She stopped at the threshold, just long enough to watch the child in action, unaware of her presence. She was on the telephone.

"I can't come just yet. I have to wait until I get out of here . . . I don't know . . . Hey, Brian, do you know anything about Teddy Roosevelt? I have to write a paper on him . . . Yeah, but the library isn't great. I hate to ask my Mom to do it for me . . . I'm listening . . ." Suddenly Suzie looked up from her note pad and saw Ruth standing at the threshold with a grin on her face. She dropped the phone. It thudded as it fell to the floor.

Poor Brian, Ruth thought.

"Dr. Simson!" Suzie cried with delight. "Am I glad to see you!" She threw her arms around Ruth's neck. They held each other in a long, warm embrace. "How I missed you . . . how I missed you!" Suzie sighed.

"And how I missed you," Ruth whispered. And how I wish you had been as lucky as I was, she thought. But I shall never leave you, Suzie, never abandon you. You are one of the dearest people in my life.

"Oh, Dr. Simson. I left Brian hanging! There, on the telephone."

"Well, get him back for a moment. I need to speak with his mother."

Suzie ran for the phone. "Your auntie is here, Brian. She wants to speak with your mom. Then I'll talk to you again. Okay?" She handed the phone to Ruth.

"Amy, yes . . . how are you?"

"Listen, Ruth, this affair between Suzie and Brian is forcing me to buy another phone. They call each other all day!"

"I was going to ask you about that . . . I'm going to bring Suzie out next week with me. Yes, she'll be out of the hospital . . . No problem . . . Good . . . I've got to meet mother now . . . I left Larry with all the work. I'll speak to you from home." She turned to Suzie.

"I have to leave now, honey. Just a visit with my doctor. I'll be back in the morning. Now you and Brian don't have to speak three times a day; once is enough." They kissed good-bye, and Suzie went on with her conversation.

Ruth drove to her apartment. It was almost noon. She spotted Larry's car already parked in her guest spot. Damn, she thought. Mother will have something to say. Ruth greeted Thomas quickly and took the elevator to the apartment. The door was open. They were awaiting her arrival.

"Hello, Mother," Ruth called as she entered.

"In the kitchen, Ruthie," her mother answered.

Ruth walked to the kitchen. There was Larry, exhibiting his culinary talents, preparing lunch for all of them. Mrs. Simson rushed to embrace her daughter. "My God, Ruthie, you got thin!"

"Wrong, Mother. Same weight."

"Then it's your hair. You cut it?"

"Wrong again. Same style as before."

"So what is it? You look different."

"Love, Mother."

"Well I can't say I blame you, dear. He's wonderful!"

"The best," Ruth replied, kissing Larry long on the lips.

"I ate my lunch," he replied. "Great kiss, honey. It will keep me all day. Now, do you and Mother want to eat before we go to Dr. Engelman?" Larry asked.

They ate amidst much talk. The getting together of the two families for the holidays required planning. The wedding required planning. Mrs. Simson seemed to delight in the busy events. Ruth felt almost elated that her mother had a happy event, a *mitzvah,* to focus on. There had been nothing but emotional voids in her life for so many months.

"It's almost one-thirty, Ruth. We'll have to get going." Larry told her as they sat in the living room looking at gifts Mrs. Simson had brought.

"Mother, everything is lovely. And thank you for the necklace. I really love it. Are you going to wait for us here?" she asked.

"Yes, of course. And look, Ruthie, Larry said he wouldn't mind taking me to Amy's tonight. I want to see the children. So when you get back we'll all take a ride. Okay?"

Ruth looked at Larry. He winked. "Fine, Mother. Larry hasn't met Amy."

"Good, then I'll call her and tell her we'll be there. After dinner?" she asked.

"Yes. That would be better; we'll go out."

"See you later, Mom," Ruth called as she and Larry left.

They were parking in the hospital lot when Ruth turned to Larry and finally spoke. "I guess you made a big hit with my mother."

"I was wondering when you were going to say something."

"I've been thinking, Larry. She and I got along so well together today. I can't believe that the reunion was so perfectly pleasant."

"She's a good woman, honey. But mothers can be difficult at times. It was easier because I was there, too, and I think she wanted me to have that first great impression."

"Maybe you're right, Larry. But still it was very unusual for her."

Larry opened the office door and spoke to the receptionist. Dr. Engelman would be with them in a few moments. They took seats and waited.

He came into the room smiling at them. "Come on in," he said, opening the office door. The two men shook hands. "How's the lady been behaving?" he asked Larry.

"Beautifully. Hasn't gone to work at all. Just rested. Followed all orders."

Ruth chuckled to herself.

"Well, my dear, all the pathology reports are in. As I said before, everything was negative. You are home free. Now, if you'll climb up on that table and take off your blouse I want to remove the stitches."

Larry rose from his seat to leave. Dr. Engelman assured him that he could stay. He wanted him to see the beautiful stitching work. No scarring. Ruth blushed. She felt relieved that Larry did not say anything. It would have embarrassed her. When Dr. Engelman completed the work he said, "Now, you're as good as new. And I've heard from Dr. Hayes that you're ready to begin work with us in the protocol study. I'm delighted, Dr. Simson."

"And so am I. Did Dr. Hayes tell you that I am going to study the implant procedure with Dr. Hillman?"

"Yes, he did. And we shall miss you while you're gone. But what you'll be doing there with Hillman will be extremely important for the future of breast cancer treatment. I wish you luck."

"Thank you, Dr. Engelman. Dr. Ray and Dr. Kresh will be the cooperative physicians in the therapy unit at Memorial. They're extremely competent."

"Yes, so Hayes tells me. And if they trained with you I have no doubts, either."

"Will I need to come back again?" she asked.

"No, just a six-month check-up will be fine. I don't foresee any problems. Go, again in good health. And keep in touch with us." He walked them to the door. Ruth felt compelled to plant a kiss on Dr. Engelman's cheek. "Now, that's a fine reward!" he told her, hugging her back.

Chapter 23

Ruth looked out of the car window, watching the rain hit the streets and splash under car wheels. She wondered how Amy would feel with all of the children locked into the house for a full day. They had hoped to have the kind of weather that would permit the children to run free while the adults went about their preparations. Weather was so unpredictable. They drove down the Belt Parkway. It looked gray and abandoned under the heavily clouded sky. Larry exited at the Flatbush Avenue sign.

"Why so quiet?" he asked.

"Just thinking about the kids today. They hate being cooped up in the house."

"It's a family holiday. They'll just be a little more close than usual. Don't fret."

"I hope Suzie enjoys herself. And I hope the kids do get along."

"Of course they will. It will be a good experience for all of them. Inviting a stranger to a seder is a long-established custom," Larry reminded her. "Well, here we are; and look over there . . . across the street . . . my mother, waiting outside in this weather!"

"I'll bet she's been there for a while, Larry. And my God, she's got packages with her, too."

"You can't invite my mother expecting her to come empty-handed. That's her nature." He drove up to the sidewalk to let her into the car. He got out quickly, took her packages and put them in the trunk.

"Hello, darling," she said to Ruth, reaching over the seat to kiss her. "I spoke to your mother yesterday and she sounds very happy."

Larry jumped back into his seat, wiping his hands on a rag in the glove compartment. "How long have you been standing there, Mom? I'm soaked from those few seconds."

"Only a few minutes. But I have a raincoat and hat on, Larry. Look at you! Where's your hat?"

"Okay, Mom. Enough."

"So, Ruthie, tell me the plans for the wedding. . . ."

By the time they arrived at Amy's house, Mrs. Stein was involved in preparations for their wedding. Ruth and Larry would have little to do with their mothers at work. Their only duty would be to show up. It was almost a relief. And they had resigned themselves to allowing the two widow mothers to have the honor of all the arrangements.

"Put the car in the driveway, Larry," his mother said. "You don't want Ruthie getting soaked. She doesn't need to be in the hospital again."

"Mother, don't worry. Ruth won't melt. And I *will* put the car in the driveway; I *won't* have her in the hospital again; and I insist that you not make a Jewish Princess out of her!"

"She deserves to be a princess. Don't forget that," Mrs. Stein added, barely listening to her son.

Ruth sat in her seat chuckling to herself. Indeed her mother-in-law-to-be would be a friend, an ally. It was fair, she reasoned. Her own mother was taking to Larry in much the same fashion. The teams were evenly divided.

Larry took the packages while the women walked ahead of him. They were greeted at the door by a block-bustering crowd.

"Aunt Ruth . . . Aunt Ruth . . . Aunt Ruth is here!"

"Aunt Ruth is here with that guy!" they heard Paula shout.

"What's his name?" Brian yelled.

"Larry," Ruth said, smiling as she tried to make her way into the house. "Move kids, Uncle Larry has his hands full." At that moment Suzie came running. She and Brian had been somewhere.

"Dr. Simson, you're here!"

"And you're here!" Ruth replied. "Now wait a minute, kids. Let us put down all these packages before anything breaks."

"Anything for us?" Jeffrey asked. He was Amy's youngest son.

"Need any help there?" Joe called as he made his way from the kitchen. Turning to Larry, he said, "Here let me take those bundles off your hands. And kids, clear the way. Go to the den and play something . . . anything, for a few minutes."

The children went off. Joe led them into the dining room where Amy was finishing the seder plate. Mrs. Thomas was helping her.

Ruth went to greet Mrs. Thomas. "You look wonderful, indeed! And I am delighted that you were able to come. Really, I have wanted Suzie to meet these children, and for you to share our holiday with us."

"We wouldn't have missed this. It's all Suzie has been talking about since she came home. I guess that she and Brian have a very thick friendship."

"Yes, and it's good that they were each able to help the other through their illnesses," Ruth added.

"And you wouldn't believe how many tootsie rolls were consumed! Ruth, I thought his teeth would rot under my eyes. But at least he's preserved that lovely complexion. No pock marks," Amy declared.

Joe and Larry and Mr. Thomas took care of their own introductions. They were already drinking together in the living room when they were joined by the women.

"Well, here comes the bride," Joe stated loudly as he stood for her entrance. "And here's to the groom," he toasted, as he raised his glass in the air.

"I'll drink to that one, Joe," Larry said, walking over to Ruth.

The adults crowded together and were soon lost in conversation, like old friends. Ruth and Larry, though the center of their talk, by no means monopolized the day. The children ran in and out, showing the presents they had received from each of the adult visitors.

"And look, Dr. Simson," Suzie said, showing her a book. "Brian gave this to me. Remember when I had to find out about Teddy Roosevelt? Well he went to the book store and bought this one for me."

"And it wasn't easy to find, either," Brian told them.

"And Suzie bought me a puzzle, Aunt Ruth," Paula stated. "Now you can help us after the meal. Suzie says you're pretty good, but not as good as Dr. Fenster."

Just then an infant cry was heard. Ruth rose from her chair and went to the nursery. Both cribs were occupied. Carrie, her little niece, was in one; Barbara, Suzie's sister, was in the other. She saw little Carrie rubbing her eyes, tears falling to her cheeks. Quickly she lifted the infant so as not to awaken the sleeping child. "Well, little girl, you've certainly grown!" she exclaimed. At that precise moment, the other child awakened, and a small whimper was heard. "Now, look what you've done, Carrie. And I don't have four hands." She walked toward the stairway and called, "Larry, I need your help!" He came running.

"Hey, you look good with that baby. She's adorable."

"There's another one crying in the nursery. Pick her up," Ruth directed.

"Hey, this one is cute, too. Now, what do we do?" he asked.

"I guess we change their diapers," Ruth said.

"All right, you first."

"Here, watch me," Ruth said, showing him her expertise in motherhood. Larry noticed the quiet confidence that Ruth displayed in the art of diaper-changing, and the loving expression on her face as she held and fondled the child. She took to this aspect of her feminine role in the same way as she did her professional life. She looked completely content. When she finished dressing Carrie, she gave him the changing table for Barbara. In a few seconds he had completed the change; the child in his arms was gurgling with delight.

"What do we do now?" he asked.

"I think we should take these tykes to the seder table."

As they took their seats at the table, children in their laps, Joe began the prayer:

"Blessed art Thou, Eternal our God, Ruler of the Universe. . . ."

Larry whispered in Ruth's ear, ". . . Who brought you to me."

Chapter 24

Epilogue

July 26, 1979
Atlanta, Georgia

The auditorium was packed. It was the opening address, to be delivered by Dr. Engelman, which had attracted the vast and diverse crowd to the National Breast Cancer Conference. Karen and Jim Hayes, and Ruth and Larry Stein, quickly took their seats in the front row. The audience fell silent as the powerful man walked to the podium and began to speak.

"My fellow colleagues, honored guests, members of the media: It is indeed a pleasure to welcome you all here today for the first National Congress on Breast Cancer. This event hopefully ushers in a new era in the treatment of localized breast cancer. Our studies on the value of limited surgery, begun five years ago, now have firm base on which we may report data and draw deductive conclusions.

"In 1974, we began enrolling women in our protocol study. To date there are six hundred and four women participating in this trial, which employs a multimodality approach to a systemic disease. The combination of limited surgery, radiation therapy, and chemotherapy, has yielded a cure rate equal to the dreaded radical mastectomy.

"It is our desire to present this program in its full scope in the forthcoming sessions. . . ."

Karen Hayes turned to her husband, who was attempting to set his tape recorder. "What the heck are you doing, Jim?"

"I'm making myself a record," he whispered.

"But this is *your* study. Why do you need a recording?"

"This way I'll have a second opinion ready and available for my patients!" he replied.

Karen succeeded in keeping her laughter to herself. "Sometimes I wonder about your sanity!"

"So do I. But I figure I can afford to be a little eccentric today." Jim put another tape in the recorder and set the microphone in place. They turned their attention to the speaker. Dr. Engelman was now addressing the role of radiation therapy.

"Radiation therapy has long been the dark sister in cancer therapy. For many years it was employed without sufficient knowledge of its potential lethal powers. This set the stage for the slowdown

340

in its use during the Sixties and the early Seventies. However, with greater technical efficiency we have seen that radiotherapy can be used as both a primary and adjuvant therapy in the treatment of carcinomas of the breast. . . ."

Larry Stein looked adoringly at his wife. Dr. Engelman was building up to her introduction. "You're next, honey," he whispered. He gave her hand a gentle squeeze.

His concern for her today was hardly ill based. She would have to deal with her emotional reactions to her personal crisis while speaking to a very large audience. Difficult at best; nearly impossible when pregnant! And now Ruth was a mere few weeks from her delivery. But Larry felt confident about her emotional state. Although Ruth's first reaction to the crisis had been normal, the anger, fear, and tension had been greatly reduced as the days passed. They had seen Dr. Engelman. They had spent an evening with Karen and Jim Hayes. Dan Driedan was at their beck and call. All felt that she was in no position to take diagnostic tests or a biopsy at this point. "While I feel that Ruth is merely undergoing some changes in the breast tissue due to her pregnancy, Larry, I realize that this small mass does feel somewhat suspicious." Those had been Jim's words to him the day after Ruth had gone to his office. "If there are no changes after the baby is born, Larry, we'll have to go in and biopsy the lump." That was Dr. Engelman's opinion. And Larry greatly admired Ruth's strength. She continued to prepare for the conference. She carried on with tying up the loose ends at the office with Sam so that she did not have to worry about their patients. She also spent a lot of her time with him. They shopped for the baby clothes, nursery furniture and Ruth's prize, a rocking chair.

"That's perfect for nursing, Larry. That's exactly what I want," she told him plopping her very pregnant body into the chair.

Larry was brought back to the reality of the moment by Jim Hayes. "I'm going to put Ruth on a separate tape. Then we'll be able to remind her of her long suit whenever she gets too humble."

"My wife humble? Jim you're joking."

"No, I'm not. She never takes full credit for the work she's personally supervised."

"I have a bad habit of making long stories even longer," Dr. Engelman was saying, "but this one needs to be told. There are many among us who will be inspired by the courage of this very inquisitive and persevering physician. When the interstitial implant was first studied some years ago, much of the news was masked by negative reports resulting from fear of radiation. It was at that time that Dr. Ruth Simson-Stein began her studies with Dr. Hillman. The fine results achieved from that trial enabled us to assess the worth of the interstitial implant and begin enrollment in that protocol. For this address, may I present to you, Dr. Ruth Simson-Stein. . . ."

Ruth's heart was pounding as she rose from her seat to walk to the podium. And now she, Ruth Simson-Stein, would present her paper, a theme of *hope*. Hope—that was the true meaning of this meeting. She leaned over to Dr. Engelman who was about to greet her. "You're a woman of great courage," he whispered.

"I have great hope," she told him.

"Good girl. Now, let them know why you have that great hope." Dr. Engelman left the podium. For a moment Ruth felt nervous and excited. Would the words come out as she had planned? Or would she stammer and fumble? Ruth looked out into the audience, found Larry's face in the crowd, and began to speak as if he were the sole listener.

Dr. Mark Fenster walked into the auditorium with a quick step. He was late because of long-distance calls from the hospital. Constant crisis intervention had been his job since the hospital began the Cancer Rehabilitation Program four years ago. Although he now employed a very able staff of assistants, the new crises were always brought to his attention. He quietly took a seat next to Janet and Woody Doyle. "Has Dr. Driedan spoken yet?" he asked Janet.

"No, Ruth is just beginning now," she answered.

"You're looking marvelous, Mrs. Doyle. And you too, Mr. Doyle," Mark said, extending a hand to Woody. Then he looked at Janet.

"How's the work going on your personal experience article? From the parts I've read, any of the women's magazines should want to run it."

"When you complete the reading, Dr. Fenster, it will probably be the first time you'll resort to calling me Janet!"

"Is it that shocking?" he whispered.

"It was very therapeutic for me . . . let's listen. . . ."

Ruth was speaking:

"Breast cancer stands as a source of concern to all healthy women, and a particular reason for terror for the woman who finds herself afflicted. I know, for as a woman, and as a physician, I have experienced the realities of the crisis. . . ."

As she spoke those words, Ruth felt a tightness in her throat. She paused briefly and took a sip of water, then continued.

"The time which elapses between discovery of a lump, and the biopsy procedure is extraordinarily traumatic and critical. Five years ago we physicians were faced with a decision-making problem that would alter the course of breast cancer treatment; that was the problem of the reassessment of a newer theory of the biology and treatment of this disease. Unfortunately the dilemma was masked by many pointless issues. Physicians were continually engaged in heated debates over the adjuvant therapies.

"For many years I had seen patients who refused to be surgerized. Many of these women elected to do nothing. The treatment, to them, was more devastating than the disease itself. Others came to radiation therapy, and/or chemotherapy, seeking an alternative treatment. Women, like Janet Doyle, who is out there in the audience today, forced physicians to seek these logical alternatives and treat women with dignity according to personal preference. These isolated cases were the catalyst that spurred us on, to look toward new horizons, to take new direction."

Alvin Donovan stood at the threshold of the auditorium. He was shaking hands vigorously with each guest who arrived; with each speaker as they left the podium. He was, one might say, proud as a peacock. He felt responsible for the participation of the Memorial Hospital staff in what was considered to be one of the medical triumphs of the decade. And it was he, Alvin Donovan, who had been responsible—to some degree. He had had many differences with this group of rebels; yes, he remembered them well. But he had served both camps of thought. And each group had kept a quiet but fierce check on the other. That was the beauty of the battle. And the conservatives were still holding on to their theory; Davis and Thompson, and those like them, held their own conferences. However, this was the system of checks and balances in medicine. And Alvin Donovan could float from one side to the other at will. He only hoped that no one would cut that rope in the middle, that median line which he so carefully walked. His thoughts were interrupted by Dan Driedan.

"Good to see you, Al," he said quietly.

"I didn't know you were back already."

"Too much excitement. And we wanted to spend some of the holidays with the grandchildren," Dan told him.

"When are you speaking?" Donovan asked.

"After Ruth. Just a short report. The press has covered us well."

"Yes, I saw your picture out there on the front pages of the papers. We're mighty proud, Dan."

"Thanks, Al. We'll see you at the dinner," Dan replied as he walked toward the front of the room. He listened to Ruth's concluding statements:

"Today we stand on the threshold of a new and exciting era in the specialty of oncology. The results of the multimodality approach to breast cancer is yielding a cure rate which would have seemed impossible five short years ago. Respect for individual differences among our patients is an issue which must be addressed. Treatment choices are now numerous for those women presenting early and localized cancers. The aim of this conference is to disseminate information throughout the world, to best serve the physical and psychological needs of our patients. Thank you for your kind attention.

"May I now present to you Dr. Dan Driedan, recipient of the Nobel Prize in Medicine. . . ."

Lights began to flash in the auditorium. Pictures of Dr. Driedan were appearing everywhere. This was one more occasion to put him up front, exactly where he belonged. Dan approached the podium and thanked Ruth, who stepped down and took her seat next to her husband.

"That was beautiful, honey," he told her as he held her chair.

"I'm glad it's over. It's difficult making public speeches."

"Donovan's back there shaking hands," Larry told her.

"He loves this exposure, Larry. The more we

346

put him up front, the more easily he complies with our wishes," she reminded him.

Dan began to speak. Every-eye was focused upon him:

"It is certainly a privilege and an honor to stand here before you today. And I might say that it feels very good to be home again. My wife and I have made many miles this year; speaking engagements for Nobel Laureates are numerous. The guesswork of chemotherapy may now be stricken from the record, as the medical tribunal would say. The key to the new test, known as the human tumor stem cell assay, is the rediscovery of the double-layer soft agar plating technique. The use of this technique, which employs a nutrient-containing one-milliliter agar 'feeder layer' on the bottom of the plate in addition to the tumor-cell-containing layer, has made it possible to grow human tumor cell colonies in vitro, a previously difficult task.

"I should like to cite the many people involved who were instrumental in making this discovery with me. For without a grant from the Memorial Hospital, my continued studies in Germany would have been impossible. I should like to recognize Dr. Alvin Donovan, chief of staff, for his ability to extend my research grant. . . ."

Dr. Donovan stood and took a bow. The audience applauded loudly. A short "thank you" was heard.

". . . Dr. Von Hoffmann, my counter-part, and partner in study. . . ."

Dr. Von Hoffmann rose and took a bow to the applause.

". . . And Dr. Mark Fenster, the chairman of the Cancer Rehabilitation Coordination Team. Dr. Fenster's untiring drive, his unending devotion to every aspect of cancer treatment, has made possible the finest quality of holistic cancer treatment in the country. May I introduce to you, Dr. Mark Fenster. . . ."

Janet saw that Dr. Fenster did not rise from his seat immediately. She gave him a nudge. "Go ahead, Dr. Fenster . . . they're waiting for you!"

"Now how can a fellow follow a Nobel Laureate and feel comfortable?" he asked her, getting up.

"Well, you're the shrink who's always telling people that self-esteem is based upon small areas of personal competence. Now get out there and expound upon your small area of personal competence," she told him.

"I'd laugh if I weren't so goddamn nervous, Janet."

"You called me Janet!"

"I guess I did. This must be the long-awaited crisis!" Mark said, and he walked toward the front of the room and stood nervously behind the podium.

"Good morning fellow physicians, honored guests, and the press: It isn't easy to follow a man like Dr. Driedan. So bear with me while I gain composure and the words I need to make much the same impact upon your thoughts. . . ."

Ruth turned to Larry. "I think Mark is overwhelmed. I never saw him like this!"

"He'll be fine. What time is the session over today?" he asked her.

"We have to be at the luncheon at noon. We're

all honored guests. Conference resumes at two; and then at five we have the cocktail party. I managed to get tickets for Janet and Woody. I want her to meet all these people. . . ."

"You need a rest, honey, if you expect to go to the cocktail party this evening," Larry advised her. "Why don't you try to get out a little early?"

"I think I will. . . . Listen. . . ." Mark was now composed.

"A comprehensive psychiatric service that aims to prevent psychological battle scars among cancer victims was begun at Memorial Hospital in conjunction with the research in the oncology units four years ago. Until that time psychiatric counseling for the cancer patient was sporadic at best. With the institution of this service, we are now able to serve the community at large.

"Our service reflects a new and growing concern for the quality of life experienced by cancer patients both during and after illness. With higher cure rates and more patients living longer than ever before, psychiatric counseling and support for such individuals is becoming increasingly important.

"A major part of our work with patients is to keep them functioning psychologically. The fact of having had cancer or undergoing treatment for it can cause some people to lose their self-esteem and develop psychological sequelae, including severe depression. Moreover, many individuals, once cured, desperately fear recurrence of the disease. This experience can be incapacitating. . . .

"Increased attention should be paid to living

with the uncertainty that cancer generates. Anyone who's had the disease can never feel invulnerable to it again. . . ."

"I hope this program goes over well, Dan,"
Ruth remarked, as he sat down next to her.

"Yes. I think it's going to be the hardest one to
sell, Ruth. There's no doubt about it. Where you
can't make scientific measurement it's difficult to
gain the sympathy of the medical community," he
said.

"I think the seminars he's going to give will
help. And, of course, the journal he's working on
will begin to focus on these needs."

"I spoke to Janet and Woody," Dan commented.
"I was happy they could make it. She looks grand.
She has quite a story to tell, thanks to your giving
her a second lease on life."

"May we all have a second lease. . . ." Ruth
added pensively.

"You will, sweetheart," Dan said. He squeezed
her hand tightly.

Today, Ruth realized, it was almost inappropriate to be fearful. . . .

August 16, 1979

Larry Stein and Jim Hayes walked down the
corridor of Memorial Hospital's maternity ward.
As they approached Ruth's room, Jim spoke.
"You go in and see her alone, Larry. I can
remember how hectic things got for Karen and me
shortly after the kids were born. Mother, mother-

350

in-law; the whole family will be descending upon you soon."

"You're right, Buddy," Larry answered looking at his watch. "I'm sure they'll all be here as soon as visiting hours begin."

"Which leaves you just about half an hour. . . ."

"I'll need that time," Larry told him. "But I want you to know how grateful Ruth and I are for everything. . . ."

"Hold the thanks. I'm godfather. That makes up for all," Jim said proudly. "And Larry, I've decided to do the biopsy on Ruth's breast just before she leaves. We've got a few days so I'll let her get adjusted to motherhood." Jim walked away quickly, leaving Larry alone. He rapped on the door. No response. Slowly he opened the door and let himself in. Ruth was sleeping peacefully in her bed. A small lock of hair had fallen over her eye. Quickly he peeked into the bassinet. There, his beautiful daughter Jennifer lay asleep. "God, she's the image of me!" Larry said aloud.

"She is not!"

It was Ruth. Her eyes, glazed with sleep, were half open. He walked over to the bedside, brushed the hair from her face, and planted a kiss on her cheek.

"Ruth, I concede. She's the image of you," he whispered.

"She's both of us, Larry. Jennifer's our miracle." Then Ruth closed her eyes again and seemed to drift into slumber.

Larry sat down next to Jennifer's bassinet. "Now, my little one, *we* must pray for another

351

miracle." He was thinking of Ruth and the biopsy.

"The next one will be a boy, Larry," Ruth whispered. Was that the miracle he was asking for?

"Are you observing me with closed eyes?" he asked lovingly.

"Come closer and I'll tell you. . . ." Ruth was drifting again.

Larry sat on the bed and held Ruth in his arms. "Did you want a son?" she asked.

"Is that what you thought I was praying for?"

"I don't know," she responded.

"I was wishing for another miracle, honey. The miracle that would make this happiness last a lifetime," Larry said with emotion.

"Sometimes when we're so happy we're afraid of that happiness, Larry. We think that if we blink our eyes it might disappear from view. Then all bad things would happen to take its place. But I don't feel or believe in that anymore. . . . It's—well, it's dumb!"

"Perhaps you're right, honey. But I guess I've never had so much happiness in my life. It's hard to believe that it can last . . . even though it's lasted."

"Don't be afraid, Larry. I'm not afraid anymore," Ruth said as she kissed him. "I have you, and now we have Jennifer . . . I have everything in the world to fight for."